A Fair Chance of Murder

A Maiden Harlow Mystery - Book 2

Camille Sharp

CONTENTS

CHAPTER ONE

"Can you believe how good murder is for business?" Alfie Harlow shook his head in wonder as he looked over the next few weeks' worth of bookings.

"Yeah, I wouldn't have thought so, but here we are," Maiden peered over her father's shoulder to see the computer screen.

Their elegant little inn, Harlow House, was heavily booked for months. This was partly because Golden Glen, Michigan was a tourist retreat that didn't skimp on special events, but their business' recent success was due to a couple of brutal killings that took place on site. The rooms that had been occupied by those involved continued to be the most requested; there was even a growing waitlist.

"At least we aren't on the front page today," she said as she sipped her coffee and pointed at the morning paper.

"I didn't mind being on the front page," Alfie chuckled. "Like I said, it's good for business. You can't stop people from being curious, however morbid it might be."

"I guess, but that woman who asked if there were any bloodstains left that she could look at was a bit much." Maiden wrinkled her nose and started reading the paper again.

The Golden Glen Gazette wasn't exactly a pillar of journalistic integrity, but it excelled at keeping the town's residents entertained with sensationalized drama and shameless exaggeration. Sometimes at least. Other times they just persistently hounded people for interviews no matter how firmly that person had turned them down. An annoying truth that Maiden had learned all too well.

After solving the two murders that had taken place at their inn, Maiden became the talk of the town. As the police built the case, the headlines were continually focused on what was dubbed the 'Harlow House Killings'.

She must have turned down at least a dozen calls for interviews. Not only because she didn't want the attention or to add to the general frenzy, but she wasn't free to discuss much of it. The assortment of trials hadn't started yet, and a lot of information was still confidential.

Of course, that made no difference to the local gossips, with the Harlow's friend Amelia Ferris being their undisputed queen. Her son, Tony, also did his part to share everything he knew about the case with anyone who would listen. Thanks to their enthusiasm, the stories spread through town like wildfire.

Despite the constant chatter, Maiden had done her best to avoid discussing any of the dirty details with strangers, or so-called friends who'd all but forgotten she existed until seeing her name in the papers.

Unfortunately, even this had backfired on her. Maiden's persistent silence about the case lent her an air of mystery. While it had all been flattering and rather fun at first, it was quickly becoming tiresome. Maiden could only hope that the fuss would calm down at last.

It actually wasn't the first time she'd made the papers, but solving two murders and a bank robbery sounded far more impressive than being barred from the school spelling bee because of an unusually sharp memory. And collecting the $5000 reward for identifying and helping capture the masterminds behind the heist, which led to the recovery of the stolen money, had been an unexpected perk.

Maiden felt proud of herself for having outfoxed some very frightening people, but she was genuinely pleased to read a headline that didn't include the words 'murder', 'psychopath' or 'hotel-of-death'.

"Things should brighten up now, at least," she mused as she held up the paper for her dad to see.

Summerfest Has Come to Golden Glen!

The annual Summerfest fair had hit town, and that always made her happy. Banners and balloons adorned every storefront, and the smell of incredible food filled the air. People poured into their quaint community in droves and provided a nice boost to the local businesses, theirs included.

Golden Glen was abuzz with excitement. The main streets were already closed to road traffic and transformed into one of the most beloved outdoor markets in the state. Countless market stalls and tents popped up, featuring goods from local artisans as well as offerings from around the country. There would be plenty to see and do throughout the two-week festival, and everyone seemed to be in a jovial mood.

"Ah yes!" Alfie brightened, rubbing his hands together happily. "Triumph awaits! Not only am I opening my biggest woodworking stall to date, but I have a little surprise planned for Gloria too."

The gleam in her father's eyes filled Maiden with suspicion, but she decided not to risk becoming an accessory to his mischief by asking about it.

Instead, she let her thoughts drift to Captain McAlister, the new head of the local police department. Considering he had recently moved from a much larger city, she wondered if he liked small-town fetes, or if he'd ever even gone to one. She admitted to herself that she really knew little about him, and that didn't look likely to change.

She hadn't seen much of him in the past couple of weeks, and not at all since forensics collected the last shreds of evidence and he took her final statement. There was no reason for him to come by or to contact her anymore. So, that was that.

While they had parted on good terms, she worried he might be angry with her over the publicity she'd attracted. It was hardly a dream start to his new job. Maiden knew she had stolen his thunder, but it hadn't been done on purpose, and she'd made a point of commending the police whenever she could. It would be cold comfort, though, when almost every article crowed about the local woman who picked up the clues that the cops missed.

Despite those stark realities, Gloria, her mother, genuinely wondered why Captain McAlister hadn't invented an excuse to visit again. The boisterous southern broad strongly believed that her youngest daughter had caught the policeman's eye.

To save face and stop herself from growing disappointed, Maiden had quickly reverted to her old defense of insisting that McAlister wasn't interested in her and never had been. While mystified, Gloria couldn't argue it since the man in question hadn't been back.

Maiden set the paper down and glanced over when she saw her mother emerge from the dining room, followed closely by Kylie. They were both scowling thunderously.

Kylie Abrams was their chef. She had worked at Harlow House for several months now and produced amazing dishes, but her personality left a lot to be desired, in Gloria's eyes at least.

But at present, Kylie's usually painful shyness was warring with obvious temper. From the way the two women started almost sprinting towards the reception desk the moment they spotted Alfie, Maiden easily guessed that her father was their common enemy. Alfie met her gaze and barely smothered a pleased smirk as he hurried to duck behind her.

"I take it Mom's learned about the surprise you arranged for her?" she whispered dryly.

"Everything I do is for the good of others," he promised, even as a wicked grin slipped free.

"Whatever you say, but if this turns violent, I never met you," Maiden hissed before facing the angry women with a wary smile. "Hey, what's up?"

"Your father!" Gloria pointed in her direction with a bright yellow acrylic nail that matched her flouncy polka-dot sundress. "Your selfish, thoughtless father has thrown us to the wolves! And he isn't even sorry!"

"That's true," Alfie chuckled as he peeked out from behind his human shield. "I'm not."

"Really, Mr. Harlow!" Kylie's gaunt cheeks were pink with anger. Her immaculate chef's whites almost glowed in the early morning light; that somehow made her look scarier. "I didn't sign up for this sort of spectacle! I was never even asked!"

"Maybe we could all stop arguing?" Maiden held up her hands soothingly. "Now, please tell me what's happened. What has Dad done?"

"Alfred Francis Harlow has gone behind my back and entered us into the 'Best Pie' category of the Summerfest Food Extravaganza!" Gloria's normal southern drawl was tightly wound and grew higher with each indignant word. "Without consent or even a hint of warnin'! And not just the inn, oh no! Kylie and me specifically! *By name!*"

"Why all the fuss?" Alfie shrugged and waved away his wife's nearly hysterical screech. "All you have to do is throw together a stupid pie and chuck it in with the rest. No one cares if it's any good; it's free publicity."

Gloria and Kylie were incoherent for a moment while they tried to put their fury into words. Maiden busied herself pretending to wipe a speck of dirt off the desk as she waited for them to calm down or at least pull in a full breath. At this rate they'd both pass out in the middle of the foyer.

She understood the annoyance of being entered without agreeing, but they were carrying on a bit for a pie contest. She suspected it was the prospect of having to work together that was bothering them. Her mother had made no secret of the fact that she found Kylie cold and unpleasant, and Kylie doubtless found Gloria overbearing and intrusive. Not a match made in heaven.

"Well..." Maiden began cautiously, knowing that any encouraging suggestions would only irritate them further. Finally, she propped her elbows on the desk and smiled brightly. "What are you going to make?"

"Yes!" Alfie grinned and patted her on the shoulder. "Positivity! That's the spirit, my dear."

"I'm not bakin' a dang pie!" Gloria said defiantly and pointed her thumb in Kylie's direction. "And certainly not with Miss Fancy-pants here. She'd plaster the whole thing with gold leaf and those stupid little sugar beads that look like grapeshot!"

"Firstly, they are called dragees, and I would *never* put them on a pie! Secondly, it is not my fault if you're intimidated by my culinary training, Mrs. Harlow," Kylie said tightly. "But there's no need to insult me."

Maiden hid an impressed smile; only a month ago Kylie wouldn't have dared respond to Gloria's jibe. The meals her mother forced the shy cook to share with their family had toughened her up a bit. That's not to say the poor woman had enjoyed the experiences, but at least she'd grown stronger.

The two women would not even look at each other now; they both stared in opposite directions and seethed. The collaboration was a stupidly horrible idea; they'd hate every second. Maiden decided to try to be positive anyway.

"Mom, you and Kylie both have different strengths and talents. Together you two could come up with something genuinely incredible," she pointed out optimistically. "It would be kind of cool. If you win a ribbon, we could add the pie to the menu as a special feature."

The irate pair glanced at each other warily as they both stopped to actually consider the idea. Alfie met his daughter's gaze and winked. Maiden smiled and looked back at the article she'd been perusing. As she turned a page, she cleared her throat delicately.

"I've always loved cherry pie myself," she offered.

"Everyone will make cherry pie, Maiden." Kylie frowned and rested her chin in her hand. "Or apple. This is Michigan. It's too predictable and would be too hard to distinguish ourselves from the rest."

"Maybe," Gloria conceded with a tiny nod. "But we can't be too wild either; the judges would dismiss us as a novelty. We need to find a middle ground."

They turned to face each other; Gloria's soft brown eyes met Kylie's piercing blue. They both eased back a step, but nodded in silent agreement.

"It's settled then. I'll go and dig through some of my old family recipes," Gloria said guardedly.

"That's fine." Kylie raised her chin a fraction. "I'll look through my notes from culinary school."

"Dandy," Gloria murmured. "This'll be good; we'll do it for Harlow House."

"Yes," Kylie said enigmatically, "for Harlow House."

The women watched each other warily as they backed away. They both looked ready to draw their six-shooters and find out once and for all who was the fastest gun in town. Maiden smirked at the mental image but waited until Kylie skulked back into the kitchen before she spoke up.

"Mom." She gave Gloria a serious look. "Play nice!"

"Oh hush, you." Gloria waved her away. "I'll be the picture of grace and charm...but I'm not gonna have some skinny little girl tell me how to make pie!"

"Darling, I've presented you two with the opportunity to bond at last," Alfie said magnanimously, and then arched a bushy brow. "Try not to ruin it, please."

Chapter Two

The inn was busy, as it typically was when a big event hit town, but this felt like their busiest season yet. Maiden marveled that last month's murders boosted their business so much. It was gruesome, but a distinction was a distinction.

Many of the guests who checked in asked to meet her, and that inevitably turned into a flurry of questions about the case. She understood people being curious, but she was getting tired of repeating the same information.

It didn't help that Alfie had pinned a collection of newspaper clippings about the investigation on the notice board in the foyer. Maiden passively retaliated by avoiding the busier afternoon shifts. She was a morning person anyway.

None of it mattered today, however. It was the first official day of Summerfest, so despite the increase in guests, Maiden and her older sister followed their annual tradition and took the day off to visit the fair. This was always the most exciting time to go; everything was new and fresh and bustling.

Maiden only felt a little bad that she and Vonny were leaving Gloria to watch the desk while they went to have fun. Alfie would be running his woodworking stall at the markets. He spent much of the winter off-season in his workshop making things to sell at the annual festivals or to give as gifts to friends. He had a store at Summerfest every year, and he had built a good reputation for himself.

But Maiden and Von always worked hard, and Gloria wasn't fussed. She said she would rope Billie, their long-time house-keeper, into helping her. She was also a reliable worker, but she'd never been recruited to the reception desk before. Maiden had been concerned when Gloria mentioned having the plain-spoken woman help out; she could only hope that Billie wouldn't be allowed to answer the phone.

Pushing those concerns aside, Maiden felt her excitement grow as they drove downtown. It wasn't long before they could see the top of the Ferris wheel coming into view; she smiled happily at the nostalgic sight.

The city council had arranged for several parking lots to be available for fair-goers. Maiden slid her dark green sedan into a surprisingly close space. The parking lot was already two-thirds full; she was glad they hadn't left any later. She and Vonny wrestled with the expandable sunshade—she only got smacked in the face with it once—before finally pinning it against the windscreen with the sun visors. They climbed out and gazed at the crowds of people walking towards the heart of town; with cheerful smiles, they joined the throng heading for the fair.

It was a warm day; Maiden had slipped into a pair of denim shorts and a blue gingham blouse. Vonny wore a fitted peach romper and pigtail braids; it looked sweet on her but gave an unfair illusion of bashful innocence. Von was quite nice when she wanted to be, but she could really bite back when provoked.

They came to the markets first; the stalls were lined up in tidy rows through the main streets. Some had signs out front displaying the name of the business; others had tables arranged with merchandise designed to lure people inside.

Among the various offerings were handmade jewelry and crafts, scented candles and soaps, toys, and an extensive collection of tie-dyed t-shirts. They even saw a tent that specialized exclusively in embroidering personalized baseball caps.

The sound of happy chatter and the distant laughter of children filled the air. Maiden smiled and took a deep, relaxing breath as she soaked in the atmosphere. Summerfest always brought back good memories for her.

She and Von spent a peaceful hour wandering through the market stalls, stopping once in a while when something caught their eye. Vonny picked up a pair of fashionably oversized sunglasses, and Maiden spotted a lovely silver pendant shaped like a swan that she debated about going back for.

When the smell of fresh waffle cones wafted over them, they promptly decided to go for ice cream and then explore the carnival. They followed their noses past clusters of colorful balloons and on under an enormous banner that proclaimed the name of the travelling company; *Spencer & Spencer*.

Maiden thought back to the carnivals that came to town every year; they had been a highlight of the summer for as long as she could remember. The sights and smells were both familiar and welcome: cotton candy, popcorn, and funnel cakes in a delicious medley.

She glanced up when she heard delighted screams from the faint-hearted patrons at the peak of the Ferris wheel. Maiden felt a little wobble in her stomach, even standing safely on the ground looking up at them. She was grateful that Vonny was no more inclined towards heights than she was.

It's just a merry-go-round that fell on its side, Maiden thought uneasily to herself and edged away from the huge metal edifice. Judging by the long line of people waiting for their turn, few others shared her concerns.

She and Vonny walked on, passing clusters of giggling teenagers and young families excitedly exploring all that the fair had to offer. Most of the children they saw were carrying bags of candy or popcorn as they ran around with their friends. It was all dazzling and cheerful, but as they walked deeper in and neared the food trucks, the sound of angry voices cut through the bliss.

She looked over as subtly as she could and saw two men tucked away in a small corridor formed by the flavored popcorn wagon and the bumper cars. Despite the festive surroundings, they were clearly in the midst of a heated argument.

Maiden recognized one of them; his name was Sam Chalmers. He worked for the town council as an event coordinator. She had met him the day before when she'd helped her father set up his stall. Chalmers had stopped by to meet him and congratulate him on being one of their more successful local vendors. Alfie was now well known for his woodworking, and particularly his birdhouses.

The man arguing with Chalmers was a stranger to her, but he seemed like a nasty piece of work. He wasn't overly tall, but he was brawny and stood with his arms crossed and an unyielding look on his suntanned face. His hair was a sandy blonde that was heavily grayed at his temples. He had cold eyes and a long nose that looked like it had been broken a couple of times.

His expression was one of derisive contempt, while Chalmers appeared frustrated and indignant. She watched as the brawny man took a step towards the far doughier Chalmers and pointed a finger in his face. He then gave a dismissing wave of his hand and stalked off with a smirk.

Chalmers glared as the other man disappeared around a corner. He then turned on his heel and stormed off in the opposite direction. Maiden couldn't help wondering what they were fighting about.

"Come on." Vonny nudged her impatiently, disrupting her wandering thoughts. "Let's get in line before it gets any busier. And then I want to ride the merry-go-round."

"It's like escorting a very tall 10-year-old," she chuckled but followed her sister to the end of the long line that was snaking out from in front of the ice cream truck.

As they waited, slowly inching forward, Maiden took the opportunity to study the crowd. It was summer break for the local schools, so there were children everywhere. They were noisy, but she couldn't begrudge them the same fun and excitement that she'd enjoyed at their age.

She spotted a family that was staying at the inn, the Jensens; it looked like the two young sons were trying to talk their mother into braving the funhouse. Mrs. Jensen shook her head vehemently until the boys gave up and started on their dad instead. Maiden smiled faintly and glanced over at the attraction they kept pointing to.

The funhouse was quite large, certainly the biggest one she had ever seen. Most of it sprawled out across the promenade, but another section rose high into the air behind it. The upper deck sat on heavy scaffolding and wound its way to a big, twisting yellow slide. As she watched, several kids emerged and plunged down it with delighted squeals.

Her eyes shifted back to the Jensen family, but she saw only Mrs. Jensen now, standing there waiting patiently. Evidently, her husband lost the argument. She glanced around and spotted him and the boys at the ticket booth.

The woman sitting behind a flimsy plexiglass barrier caught her attention. She looked like a cross between a medieval reenactment and a children's puppet show.

Her curly hair was a deep shade of vibrant purple, a color that was mirrored in her heavy eye makeup. What Maiden could see of her outfit consisted of a linen tunic with a black leather corset laced up over the top. It was unusual, but at the same time entirely appropriate for the setting.

The interesting woman took the money Mr. Jensen handed her and slid three tickets across the counter with a polite smile. The kids waved to her as they ran excitedly toward the large entrance. The fiberglass archway was fashioned to resemble a huge clown face, obliging the patrons to walk through its gaping, grinning mouth. Mr. Jensen looked it over and followed his sons inside, but far more sedately.

Maiden smiled at him and glanced away. Their line had barely moved; she drew her brows together and stood on tiptoe to peer at the truck in the distance. There seemed to be only one person working. No wonder it was taking so long; she pulled a face and went back to studying the crowd.

She enjoyed people-watching; covertly studying total strangers and trying to invent stories about who they were and what they were doing. Her attention once again strayed to the purple-haired woman in the ticket booth.

She was holding a magazine in front of her, but Maiden could see her gaze was subtly fixed on the long lineup. The woman shook her head irately before giving an unconcerned sniff and going back to whatever she was reading.

Maiden wondered at her but held her breath involuntarily when she looked further on and spotted Captain McAlister milling around through the growing crowd.

He was walking with Greg Smith, an eager-to-please deputy that she'd been friends with since elementary school. Greg was in uniform, so she assumed they were on duty. McAlister always wore plain clothes but still managed to look imposing and au-thoritative...and really hot.

Maiden shut her eyes. It embarrassed her a bit that she was so attracted to him, mainly because a few people had picked up on it, but she was gradually coming to accept the fact.

She couldn't help it anyway; McAlister was very handsome. He was tall, at least six foot three, and quite fit. The dark slacks and button-down shirts he favored did nothing to hide his broad shoulders and narrow hips. He also wore a tie, but let it hang open around his neck.

She wondered what they were doing there. They didn't look like they were in a particular rush, so it mustn't have been anything urgent. She allowed herself a quick moment to admire the sunlight glinting off his thick brown hair and then made herself turn back to Vonny.

"How badly do you want this ice cream?" she sighed, checking the time on her phone. "This is taking forever."

"Listen, there are fresh waffle cones dipped in chocolate at the front of this line." Von pulled down her large sunglasses enough to look her little sister in the eye. "This is happening."

"Fine," she grumbled, but looked over sharply when she heard her name.

"Maiden!"

It was Greg. He was waving and smiling at her, as usual he all but ignored Vonny.

Maiden smiled back and returned the wave. Vonny pushed a finger up the bridge of her nose, smoothly sliding her sunglasses into place and folded her arms over her chest. The pair had never gotten along well, not when they were kids and not now that they were...taller kids.

Maiden tried to keep her expression friendly, but when McAlister glanced over, he spared her only the slightest inclination of his head before walking away. Her smile faded a little.

"Brr!" Von pretended to shiver. "He's cold enough to stop your ice cream from melting."

"Yeah, I guess. Whatever." She shrugged and waved once more to Greg as he followed the captain.

She wouldn't dare say anything in front of Vonny, but she found his tepid reception disheartening. They had shared an undeniable attraction when he'd worked on the murder case at the inn, although she had denied it anyway. Enough other people had noticed that she knew she hadn't imagined it, but McAlister looked at her now as if they'd barely met.

She wondered if he really was irritated by the attention she'd received for solving those murders. It seemed likely. She could understand why, but it still stung. It's not like it was her fault that she had figured it out. Was she supposed to have kept it to herself and let the murderers get away?

By the time they'd neared the front of the line, the scent of fresh waffles was enough to take her focus off fickle and confusing men.

She glanced at the menu, but already knew what she wanted. She felt fortunate that it was available; half the flavors on offer were marked as sold out. That seemed odd, considering it was relatively early and only the first day of the fair.

While Vonny dithered and debated whether to get rocky road or marshmallow fudge, Maiden glanced to the side of the truck and saw a plume of smoke curl and twist into the air like an exotic dancer. A moment later, a woman holding a cigarette stepped into view; Maiden looked her over curiously.

She was at least part Asian. Her expertly painted, al-mond-shaped eyes turned up slightly at the corners like a cat's. She was small in stature; her slim but attractive figure was wrapped in a tight leopard-print jumpsuit. Her hair was platinum blonde and pulled into a messy bun on the top of her head. She was gorgeous.

"Hey, Janet!"

The woman glanced at the truck and rolled her eyes when the man serving the ice cream called out.

"Could I trouble you to come and do some work, princess?" he said it lightly enough, but he looked annoyed and frustrated as he slapped a scoop of chocolate ice cream into a small paper bowl.

Janet smiled ruefully and stubbed out her cigarette with a thoroughly put-upon sigh. She vanished behind the large truck but soon appeared beside him at the window.

"I told you," she responded in a flat mid-west accent, "if you're going to call me names, I prefer 'queen'."

The man gave her a look but said nothing; the people in line behind them laughed. The lady walked over and beamed down at Maiden and Vonny.

"Hello there, beautiful girls." Janet smiled. "What can I get for you?"

"Chocolate chip cookie dough in a waffle cone, please," Maiden said nicely, and then slid her sister a wry look. "Have you decided yet? It's the last taste of ice cream you'll ever know, after all."

"Don't pressure me!" Von scowled and was still biting her lip uneasily when Janet handed Maiden her cone. "I can't decide between raspberry swirl or mint chip."

"What?! You weren't even thinking of those flavors in line!" Maiden said with exasperation. "What happened to marshmallow fudge?"

"Tell you what, doll face," Janet smirked, "I'll do a bit of both."

"Thank you!" Vonny clasped her hands together like a child and bounced happily.

Waiting for Vonny to order food had always been a needlessly frustrating ordeal. No matter how long she was given to look at a menu, she was never ready to commit. And if by some miracle she ordered first, she changed her mind every time someone else said what they were getting.

After Von accepted her ice cream, they paid, left five dollars in the tip jar, and walked away to make room for others. Maiden glanced back and saw that the line moved much faster with two people working.

She shrugged it off as they wandered further into the promenade. Vonny dug her tiny wooden spoon into her dessert and took a large bite as she looked around at the strings of pennants and clusters of brightly colored balloons.

"Have you ever wanted to work at a carnival?" she asked with a dreamy look in her eyes.

"No," Maiden scoffed. "Have you?"

"Well, not especially, but it seems like such a fun place to be." Von shrugged.

"Yeah, when you're a patron," Maiden chuckled at her. "It wouldn't be that great to spend the day watching other people enjoy themselves and then have to clean up the vomit and candy wrappers they leave behind."

"Oh yuck." Von wrinkled her nose at her. "I should have come with Tony; you're no fun."

Tony Ferris was another friend they'd known since childhood. He worked as a postman now, which gave him and his mother, Amelia, ample access to the latest and juiciest rumors in town. Maiden also knew that her sister had been nursing a secret crush on him almost since the moment they met. She smiled at her.

"I'm plenty of fun, thank you very much," she said in a teasingly haughty, voice but then sighed down into her ice cream. "But, if I'm honest, I wouldn't mind being here with a man either."

"Ooo! Anyone in particular?" Vonny gave her a smiling look.

"Well, not Tony," Maiden replied dryly, and then made a point of being distracted by more raised voices.

Two men and one woman stood in a small huddle, but one of the men started shouting as if they were miles apart. Maiden recognized him as the same angry guy who had been fighting with Mr. Chalmers earlier.

"Listen, Haynes," the other man, a tall and burly red-head with an impressively bushy beard, said steadily, "I know my job, I know more than my job, it's perfectly sound."

"Sure, that's what you say now," he retorted harshly. "You think you're so clever; of course you won't admit to negligence!"

"Keith, please!" The woman stepped between them and nodded towards the handful of people watching them curiously. She lowered her voice. "This isn't good for business."

Keith still looked furious but quieted. Despite the added care, Maiden and Vonny were standing close enough to hear their conversation. He turned on the larger, calmer man and stuck a finger in his face.

"I'm serious, Armstrong," Keith grated. "If anything goes wrong here, it's on *you*."

"No it isn't, Haynes," he replied placidly. "I have all the maintenance schedules, logbooks and documentation. Nothing's going to happen but, if it does, it's on whoever *makes* it happen."

The woman let out a startled gasp but clapped a hand to her mouth in an attempt to hide it. The redhead still looked as undisturbed as a glassy lake, but Keith was glaring viciously at him.

"We'll see about that!" he spat and stalked away.

Maiden and Vonny watched him go and then turned and met the uncomfortable looks of the remaining two. Maiden managed a smile and took a step closer.

"Sorry, we weren't trying to eavesdrop," she said with an apologetic shrug. "But he was kind of loud."

"Not your fault, miss." The big man smiled. "Mr. Haynes has a temper, that's for sure."

"Not to lean on a sore point," Von said, despite planning to do exactly that, "but is something here unsafe?"

"Absolutely not!" the woman stated vehemently and held up a hand, but then she managed a smile. "Everything is inspected regularly according to stricter standards than are legally required, I assure you."

"Yes, please don't let his petty whining spoil your fun, ladies," the brawny red-head inclined his head politely. "The name's Oliver Armstrong. I'm head of maintenance, repair and the fixer of everything that breaks. These rides are as safe as can be."

"Nice to meet you." Maiden smiled and gestured to herself. "I'm Maiden Harlow and this is my sister Vonny."

"Lovely." Oliver nodded to them both and then to the lady at his side. "This is Gabby Lopez, office manager extraordinaire."

They exchanged polite smiles. Gabby stood in striking contrast to the tall and well-muscled Oliver. She was five feet tall at most and was swamped by an oversized floral peasant top, with a baggy pair of beige capris underneath. Her hair was dark, glossy, and incredibly thick. It fell to her sloped shoulders in a heavy curtain.

"Well, as Oliver said," Gabby's voice held a trace of a Spanish accent, "please enjoy yourselves without fear. Unless you go in the funhouse, of course, a little fear is part of the fun."

A giggle that ended in a rather cute snort heralded her departure. She excused herself and waddled towards a large trailer with a sign that said *Office* hanging above the door. Oliver watched her go and then turned back to them and inclined his head once again.

"I'll leave you ladies to it," he said as he walked past. "Enjoy yourselves."

A moment after the man ducked out of sight, Maiden was distracted by the glint of sunshine off metal. She looked down near their feet and saw a large bolt lying in the dirt.

"Here's hoping that didn't come off the merry-go-round," she whispered to herself.

Chapter Three

As promised, Maiden and Vonny next headed for the carousel. Maiden perched side-saddle on the back of a rather regal pink pony while Von settled onto the glossy shell of a sea turtle. The happy laughter of the children who sat on the rest of the colorful animals made them both smile.

They were halfway through the ride when Maiden noticed that the guy running it was looking her over. The man's blatant study of her bare legs rudely interrupted the carefree journey into childhood memories. She did her best to ignore him as the carousel twirled her and Vonny out of view.

As they swirled past again, he made eye contact and smiled at her. He had a greasy, unkempt appearance that was instantly off-putting. She wasn't a snob, but she liked a man who showered regularly. His jeans were stained, as was his sleeveless shirt, and he had a cigarette tucked behind his ear.

Maiden didn't return the smile but looked at the trail of tattoos that covered his left arm from shoulder to wrist. When she made out the form of a scantily clad woman on his forearm, she glanced quickly away again.

The carousel at last glided to a reasonably smooth stop; neither she nor Vonny dropped their ice creams, at least. Maiden slid to the checker-plate floor and gave her pony a pat on the head before stepping off the ride.

"How's it going?"

Maiden glanced over to see that the guy had left his post and sauntered over. A moment later Vonny was by her side and studying him critically. He didn't improve on closer inspection, but she could now see 'Timmy' embroidered on his shirt.

"Fine, thanks," she said with a polite nod and started to turn away.

"You ladies from around here?" he asked inventively.

"Kind of," Vonny replied in a grim, discouraging monotone. "You?"

"No, honey," Timmy chuckled and pointed to the carousel with his thumb. "We travel to you."

"Cool," she said flatly. "Your line's not moving much."

"They'll get by for a minute." He shrugged it off. "I just wondered if you ladies would like another ride? No charge."

"Gibson!" a now familiar voice snarled.

Maiden and Vonny stepped away subtly as Keith Haynes stalked over and grabbed Timmy by the collar and pulled him back a few steps. A handful of people looking on gasped at the needless physical confrontation.

"Stop harassing the patrons and get back to work!" he ordered loudly.

Maiden felt the stares on her and Von as well as a furiously red-faced Timmy. Riding the carousel was officially in the top three most terrible ideas Vonny had ever had—right next to the time she gave her goldfish some orange juice when she was seven and the perm she got in high school.

"Move it!" Keith pointed Timmy back to his station at the front of the long and quietly amused line of people enjoying the drama as they waited for their turn.

Timmy set his teeth and did as he was told, but he threw his boss a look of sheer hatred. Maiden watched the exchange in mortified silence. She realized Keith was coming straight off an argument with Oliver, but this was one of the worst ways he could have chosen to vent his frustration. There had to be some kind of rule on the books somewhere that prohibited using public humiliation and barroom brawl tactics against even the laziest employee.

She grasped Von's arm and nodded for them to go. Her sister didn't argue, and they slipped away before anyone could say anything to them. She doubted that Keith Haynes had the savvy to offer a polite apology to the innocent patrons he'd just embarrassed, and she certainly didn't want to hear him try.

"Well, that was loads of fun," Vonny said dryly.

"It was your suggestion," Maiden reminded her as she dug a chunk of slowly thawing cookie dough from her ice cream.

"Yeah, you're right, I should've seen this coming." She rolled her eyes and sighed. "At the risk of sounding like a little kid, let's go find Dad."

Maiden and Vonny skulked out of the carnival and again wound their way through the markets. They knew vaguely where to find their father's woodworking stall and soon saw a hand-carved sign that read: *Alfie's Woodworking Wonders*. As he had promised, his tent was much bigger than last year's.

They spotted a fair few people milling around and several walking out carrying one of Alfie's handmade pieces. Summer and spring were always his busiest seasons, as he specialized in birdhouses and the warmer weather helped turn people's attention to the outdoors.

They stepped into the tent and found him seated at a small table with his set of good chisels. They'd been expensive, and he took excellent care of them; Maiden wondered if he had them out to show them off a bit. The thought made her smile, as it seemed unlikely that many people would recognize premium tools to the point of actually being impressed by them.

She shifted her eyes to the shelves on the rear wall and saw that more than a few of his birdhouses were already marked as sold. Alfie appeared quite content as he carved something into a piece of pine while a few people looked on and chatted to him. Maiden loved seeing him so happy and opted not to interrupt. Vonny clearly had no such inhibitions and led the way straight to him.

"Wow." She glanced around owlishly as they reached his side. "You're really busy this year, Dad."

"It's about the same as usual." He flicked her a patient smile as the handful of observers wandered off. "You don't pay much attention to what the rest of us are up to, do you, my dear?"

"I manage all right, thanks a lot." She pulled a grumpy face and fell silent.

Maiden finished the last few bites of her ice cream and avoided her sister's eye. Vonny had never bothered to be terribly attentive. It wasn't that she didn't care about others; she did, but she tended to disregard things that weren't of particular interest to her.

Maiden ignored her quiet sulk and took a moment to admire the birdhouses displayed on the wire shelves that lined the walls of the tent. Her father's woodworking skills had come a long way since his first efforts when she was a kid.

What had started as the simplest of boxes with a bird-sized hole in the front were now intricately carved and carefully painted tiny houses. Alfie had even recreated Harlow House in miniature; the clever creation sat in the big oak tree outside the inn and rarely went unoccupied by birds or unnoticed by passersby.

What caught her notice at the moment, however, was the number of sold stickers that were stuck on the offerings. It was pretty typical for people to make a purchase but leave it there to pick up later; it saved them the hassle of carrying it around for hours. At least a quarter of the inventory was already spoken for.

She wondered if he had enough items back in his workshop to keep the stall open for two weeks. She knew he loved what he did, and that showed through in every piece he made. She smiled again but was distracted when a large shadow briefly blocked the sun from the tent's entrance. She glanced over and saw a very brawny and familiar man.

It was Oliver Armstrong, the carnival's ginger-haired head of maintenance. He strolled in and scanned the table beside the doorway, which displayed signs that Alfie had carved with a variety of cutesy sayings and affirmations.

Oliver's expression was reticent until his eyes shifted to the birdhouses; he stopped in his tracks and let out a low whistle before walking towards the nearest shelf. He picked up a rather handsome specimen in teal green, accented with glossy black trim. He turned it over and examined each side with an air of someone who knew what they were looking for; Alfie also noticed his perusal and approached.

"You have a good eye, that's one of my better efforts," he said with a pleased smile.

"Nice dovetails," Oliver agreed with an admiring nod. "I heard a few people talking about Alfie Harlow and his famous birdhouses. I wanted to see them for myself."

Maiden grinned at the term 'famous', although her father was certainly known for them and, while she might be biased, they were beautiful. Oliver started asking him which chisels he preferred. This descended into a dissertation on sharpening tool steel by hand and whether water stones were better than oil stones.

As the two men enjoyed a discussion that soon turned boring for almost everyone else, Maiden and Vonny began edging towards the door. Before they could make their escape, however, Janet walked in on Keith's arm.

The platinum-blonde beauty had thrown a shimmery gold shawl over her leopard jumpsuit and slid on a pair of horn-rimmed sunglasses that she now whipped off to stylish effect. Judging by the strong smell of tobacco mixed with exotic perfume, she must have hastily finished her last cigarette just outside. She ran her gaze over the room but stilled, and her lips parted slightly when she saw Oliver.

Admitting to herself that she was being shamelessly nosy, Maiden watched subtly as Oliver and Keith spotted each other. They both looked coldly annoyed, but Oliver cleared his expressed and turned back to Alfie with a smile.

"Well, thank you for the chat, but I can see you're busy," he said nicely. "I'll let you get back to it; I might browse a bit longer."

"Certainly, young man," Alfie said pleasantly. "And thank *you*. I'm always happy to talk to someone with a technical mind."

Keith gave a derisive scoff at that comment and then made an obvious point of ignoring Oliver as he and Janet toured the remaining wares in the tent. Janet was obviously uncomfortable over the friction but seemed to be trying to ignore it as she walked over to the nearest shelf of birdhouses. She looked them over with a serenely admiring smile, running a finger over a few of them as she passed.

As she moved along the row, she stopped suddenly and pressed a hand to her chest. She exhaled softly and stared at an ornate pink birdhouse accented with cream and gold.

"How lovely!" she breathed as she gazed at it wistfully. She very gingerly touched a finger to the glossy trim on the roof, as though afraid it would shatter if she weren't careful. "It reminds me of when I was a kid and lived with my grandma, she had one very similar...those were her favorite colors. Oh, she would've loved it."

"Yeah well, it's all right if you like birds, I guess." Keith sounded bored until he saw a tray full of hand-carved bottle stoppers. "Hey! Now there's something that's actually useful!"

Janet gave him an incensed look that faded into a disappointed shake of her head. Keith didn't appear to notice; he looked over the options and selected an oak stopper that was fashioned to look like the knob of a gear stick. After paying, he stuffed it in his pocket and glanced around for Janet. She was standing quietly beside him but kept glancing back at the pink birdhouse.

"Come on, it's getting late," he said gruffly and grasped her slender arm, his calloused fingers closing around it completely. "Time to get back to work."

As Keith led her out, Maiden couldn't help noticing the way Janet and Oliver's eyes met for a long, intent moment before she was dragged out into the sunshine. Oliver stared wordlessly at the doorway for a moment and then walked out as well.

Wow. Soap opera stuff, Maiden thought with a slight shake of her head. *Old Keith sure gets around.*

Her mind was ticking over all sorts of possible meanings behind the looks exchanged by the members of that unhappy trio. It appeared complicated, to say the least. From what they'd seen of his harsh behavior towards Timmy and Oliver, it was obvious that Keith was awful to work for. She couldn't imagine how miserable it would be working for him *and* dating him. Maiden was distracted from her musings when her father spoke up.

"You'd think a man with any sense would look after a lady like that a bit better," Alfie grumbled as he dropped Keith's money in the lockbox.

"You mean Janet?" She glanced at him. "Yeah, he wasn't especially nice to her."

"I was tempted to just give her that house," he sighed. "It's not even one of the more expensive ones."

"That's probably not the point, though," Maiden remarked. "It's the lack of interest that cuts deepest, I'd say."

CHAPTER FOUR

Maiden and Vonny left their father to bask in the glow of admiration that his birdhouses had garnered. They talked, laughed and wandered contentedly around the fair for hours.

They'd agreed weeks ago that they would have a whole day at Summerfest alone together. That was the real reason they hadn't invited Tony or anyone else.

While neither of them said it outright, they both knew that someday one or both of them would have a serious relationship and they'd never have as much time for each other as they did now. Neither of them wanted to waste the opportunities they had left.

They had both dated guys in the past, but nothing had progressed or even lasted for long. For Vonny, this was mostly because of her persistent, and so far unrequited, crush on Tony.

As for Maiden, she'd already been hurt more than once. She had gone out with a few men who had been attracted to her physically, but when it came to building a relationship, they'd turned out to be selfish and disinterested. She didn't like being used or disrespected and ended up dumping all of them early on.

She had done her best to learn from the painful and disappointing experiences and be more careful about who she let get close to her; she'd been single for a while now.

Maiden didn't overly mind. She got lonely sometimes, but she knew that was better than being stuck with some creep who would treat her badly. Her thoughts drifted to Janet; she wondered if Keith was any nicer to her when they were alone. Maiden pushed the somber concern away; Janet had looked disappointed, not scared. It was none of her business anyway, and she was not going to put a damper on the end of her special day with Vonny.

It was almost 6 o'clock; plenty of time for one more treat, and then they'd find some place to have dinner. It would be a perfect way to round out their sisterly outing. Despite the carousel disaster, Maiden had agreed to let Von choose their last stop; she had already guessed what it would be.

"Here we are!" Vonny twittered as she gestured with a flourish at the building that spread out before them. "The mirror maze!"

It had always been an absolute favorite for both of them. Somehow looking into silly distorting mirrors while bathed in psychedelic lights never got old. As they approached the entrance, Vonny turned to her with a pointed finger and a warning look; Maiden blinked at her.

"Do *not* look at the map before we go in!" she said sternly. "You ruined the corn maze last year by memorizing the way out before we even started!"

"I didn't mean to!" Maiden protested with a sigh. She *had* ruined it; they were in and out in five minutes because Vonny told her to lead the way. "You can take charge this time, all right?"

Von gave her the stink eye until Maiden held up her hands in mock surrender and shielded her face from the diagram posted by the door as if it were as bright as the sun. Von snorted and gave her shoulder a teasing swat.

Maiden had a peculiar memory; she could recall sights and sometimes conversations in startling detail, but only when she really took notice of them. This dubious 'gift' seemed to work against her as often as it did for her, so she rarely tried too hard to put it to any use.

The guy at the door smiled warmly as they approached; it only took a second to recognize Timmy. Judging by the way he was leering at them, he hadn't learned his lesson, despite Keith Haynes almost taking his head off for flirting with them earlier.

Maiden kept her expression polite, something Vonny didn't bother with. She handed him two tickets and breezed through the turnstile, grasping Maiden by the wrist and dragging her along behind her.

"Have fun ladies," Timmy called after them. "I'm jealous of how many times you'll get to look at yourselves!"

"Don't reply, you twit!" Von muttered when Maiden glanced back at the door. "Just keep walking."

Maiden followed her advice and shook off the moment's awkwardness. They stepped through a double row of heavy curtains and found themselves instantly enveloped in dim lights and whimsical, medieval music. Vonny grinned and bounced as the nostalgia washed over them both.

"Yes! This is perfect!" she squeaked excitedly. "It feels like we're teenagers again!"

"It'll be even better when we can see where we're going," Maiden laughed.

She waited a moment for her eyes to adjust to the darkened room. The show then began, bathing them in colorful lights. They headed towards the start of the maze and giggled when Vonny almost walked into her reflection.

"I'm very observant," she chuckled.

"Kind of like a parakeet." Maiden smirked. "You must have thought you'd found a new best friend."

"Whatever, brat." She wrinkled her nose at her.

The mirrors were angled perfectly to create the illusion of endless corridors. The lights shifted from purple to orange and then green, making every path look as though it led to a strange and otherworldly place. It was disorienting but fired the imagination at the same time.

They pressed on down a few long paths that turned so sharply that they both ended up bumping into the walls a few times. After another turn, the mirrors changed. Maiden walked down a row of the highly polished panels and grinned as her reflection twisted, stretched, and spread. Vonny stopped and pointed her backside at a rippled mirror that made it look as wide as the room.

"Hey, I finally have a bottom as juicy as yours, Mae," she said, giving it a little wiggle.

Maiden deployed the childhood codeword they'd agreed on to call each other a cow without getting in trouble for name-calling.

"Moo."

Maiden's more voluptuous figure used to be a source of frustration for her svelte sister. There had been a couple of unhappy years where they struggled even to be friends. But their relationship had mellowed to the point where Von could now tease Maiden without being mean.

They wove through the maze until they were effectively lost. Vonny appeared pleased by the novel experience; it was exactly what she'd insisted on. The lights and the music swept them away with the promise of whimsy and adventure.

After another ten minutes, however, the thrill had worn off. They weren't in a faraway land, and they'd been on their feet all day. As was often the case, Vonny was abruptly and completely over the situation.

"Okay, this was good; I have no idea where we are." Von turned to her with a satisfied nod. "I'm bored and hungry, so you can get us out now."

"What?" Maiden gaped at her. "This is what you demanded! A real, full-sized maze to get lost in! Don't you want to figure it out for yourself?"

"What did I just say?" Von asked patiently as she folded her arms.

"You're such a pain in the neck." She shook her head and ran an assessing eye over their surroundings.

With a forbearing sigh, Maiden took over leading the way. She wasn't sure where they needed to go, thanks to Vonny's insistence, but she knew roughly where they'd already been.

They wandered down a few dead ends before she got her bearings. The constantly dimming and color-changing lights didn't help much. It took a couple of twists and turns, but she was confident they were nearly at the exit when she rounded a corner and gasped loudly.

Vonny whipped around the bend to make sure she was all right and choked back a scream.

Keith Haynes was lying on the floor at the end of the maze; he was pinned beneath one of the heavy mirrored panels. He didn't move despite their noisy arrival, and a pool of blood had spread from underneath his head.

The multicolored lights shone down on his blank expression. His eyes were shut, but his mouth was open as if he'd been gasping for air, or screaming in terror.

Maiden's heart was pounding. She took a shaky breath and motioned for Vonny to stay back. Von paled, and her expression was anxious, but she pressed her lips together and nodded.

She looked around cautiously as she approached but saw no one except herself and Vonny, shaking and terrified, reflected hundreds of times over in the mirrors that still sat upright. It was disorienting and disturbing.

Maiden forced herself to keep moving and knelt beside Keith, taking care to avoid the spill of blood. Pushing away unpleasant flashbacks of the first time she'd found a body; she gave his shoulder a nudge. Nothing.

She steeled herself to touch him and pressed her fingers to his throat, searching for a pulse. Again, there was nothing, and his skin felt cold.

Maiden jerked her hand away and stood, pulling her phone from her back pocket. As she did so, her eyes stole over a small, boxy object that sat near the body.

She frowned in confusion. It was that pink and gold birdhouse that had been in her father's stall, the one Keith could've bought for Janet but ignored. Now it was sitting beside his cold, dead body.

She didn't take the time to consider the implications of that; she just dialed the police station. She grasped her phone in both hands to try to stop it shaking as she held it to her ear. A moment later she heard Nancy the receptionist's tranquil voice on the line.

"Golden Glen Police Department," she said. "How may I direct your call?"

"This is Maiden Harlow," she replied quickly and took a deep breath as she tried to keep her own voice steady. "My sister and I are in the mirror maze at the town carnival and we've found a dead body."

Maiden frowned and glanced over at Vonny and shrugged helplessly. On the other end of the line, Nancy had gone quiet for a heartbeat, but soon recovered.

"Could you repeat that, Miss Harlow?" she asked.

"We are in the middle of the mirror maze at the Spencer and Spencer carnival and we've found a dead man." She forced herself to speak slowly and clearly.

"All right, I'll just hand you over to the captain," Nancy murmured.

"No! I don't need to—"

"Miss Harlow? Is that you?" McAlister's deep voice cut off her complaint. "What's up?"

"Dead body," she said tightly, not certain why Nancy couldn't have relayed the message herself. "There is a dead body in the mirror maze!"

"Okay, take a deep breath. Now are you sure he's dead? Or even a real person?" He spoke very patiently. "It's a carnival after all, are you positive that it isn't one of the dumb gimmicks?"

"What?!" she demanded incredulously, feeling distinctly chilled as she stared back at the corpse that was bleeding out in front of her. "Are you serious?!"

"Are you sure it's real?" he repeated.

"I *highly* doubt that leaving the manager of the carnival crushed to death under a chunk of the demountable wall is part of the show, Captain!" she grated, growing steadily angrier at his unhelpful responses. "Do you want me to find someone and ask?!"

"Okay, stay calm, Miss Harlow." He sounded more serious now. "We're on the way. Where are you exactly?"

"*In the mirror maze!*" she said loudly and hung up. "Honestly! Am I speaking in code or something?!"

Vonny stared as Maiden took a moment to steady herself and then started furiously tapping at her phone again. Von glanced around as the lights kept changing color and the music droned on cheerfully; it was all perversely sinister and dangerous now.

Greg Smith finally wrenched his phone from his pocket. He was sitting in the passenger seat of Captain McAlister's car as they, along with two more officers driving behind them, tore out of the parking lot of the police station. The captain had only just informed him that Miss Harlow had reported an alleged casualty when his phone started to ring.

Greg looked down at the screen and saw Maiden's name displayed. He shut his eyes as he felt his stomach drop. The captain had gotten on his case before when he thought he was slipping information to his childhood friend. But he wasn't about to ignore her, especially if she'd found a body. He took a deep breath and raised the phone bravely to his ear.

"Hey, Maiden," Greg answered nervously and winced when McAlister looked over sharply. "Yes, of course we're on the way, we're driving there now. Are you okay? Good, no sign of anyone still hanging around? All right. Where? Okay, right at the end of the maze, yeah, I'll tell him."

"If she hadn't hung up, she could've told me that when I asked!" McAlister said loudly as he shifted gears angrily.

"What was that, Mae?" Greg asked. He stilled as she spoke and then lowered his voice discreetly. "I can't say that to him, Maiden, he's my boss."

McAlister grinned in spite of the situation and his own annoyance; he shook his head and flicked on the sirens.

CHAPTER FIVE

Maiden and Vonny were sitting on the ground, their eyes fixed on Mr. Haynes' body. It had been less than fifteen minutes since she'd called the police, but as they'd spent that time staring at a corpse, it felt more like years.

This wasn't Maiden's first experience standing guard over a body, but Vonny was clearly unnerved. Her big sister's hands trembled, and her breathing was shallow and anxious. Maiden reached over and put an arm around her.

They both tensed when they heard several voices approaching. She hoped it wasn't more fair-goers; it would be hard to keep people calm and away from any evidence.

They hadn't met up with anyone else since they entered, which was eerie but probably best all things considered. A moment later she recognized Captain McAlister's deep voice and relaxed a fraction.

Neither she nor Von got up as McAlister, Greg, and two other officers walked in along with a confused and scowling Timmy. He looked over at her and Vonny uncertainly, but his eyes quickly found the body.

"Mr. Haynes! No!" Timmy exclaimed with a tinge of raw panic and started towards him.

"Don't touch anything!" McAlister warned as he grabbed him by the shoulder and pulled him back.

"But...it's...it's Keith," he mumbled in obvious shock. "Oh, this is bad. This is so bad!"

Maiden pulled a face and hugged her knees to her chest; 'bad' was a bit of an understatement. She met McAlister's gaze when he glanced over and spotted them; she hugged herself a little tighter and sighed.

It had been about two hours since the mirror maze was closed off and all pedestrian traffic blocked from the area. David glanced at his notes and reviewed the progress they'd made so far.

"All right, the area's cordoned off and Doc Jenkins is examining the body," David said as he skimmed over his neat and concise handwriting.

"Yes sir." Officer Smith nodded dutifully.

"Ramirez is still doing a sweep of the interior and Briggs is stationed at the door. We'll have to wait to see what the doc has to say."

Absorbed as he was in his notes and the prospect of investigating another suspicious death, David hadn't heard Miss Harlow approach them and shut his eyes briefly when she spoke.

"Did you ask the doctor if he's sure the man's actually dead?" she inquired mildly as she pulled a bit of cotton candy from the bag she was holding and popped it into her mouth.

David mostly didn't smile as he slid his gaze to her. Her expression was somewhere between teasing and unimpressed; he knew she was still miffed, but he doubted it ran too deep. He flipped his notebook closed and turned to face her.

"Go and sit down, Miss Harlow," he said as he helped himself to a large piece of the spun sugar. "I'll deal with you in a minute."

"Something to look forward to." She flicked an unrevealing glance over him and turned and walked away.

David watched her go as he put the candy in his mouth and let it melt on his tongue. His eyes drifted from her bouncy ponytail all the way down to her sandals and back again as she sauntered over in her snug little shorts and perched on the hood of his car.

He pulled in a calm and steady breath. If it had been anyone else, he'd have already advised them to move it *immediately*. But considering that she looked like something out of the Dukes of Hazzard, he decided not to make an issue of it.

The sun dripped slowly lower in the sky; the fading light kissed her pale skin and dark hair with soft shades of orange and pink. He knew that his wandering thoughts were focused on the wrong body as he studied Miss Harlow's curvy figure silhouetted in the fading sunshine. It was a warm evening, and it was starting to feel warmer.

He hadn't spoken to her in a couple of weeks, but it seemed like it had been longer. He'd been busy and really had no excuse to drop in and see her. But here she was again, sitting on the hood of his car like a model in one of the posters he had on his bedroom wall when he was a teenager.

While he admitted to himself that he wasn't sorry to see her again, it was ironic that Miss Harlow turned up with another dead body. At least there was a chance this one wasn't a murder.

"Captain?"

"What?" David turned to Smith and then remembered that he'd been in the middle of a discussion. "Right. We need to find out how Keith Haynes happened to be right underneath that panel when it fell. There's also that birdhouse that was beside the body; I want to know what that's all about."

"Yeah, that was weird." Smith looked uncomfortable but quickly rallied and pointed past David's shoulder. "Oh good! There's the doc now!"

David glanced over and felt his jaw tighten and his shoulders tense when he also spotted Jenkins. The slender man had emerged from the house of mirrors and headed straight for Harlow, as opposed to the head of the police department, who he was meant to be directly reporting to.

"How lovely to see you again, Miss Harlow!" Jenkins smiled at her as he came and stood beside the car. "If you don't mind my saying it, you look quite fetching sitting there. You're like a postcard for Summer."

"Thank you, Doctor," she replied a touch shyly. "You're always so kind."

Dr. Jenkins was a surprisingly genial man, considering the grim nature of his profession. She'd met him after the murders at her family's hotel. He'd been quite nice to her from the start and seemed to have maintained that goodwill.

Maiden wasn't a fool and knew when she was being admired, which she was, but Jenkins was never creepy or offensive about it.

"Did you find this body as well?" he asked.

"Unfortunately," she sighed. "It's really not the sort of habit I want to cultivate."

"Certainly not," he chuckled and started pulling off his gloves. He glanced to his right and smiled again. "Ah, there you are, David."

"Yeah, here I am," McAlister said dryly. "I'm assuming you've finished your examination. Can we discuss it elsewhere?"

"There's really not too much to say." Jenkins shrugged and nodded to Maiden. "Nothing she won't have gleaned from finding the corpse, anyway. He was killed by a combination of the trauma to the back of his head when he hit the ground and the impingement on his lungs and other vitals; that was a lot of extra weight added to the equation."

"Thanks," McAlister murmured. "What about that bird-house next to the victim?"

"Oh." Maiden blinked up at him. "That. Yeah, that's one my dad made. I saw it in his stall this morning. Janet fell in love with it. I guess Keith might have gone back to get it for her."

"Who's Janet?" McAlister braced his hand against the roof of the car and just looked at her.

"She works here at the carnival; she was in the concession area earlier, but she may do more than that. I'm not sure." Maiden shrugged and smiled up at him. "But she appeared to be in some sort of a relationship with Keith Haynes. Although he didn't give the impression that he treated her well." She felt herself smile wider as she pointed towards the mirror maze. "Keith is the dead guy."

"Thanks for the heads up," he said with a tolerant smirk. "And how do you know all this?"

"Right place at the right time." She shrugged but gave a helpless laugh at his skeptical look. "Well what's *your* theory, Captain? How else would I know?"

"Why make a fuss about it anyway?" Jenkins smiled quizzically at McAlister. "Our dear Miss Harlow is an absolute font of useful knowledge that you didn't have to chase after. She's perched like a benevolent dove right here on the hood."

"So, your father made the birdhouse?" McAlister plowed on, ignoring both of their semi-reasonable arguments. "Fine. Where is he now?"

"Dad?" She stared at him with wide, startled eyes. "You don't think he was involved, do you?"

"Please answer the question," he said mildly.

"Well, I don't know!" She frowned and gestured towards the mirror maze again. "I've been in that overgrown music box for the past two hours. Where's Vonny, by the way?"

"She's sitting over there at one of many empty tables," McAlister said as he pointed towards a cozy plaza about thirty feet away from them. "Which is where most people would've gone if told to sit and wait."

Maiden followed his gaze and spotted Von at a table with her feet propped up on the neighboring chair, tapping away at her phone. She knew the plaza was there; she'd sat at one of those tables earlier. Dismissing that unwanted bit of acknowledgement, Maiden turned back to him with a scowl.

"You nodded in *this* direction," she told him grimly, fairly sure that it could have been true.

"No, I didn't," he replied. "I only said to sit and wait."

"So, you think I decided to wander over and sit on your stupid car for no good reason?" She exhaled loudly.

"There are many good reasons, Miss Harlow." Jenkins smiled fondly at her.

"Ease off, Doc, please." McAlister gave him a wry smirk, but his expression sobered when he turned back to Maiden. "Your interesting choice notwithstanding, could you please wait over there? I have a few details to discuss privately with the doctor."

"How strange then that you *both* approached *me*," she said as she slid to her feet and met his gaze with teasing defiance. "I should've swiped your keys and played with the siren while I was at it."

"Opportunity missed," he said with a faint smile.

David saw Miss Harlow try to hide her begrudging amusement as she walked away. The men watched her go but didn't speak until she was out of earshot. Jenkins slid him a sly look.

"Have you asked her out yet?" he murmured with a grin.

"No, of course not." David sounded as startled as he felt by the abrupt question.

"Brilliant, David. You might want to get cracking on that," Jenkins suggested dryly, but then got back to the matter at hand. "Anyway, I looked over that fallen panel. I'd say the fittings appeared damaged, not worn."

"Interesting," he mused as he picked up Miss Harlow's abandoned bag of cotton candy and pulled out another piece.

"It gets even more interesting," Jenkins warned. "I found a screwdriver and a metal file in the victim's pockets."

"Any sign of them having been used?" he asked after a considering pause.

"Yes, but not necessarily enough to cause a failure like that," Jenkins mused. "There were a few shavings, but it didn't look as though he had finished whatever he was trying to do."

"Right," David said as his gaze slid back to the maze.

He'd met Keith Haynes that morning when he and Smith responded to an anonymous tip that had been phoned in to the station.

A man called and spoke to Nancy in hushed tones, saying that someone was sabotaging the equipment at the Spencer and Spencer carnival. He warned that the patrons were in danger until the person responsible was caught.

Haynes had been annoyed when David told him about the call; he'd insisted that it was probably some crackpot that got thrills from scaring people. The closest the irate man came to cooperating was suggesting that David talk to the maintenance man, Oliver Armstrong.

He did so and found Armstrong far more polite than Haynes, but about as helpful. He had serenely assured David that any safety complaints were either false or exaggerated. He offered to show him the maintenance logs but acknowledged that the information wasn't necessarily relevant if sabotage was the issue. Armstrong insisted that Haynes was the most likely to know about any disgruntled employees or other threats to the running of the operation.

But now Keith Haynes was dead, and potentially because of unsafe equipment...or sabotage.

Maiden wandered over to the warmly lit plaza and settled next to Vonny without a word. She remained pensively silent as she watched McAlister and Jenkins talk. She wondered what had happened that the stubborn captain didn't want her to over-hear.

His secrecy annoyed her. She'd found the body after all; it's not like it had nothing to do with her. Admitting to herself that she really had no right to the information, and that sulking was futile at best, she shifted her thoughts to what she *did* know.

Keith Haynes had been crushed to death a few hours after publicly arguing with the head of maintenance about safety concerns.

Oliver Armstrong hadn't seemed at all worried about Mr. Hayne's claims, but now the man was dead. She wondered if Oliver would feel less confident now. What was it he'd told Keith earlier? That if anything happened, it was the fault of whoever *made* it happen. Was he suggesting that someone was deliberately damaging the attractions to make them unsafe? In light of what had happened to Keith, it was a very real and frightening possibility.

Her thoughts drifted to Janet. Would she have learned about Keith yet? It was obvious that the police were there, but not many people would know why, except for Timmy, of course.

The thought had barely crossed her mind when she heard raised voices approaching fast. She glanced over and saw both Janet and Gabby running towards the mirror maze. Maiden stared helplessly as they gasped and shook their heads in horrified disbelief.

A part of her wanted to rush over and try to help, but that felt intrusive somehow, perhaps because she barely knew them. She doubted that McAlister would welcome her interference either.

Officer Briggs, a shy but well-meaning young policeman, was stationed at the door. He spotted the pair plowing towards him and stepped courageously forward. He held up his hands to stop them, but it took him and Greg together to prevent the women from pushing him down and charging inside.

Janet was shaking, and tears streamed down her cheeks, leaving trails of blackest mascara in their wake.

"Is Keith in there?" she demanded as she pounded her small fists on her thighs. "Is he?!"

Maiden felt her chest tighten at the sight of the other woman's distress, but she was quickly distracted when she saw someone else approaching from the corner of her eye. She arched a brow.

In the few minutes since she'd seen him, McAlister had rolled his sleeves up to his elbows and undone another button on his shirt. The evening was warm, but it wasn't *that* warm. He looked really good too; his chest and forearms were well-toned and dusted with dark hair.

"You jerk," she whispered under her breath. Her eyes widened and flew to Vonny. Thankfully, she was watching the unfolding scene with a scowl. Deeply grateful that her sister hadn't heard her, Maiden also pulled her focus back to the drama.

"Settle down, ladies." McAlister walked over and started murmuring patiently to Janet and Gabby. His voice was like warm honey, smooth and soothing.

He sounds a heck of a lot sweeter than when he was trying to calm me down, Maiden thought grumpily. Vonny, who'd doubtless been texting the entire story to Tony, seemed to have made a similar observation.

"Captain Cutie-pie must have a thing for zebras," she suggested.

Maiden rolled her eyes and nodded. Janet staggered forward and collapsed against McAlister, her slender body wracked with grief. He looked startled as she tucked in close to him, sobbing pitifully, and buried her face in his collar.

As Vonny had noted, she'd changed into a flowing zebra-print dress with slits cut halfway up her thighs. The high mandarin collar was subtly seductive; it covered her décolletage despite her legs being at the mercy of the fickle breeze. The contrast made her figure appear exposed and yet jealously guarded.

Neither Maiden nor Vonny moved an inch while McAlister and Gabby both endeavored to lead the hysterical woman away from the entrance to the maze. Janet could barely stand and stumbled as she tried to walk. It was disturbing and horrible, and impossible to look away.

Maiden's sympathies were further tested, however, when she noticed the way Janet clung to McAlister's broad chest, digging her dainty little fingers into the fabric of his shirt. It was too tactile considering what she was crying about; Maiden then chided herself for being unkind.

When McAlister finally tore himself free, he shook his head and rubbed the red marks on his flesh where Janet had clawed him. He glanced immediately at Maiden and looked uneasy when he saw that she was watching. His indiscreetly obvious concern was then hidden away, but not soon enough to go unnoticed.

For her part, Maiden met his gaze but made a point of keeping her expression blank. She then checked the time on her phone and tapped her fingertips on the tabletop.

He frowned and took a large step away from Janet, waving Greg over and issuing some kind of instruction to him. Greg knelt in front of the woman and smiled kindly as he attempted to quiet her down.

McAlister muttered to himself and straightened his rumpled shirt as he walked towards them. Maiden reminded herself that looking angry would only subject her to more teasing from Vonny. But she *was* angry and didn't appreciate that he let Janet maul him while she was dismissively sent to sit and wait for hours.

She knew she was being unreasonable; he had been more or less pounced on and could hardly swat the poor woman away. But she'd just had a long, cozy sit-down with yet another corpse and wasn't in the best of moods. McAlister appeared to notice and stood a bit cautiously before their table.

"You didn't exactly step in to help," he pointed out quietly, and specifically to Maiden.

Vonny noticed and glanced up at him with a hint of pleased surprise; she went back to her phone with a quiet little smile and started typing again.

Maiden had locked eyes with McAlister and frowned questioningly. Was that a criticism...or an explanation? No, that was ridiculous; he didn't have to explain himself to her, and he knew it.

"You don't exactly appreciate it when I try to help," she replied as neutrally as she could.

"I'm assuming that's Janet?" He nodded over his shoulder in her direction.

"You mean the chick you were wearing like a scarf?" Vonny cut in dryly. "Yeah that's Janet. Classy of you to get her name, considering how much of her makeup is on your collar."

"That wasn't my idea," McAlister said mildly, submerging any other concerns and recovering his professionalism. "She was quite distraught."

"*We* weren't thrilled to find the body," Von retorted mercilessly as she gave him a cool look, "but I notice you didn't drive the zebra queen to frustrated shouting."

"I didn't need to get lucid information from her," McAlister said as he pulled out the chair across from Maiden and settled into it. "And since you're in such a talkative mood, Miss Harlow, you might try being more helpful. What time did you enter the mirror maze?"

"About 6 pm," Von said as she continued texting. "It was pretty empty, but there's usually a lull until evening when the night life starts up."

"And are you frequent partakers of this 'night life'?" McAlister pulled a notebook and pen from his pocket and started writing.

"No, not especially," Maiden replied, since he had looked at her when he asked it. "But we're in the hospitality industry so we see the trends."

"You didn't meet up with anyone in the maze?"

"The only person we saw was Timmy, he took our tickets and let us through the turnstile," she said, shaking her head once.

"How long were you in there before you found the body?" he asked.

Maiden pulled out her phone and checked the call log. "I called you at 6:22 so, twenty minutes or so."

"Did you notice anything else that was suspicious?" McAlister still kept his attention on her, although he flicked Vonny a glance once or twice. "Or potentially relevant?"

"We saw Mr. Haynes engaged in an argument with at least three different people throughout the day." Maiden brushed a lock of dark hair out of her face.

McAlister paused with his pen hovering above the page and met her deeply green gaze. He gestured for her to continue.

"He was fighting with Sam Chalmers this morning," Maiden began.

"Right before Greg saw us and waved." Vonny joined in long enough to stir the pot. "You probably don't remember though, you seemed too distracted to say hello."

"Very astute," McAlister said without looking away from Maiden. "Who's Sam Chalmers?"

"An event coordinator for the town," she explained, also ignoring Vonny's embarrassing petulance. "We were too far away to hear what they were fighting about, but they both looked furious. Then there was a brief snarling at Timmy, which was really embarrassing, but…"

"Don't leave me in suspense, Miss Harlow." He glanced up from what he'd been writing.

"We also walked into a sort of fight between Mr. Haynes and Oliver Armstrong, he's the head of maintenance," she murmured.

"Yes, I know." McAlister nodded. "What was the fight about?"

"Keith accused him of negligence." Maiden rubbed her arms. "He claimed some of the attractions were unsafe."

McAlister arched a brow and tapped his pen firmly on the paper. It was clear that he'd rather she'd shared that particular tidbit a while ago. Before he could voice his annoyance, a frantic Janet again descended upon them.

"No! That's not true!" she exclaimed as she ran over to them, clutching a tissue in her hands. "Oliver would never hurt any-one!"

"I also think Janet and Oliver might be having some kind of a thing," Maiden whispered deliberately loudly before sliding her gaze back to the tearful lady. "We *did* hear them fighting, but I'm not suggesting anything more than that."

"Don't get the wrong idea, please." Janet shut her eyes and put a hand to her head as though it ached. "I love Keith, Oliver is just a very nice person. We're friends that's all, but Keith still hated him."

"Did he suspect you were involved with Mr. Armstrong?" McAlister started writing again.

"He tended to suspect that I was involved with every man I met," she said wearily. "I don't know what more I could have done to convince him not to worry. I guess that doesn't matter now."

She buried her face in the tissue, and her waifish shoulders shook with renewed grief. Gabby stood behind her, very much in the shadow of the dramatically lovely woman, and seemed to be dealing with her own distressed feelings. McAlister glanced up with a carefully neutral expression when Maiden pushed to her feet.

She walked around and guided Janet to the nearest chair. She made a point of reaching over and giving Gabby's shoulder a comforting squeeze before turning a kind smile on Janet.

"Are you all right?" Maiden asked gently.

"I-I will be, thank you, beautiful." She smiled weakly and dabbed at her eyes as she sank into the seat.

"Who told you about what happened?" Maiden kept her voice soft. McAlister wasn't the only one who was used to dealing with unhappy strangers; she'd worked in the family's inn since she was a teenager.

"Hmm? Oh, Timmy did." She let out a shaky breath as she struggled to organize her thoughts. "He was pacing around and looked really upset; we asked him what was wrong...so he told us."

"I'm so sorry," Maiden said as she sat in the chair on her left, placing Janet between the captain and herself. "When did you last see Keith?"

McAlister glanced up at her only to be met by the stoniest expression she could conjure up; he kept quiet and held his pen poised above the page.

"We visited that cute little market stall. Oh, you were there!" Janet blinked at her and smiled weakly. "I remember seeing you, that's right. That was about 2 o'clock maybe? After that I went back to the concession stands to help out, and Keith said he had some work to do in the office. We were supposed to meet up for dinner, but..."

Janet trailed off and stared forlornly down at the table. Maiden decided to push the boundaries further and glanced over at Gabby, aware that McAlister might not know who she was yet.

"So Gabby," Maiden sat back a little, "you're the office manager, you must have seen Keith after Janet went back to work, right?"

Maiden slid her gaze to McAlister; she could see the storm clouds gathering when he slowly looked up at her through his eyebrows and gave him a wink. He stilled at the unexpected familiarity, and his expression regained a measure of tolerance, but she suspected it would be wise to back off at that point.

"I did, yes," Gabby replied carefully. "He came in and started going over the ticket sales, he always checked the numbers after lunch and then again at the end of the day. He liked to keep track of how everything was going."

"And how was everything going?" McAlister asked impassively.

"Good, we've been busy." She smiled a little sadly and settled her gaze on her feet. "I'm not sure how we'll go after this though."

"It's too soon to speculate about much of anything, unfortunately." McAlister shrugged. "Do you know where Oliver Armstrong is?"

"No idea, sorry." Gabby shook her head. "I haven't seen him in a while. Do you want me to find him?"

"Yes, thanks." He gestured towards Greg. "Officer Smith will go with you."

Greg stepped forward and motioned for her to proceed. Gabby looked a tad unsettled at the prospect of a police escort but turned and headed back into the heart of the carnival without complaint.

Maiden watched them leave and noticed that there was a tear in the back of Gabby's left pant leg. She thought back to when she'd met her earlier. No, the hole hadn't been there then. McAlister's deep voice returned her attention to the others sitting at the table.

"So, Miss—" He gave Janet a prompting look.

"Lee," she supplied quietly. "Janet Lee."

"Miss Lee." He made another note. "Are you aware of anyone that would have reason to harm Keith Haynes?"

"Oh, that's a tricky one." She shut her eyes and sighed. "Keith could be very hard to deal with. He didn't have a lot of friends, I'm afraid."

"How was he hard to deal with?" he asked.

"He had a temper, and he was quick to tell people off," Janet mumbled, almost as if Keith's behavior embarrassed her. "If any of the staff got out of line he could be really harsh."

"Okay, but are you aware of anyone that might have actually hated him?" he pressed. "Enough to try and harm him?"

"I don't know, the crew always treated him with respect. That may have been out of fear, though. Hate is a strong word, but it's certainly possible...you see a lot of things in this line of work." She sniffled and skimmed a hand over her pale hair. "People who live on the road like this and just chew up one small town after another, it's a different mindset, a different outlook on life. Sometimes the conventional lines get blurred."

"What about Timmy Gibson?" Maiden asked, hoping to get her focused on specific people rather than the dramatic soap opera she seemed to be trying to concoct.

I really am being nasty about this woman, she chided herself again.

"Oh no!" Janet managed a somber chuckle. "Timmy's a big dumb kid. He threatens and snarls a lot, but he's all bark and no bite."

"Did he ever threaten Mr. Haynes?" McAlister resumed, giving Maiden a warning look.

"I wouldn't go so far as to say he threatened him," Janet demurred, twisting her crumpled tissue. "But...he did mention something about us all being better off if Keith was, well, gone."

"When was this?" McAlister watched her closely.

"Last week maybe, I don't remember exactly. I didn't pay too much attention; he complains a lot, but it's just talk." She shrugged and sank wearily into the chair.

Maiden studied her subtly. Janet's eyes were reddened, and she looked drained. She thought about what she'd said about Timmy; it was certainly possible that he hated Keith. She only had to think back to their embarrassing clash at the merry-go-round a few hours ago. But he'd seemed genuinely shocked when he saw Keith dead. Her attention went back to Janet when the lady slid her eyes back to McAlister.

"Officer?" she asked softly.

"Captain," he corrected absently.

"I'm sorry." Janet sniffled. "What's going to happen now? To...to Keith, I mean?"

"The coroner will look after that," he said tactfully. "Do you know of any next of kin that should be alerted?"

"Um, no, I don't think he had any family." She shook her head and shuddered. "Gabby might know of someone, she's worked with him for the past two years. I only joined the crew six months ago."

You've only been here six months, and you were already dating the boss? Maiden's eyes widened a fraction. *Interesting. I wonder how the rest of the troupe felt about that.*

She thought back to the obvious annoyance on the face of Janet's workmate earlier and the ill-timed cigarette break that caused it. If Janet was taking advantage of her relationship with Keith, and after only recently joining, it could have ruffled some feathers. Maiden was again distracted by the captain's deep voice.

"Thank you for your time; we'll leave it there for tonight, Miss Lee," McAlister said mildly. "Let me know if you think of anything else. And no one leaves town, understood?"

"Yes, of course, sir." She pushed to her feet and gave him and Maiden a feeble smile. "Thanks."

Janet walked slowly away from the table. She shivered and hugged herself as she glanced one more time at the mirror maze before wandering off the way she had come.

Maiden watched her until she was out of sight and then turned back to McAlister. He was looking down at his notepad, reviewing what he'd already written. She was reminded of the extra shirt button he had undone as her gaze fell unwillingly to the glimpse it revealed of his hairy chest. She wet her lips and distantly wondered if this was what guys went through when they saw cleavage, but she pushed the thought aside when he glanced up at her with an arched brow.

"So, where's your dad?" he asked.

"I've been with you all this time, Captain," Maiden pointed out, trying not to get anxious over Alfie. "If you haven't seen him, how could I have?"

"I'm starting to think you're shielding him," he said impassively and without breaking eye contact.

"By voluntarily telling you that the birdhouse found by the body was one of his?" She pulled a face. "If that's what you call 'shielding' people, I'm pretty lousy at it."

"By acting like you don't have his phone number or even a general awareness of his habits, despite living in the same apartment." McAlister's tone was steady, and he kept his gaze trained on her.

"So, I'm allowed to do your legwork when it suits you?" she asked sardonically. Even she knew she was being obstinate, but she couldn't seem to reel it in.

"Pretty much." His voice rose just enough to betray his growing irritation.

"Allow me, please. Not that anyone remembers I'm here," Vonny chuckled and put her phone to her ear. "Dad? Where are you? Okay, we'll be along soon. Bye."

Maiden and McAlister were still staring each other in the eye, locked in an incredibly small and pointless battle of wills when Von ended the call and slapped her hands loudly on the table to get their attention. Maiden jumped and glared at her sister, who smiled innocently at them both.

"Dad's home already, which must be nice," she said sweetly and rested her chin in her hand. "So now what? Do you want me to leave so you two can fight some more?"

"We're not fighting," they said in scowling unison.

"Obviously not, what was I thinking?" Vonny laughed as she stood. "Well, if it's all the same to everyone, I'll head back to the car and wait for you, Mae. Try not to be all night. See ya, Captain."

Maiden tossed her the keys and stared down at her lap as she listened to Von walk away. She felt suddenly uneasy being left alone with the handsome policeman. While there were more officers on the scene now, they were several yards from where they sat with only Janet's empty chair between them.

She made herself face McAlister only to find him preoccupied with putting his notebook back in his pocket. She couldn't tell if he was as uncomfortable as she was, but he probably wasn't as affected by their being alone together.

That stark and unflattering flash of reality chased away her threatening shyness. She sat straighter and regarded him with feigned aplomb.

"Well, what are you going to do, Captain?" she asked. "Do you plan to talk to Dad tonight?"

"No, I have too much to do here," he murmured and glanced over at the mirror house. "I'll come by tomorrow morning."

"Okay, fine." She nodded and rested her hands on her thighs. "Well, was that all then?"

"No, not quite." He turned back to her with a serious look. "Miss Harlow, you need to drop this habit you have of running straight to Officer Smith whenever you don't get what you want."

And you're a complete loon, she thought to herself as her mouth fell open at the excessive suggestion. She still strove for a slightly less inflammatory response.

"It's a habit now, is it?" She quirked a dark brow. "And by 'not getting what I want', I assume you mean useful assistance during a frantic and potentially dangerous situation?"

"You hung up on me, Harlow," he reminded her, his professionalism slipping with the resurgence of his irritation. "It's not as if I refused to speak to you."

"You were patronizing, Captain," she retorted. "I don't like that so I stopped listening to it."

His dark eyes locked on hers, and he drummed his fingers on the table. "I was trying to calm you down."

"I was keeping myself plenty calm until you started treating me like a five-year-old." She took a steadying breath that did nothing to steady her.

"You overreacted," he said tightly.

"I was standing over a corpse while also having to convince you of the fact!" she said incredulously. "Why do you care if I call Greg anyway?"

"Because you're trying to get around me and that's annoying." His voice stayed even, but his drumming grew louder.

"I was yelling at you *through* him," she said. "Believe me, you were always involved."

McAlister glanced away, sinking back into the chair with a loud sigh. Maiden felt her exasperation ease off, maybe because he didn't look angry anymore. When he faced her again, he had his impassive cop expression back in place.

"Well, if you want to yell at me in future, Miss Harlow," he said dryly, "I'd prefer that you did your own dirty work."

"That sounds very fair, Captain McAlister," she agreed, but then scoffed under her breath. "Yeah right, *'if'.*"

He clearly heard her, though, and coughed in a failed attempt to cover his laugh. He pushed to his feet and stepped away without looking at her again.

"That's all for tonight, Miss Harlow."

CHAPTER SIX

Maiden walked swiftly back through the carnival. Everything seemed a bit subdued since the cops turned up, but there were still some people wandering around. The rides were running, but most people were gathered in little groups talking as they pointed in the direction of the mirror maze. She wondered how far the rumors had spread and if anyone had an inkling of what had brought the police in.

Maiden was weaving through the crowd and heading for the banner that marked the carnival's entrance when she saw Greg standing near the concession trucks saying something into his radio.

She was curious but determined to mind her own business and started walking straight past. He spotted her, however, and waved her over discreetly. After glancing around for any sign of McAlister, Maiden hurried over to him.

"Mae," he said in a low and worried voice as he grasped her wrist and pulled her towards the alley behind the trucks. "We have a problem."

"What is it?" she asked and glanced down the alleyway.

She blinked owlishly when she saw Oliver Armstrong sprawled on his back with his head cradled in Janet's lap. The lady was frowning down at him and smoothing a hand over his hair, but her tears seemed to have run dry. Gabby was standing nearby, wringing her hands anxiously.

Next to Gabby was the purple-haired woman she'd seen in the ticket booth earlier. She was looking down at Oliver with an uncertain scowl. The studded details on her tightly laced corset gleamed in the floodlights above them. Her bright hair glowed, and her heavily painted eyes were intent; she looked like something out of a storybook.

Maiden edged closer to Greg as he turned to her. She wet her lips and nodded towards the colorful group.

"What's going on?" she asked quietly. "Is Mr. Armstrong okay?"

"I've sent for an ambulance, he's alive but unconscious." He gave her an earnest look. "I had to call it in, there's not much time before Captain McAlister gets here."

"All right, what is it you want to tell me?" she asked with a nod.

"Some of the carnies heard your dad fighting with Keith Haynes this afternoon. Apparently it got a bit heated." He pulled an apologetic face. "I just wanted to warn you. I'm pretty sure the captain will follow it up personally, *please* don't tell him I gave you the heads up."

"Don't worry, I won't." She glanced around and gave his hand a grateful squeeze as she stepped away. "Thank you, Greg."

Her stomach churned as she hurried out of the carnival and then through the markets, which now felt frustratingly huge. She needed to get home and talk to her parents; she was desperate enough to jog the rest of the way back to her car. Maiden wasn't built for running and avoided it whenever possible.

She reached the car to find Vonny waiting in blissful ignorance. She had the passenger seat reclined and was still tapping away at her phone when Maiden opened the door and sat down behind the wheel.

She took a moment to catch her breath and tried to steady her thoughts. It had been a long and very strange day, and it had the potential to get much worse now. Vonny, oblivious to her sister's distress, glanced over at her with a smirk.

"Tony wants to know if Captain Cutie-pants offered to buy you dinner after keeping you out so late," she chuckled.

"Tell him to stop being stupid, and feel free to do the same," Maiden grumbled as she started the car and pulled out of the parking space. "We have bigger problems now."

"Like what?" Vonny asked as she moved her seat upright again.

"Some of the carnival crew saw Dad arguing with Keith Haynes today," she said as she turned onto the main road and headed back to the inn. "And that dumb birdhouse was by the body. It's a weird coincidence. It's potentially very bad."

"So, does your little boyfriend think Dad murders people and leaves birdhouses as calling cards or something?" Von demanded incredulously.

"He had a public fight with the deceased and something distinctly his was found at the crime scene," Maiden retorted. "My little boyfriend can add two and two!"

"All right, all right," Vonny relented, but rolled her eyes. "Sorry, Mrs. McAlister."

"Did you tell Mom and Dad about what happened, or were you only thinking of Tony?" Maiden asked, ignoring her sister's attempt to get a rise out of her.

"What's that supposed to mean?" she snapped.

"*Von!*" Maiden said sternly.

"I thought we'd tell them when we got home," she admitted quietly, and then added as a very improvised afterthought, "why worry them when there's nothing they could've done anyway?"

"Always thinking of others." Maiden smiled wryly despite the anxiety growing inside her.

It was late by the time they arrived back at Harlow House, and everything was peacefully closed up for the night. Maiden led the way to the side door and through the office. The foyer was empty and quiet. She'd forgotten all about Billie helping at reception and couldn't help noticing that the desk was cleaner than it had been in recent memory.

They went straight to their apartment on the second floor, taking care to walk softly past the occupied guest rooms. Maiden stepped through the front door and was immediately grateful to be back in the warm and familiar surroundings of their family home.

Von bolted the door behind them, and they both turned and looked into the large, open-plan room. Everything was still, and most of the lights were off, the exception being the light that hung above the kitchen table.

Maiden stilled and frowned when her eyes rested on their mother. Gloria was sitting at the head of the long table, staring sullenly at a collection of pies. Each one had a slice cut out of it and served up on a small plate. It looked like she'd only taken a bite or two of each.

"Hey, Mom," she said kindly as she and Vonny drew closer. "How's the recipe hunt going?"

"I *thought* it was goin' just fine," Gloria grumbled, "until her royal highness went on a rampage!"

"That doesn't sound like Kylie's style," Von said dubiously as she looked the older woman over. "Why are you covered in dough? Have you given up and decided to crawl into a pie yourself?"

Gloria's bouncy blonde curls were swept up in a paisley handkerchief, which was heavily dusted with flour; so was the frilly pink apron she had tied tight around her stout waist.

"Oh, hush up," she said with less gusto than usual.

"Well, what happened?" Maiden sat beside her and rested a hand on her forearm.

"Kylie knows nothin'," Gloria informed them dourly. "I pulled all these beautiful recipes out of the family archives, made them with love and care, and she picked them all to pieces."

"Even your pecan pie?" Vonny stared incredulously as she pointed to the dish in question.

"'The crust tastes like you bought it from a grocery store!'" Gloria said in a mockingly childish tone. "Her very words! I almost smacked her!"

"You don't use store-bought crust, do you?" Maiden gave her a questioning look.

"It's a prototype!" Gloria exclaimed and fisted her pudgy hands. "That's what I told the little hag, but she just turned her nose up and started blatherin' on about artistry and purity and a whole lot of other garbage!"

"Well, that's kind of her thing." Maiden attempted a reasonable tone.

"I don't know about any of that, but I'll tell you this much," Gloria glared at them, "if that girl points her wooden spoon at me one more time, she's gonna find it rammed somewhere she don't want it to be!"

"So many possible options spring to mind," Maiden whispered under her breath before turning back to her mother. "When did you have time to make all these anyway? I thought you were on the desk all day."

"I had Billie to help; it was fine," Gloria said distractedly and poked at the charred crust of an overcooked pumpkin pie.

"Does she even know the computer system?" Maiden tried not to sound as worried about it as she felt.

"I was right up here, she knew to call me if she got stuck." She waved it away. "That's irrelevant anyway, the important thing is gettin' that twerp Kylie to listen to reason and do what I say. I'm the boss, after all, not her."

"She did train professionally," Vonny pointed out. "Why not just let her do the heavy lifting?"

"*Because I know how to make pie!*" Gloria retorted sharply, but then her eyes widened and she put a finger to her lips. "Oh, keep it down! Alfie's in bed."

"Yeah, my bad for screaming maniacally about dessert," Von said dryly, but then arched a chestnut brow. "Dad's already asleep?"

"He said he had a big day, lots of customers." She shrugged.

"That's unfortunate, we kind of needed to talk to him," Maiden sighed. "The sooner the better."

"Why, what's happened?" Gloria glanced at her curiously.

"We found a dead man in the mirror maze this evening. He was crushed under one of the big mirrors." Maiden rubbed her arms against a sudden internal chill.

"What? My poor babies, that's awful!" Gloria's soft brown eyes widened. "Who was it?"

"Keith Haynes. He was the manager of the carnival." Vonny tapped on the top of the pumpkin pie with a dubious expression; it made an odd, thudding sound under her prodding. "He was kind of a sleazeball."

"Well, yeah, that's the impression he gave," Maiden said with a conceding nod.

"Was it an accident?" Gloria asked as she picked at the dough that had dried on her nails.

"No one's said yet." Maiden took a deep breath. "But...some of the crew said they saw Dad arguing with the guy earlier today."

"Well, Alfie wouldn't have hurt anybody!" Gloria looked aghast at the notion.

"We know that, Mom. We never thought he would." Maiden reassured her. "But it could make him appear suspicious, especially since one of his birdhouses was sitting beside the body."

"One of *Alfie's* birdhouses? Are you sure?" Gloria gasped.

"I suppose it could've been one of the many other handmade birdhouses floating around town these days," Von said sarcastically. "You doggone kids and your wild weekends spent carousing and woodworking."

"Anyway." Maiden ran a hand over her hair. "When did Dad get home from the markets?"

"Maybe 7 o'clock or so," Gloria guessed as she thought about it. "But are you sure this Keith guy wasn't killed in an accident? You said somethin' fell on him."

"It could have been," Maiden allowed in a tone that she knew sounded unconvinced. "I said we found a dead man, I never said he was murdered."

"Well, what's the problem then?" Gloria shook her head, sending flour sprinkling around her like a whisper of fresh snow.

"It just seems a bit weird," Maiden said pensively. "Keith Haynes had three heated arguments today, four if we count Dad, and then he's crushed to death by a mirror panel? The only one in the entire maze that fell over?"

"That is pretty odd," Gloria admitted.

The women sat in grim and heavy silence for a moment. In all likelihood, they had another murder on their hands, and Alfie had been seen arguing with the victim not long before his death. It wasn't good.

"But on the brighter side, Captain McCutie is on the case." Vonny looked at Gloria with a pleased smirk.

"Oh goody!" She clasped her hands together and turned to Maiden with a delighted smile. "Did he question you himself?"

"Yes, he did, but that's his job," Maiden exhaled wearily. "It means nothing."

"Then why did he almost apologize to you when Janet tried to climb him?" Vonny retorted, knowing full well she'd just thrown fuel on the fire.

"What? Who's Janet? Am I gonna hate her?" Gloria looked giddy and started serving slices of pie. "Oh, this is so excitin'! Tell me everything that happened!"

Maiden glared at her sister and folded her arms across her chest. Von ignored her irritation and happily took up the narrative. She described the day in minute detail, to Gloria's sheer delight. From McAlister's initial snub to Timmy's embarrassing flirting and subsequent telling off, and finally, Janet's tawdry fumbling.

"Oh, will you please stop it." Maiden rolled her eyes. "She was hysterical over losing her boyfriend, you make it sound like she was offering to bear McAlister's children."

"She's too skinny to have children. She's probably hollow inside," Vonny teased, ironically so, since she and Janet were a similar build. She then pointed a finger at Maiden. "And you weren't impressed either, I saw it and so did McAlister, that's why he tried to explain himself."

"He didn't," she grumbled, hoping she wasn't blushing.

"Maiden," Von gave her a speaking look, "come on. I was sitting right beside you. He pushed her off and immediately checked to see if you'd seen it all, and he was worried that you did."

Maiden couldn't honestly deny that, so she shook her head and busied herself with the pecan pie she'd been served instead. Von took that as a victory and gave a smug and satisfied nod.

"Well, I hope you were careful." Gloria considered her youngest daughter with a sage look and held up a finger tipped with a dough-encrusted acrylic nail. "You don't wanna come across as bad-tempered, but you can't be too permissive either. There's a delicate balance you need to maintain there."

"Can I please remind you both that I am *not* dating this man?" Maiden said as clearly as she knew how.

"Not with that attitude," Vonny said under her breath.

"*And,*" she continued loud enough to drown out Von's sarcasm, "we need to be more interested in Dad right now. This is serious, we could be talking about murder. We need to make sure he doesn't get drawn into any nasty allegations."

"Oh it'll be fine, angel. Don't you worry about that." Gloria batted her concerns away as she plopped a slice of apple pie in front of her. "You'll figure it all out."

The following morning, David stood at his kitchen window, sipping coffee and staring out at the large oak trees that dotted his backyard.

He'd been raised in a suburban neighborhood and had grown up with a small yard, but that faded into a forgotten luxury when he became a cop and moved to a bigger city. The only charm or character of his cramped apartment had been a fire escape with a view of the building next door.

What he had now was worlds away. The house he'd bought was on a large lot with thick grass and plenty of trees. It would mean a bit of yard work, but he didn't mind; it was a very welcome change. A pair of fat squirrels chased each other up the nearest tree; David smiled at their antics.

Much nicer than seeing rats scuttling around trash cans, he thought to himself.

He couldn't pinpoint the exact moment that he had started to want something different in his life. He'd loved the hustle and pace of Stanton when he first moved there; it was fast and exhilarating and very different from what he'd grown up with.

Somewhere along the line it stopped being exciting and became routine. There was never time or opportunity for much of a life outside of work. It was hard to meet people and even harder to get close to them. The friendships had taken ages to build and still seemed shallow.

He had dated a few women, but the relationships had gone nowhere. They'd all been so focused and career-driven. He respected that; he had been the same. He'd worked hard and made progress at a young age. By the time he'd made captain, he became more content. He still loved his work, but he wanted a life when he went home as well.

It didn't take long to get tired of dating someone he rarely spent time with. He knew that he'd never been in love; he wasn't even sure what that felt like. His father had taught him never to promise a woman anything he wasn't willing to give, so he never did. His interest hadn't run deep, and he never pretended otherwise, so the relationships didn't last.

After his last breakup, he had stopped trying to meet anyone. Stanton had become anonymous and lonely; it didn't feel like home anymore. He didn't want to spend another decade there.

A little time passed, and he started looking at jobs in different places. He hadn't expected to find anything anytime soon, but then the position in a small town called Golden Glen popped up and he went for it.

It had been life-changing in several ways. Golden Glen wasn't quite like the town he grew up in and was nothing even close to the coldly industrial Stanton. The people here were nicer; they'd make eye contact and smile when they passed by on the street. And some of the women were...extra nice.

He sipped his coffee and considered the prospect of another case involving Maiden Harlow. It had been a bit embarrassing that she'd picked the killer for his first big case, but he wasn't that broken up about it. She had seen things that he hadn't, and she was clever enough to put it all together. He was okay with that.

She had been classy about it, too. She didn't make a big deal of what she'd done, even though others did. He'd read the glowing articles the Gazette had written, but noticed that never once was she directly quoted; she hadn't spoken to the press.

And now, here they were again. She had found another body, and he wasn't entirely sure how he felt about it.

He hadn't officially stated whether they were treating Keith Haynes' death as a homicide. It could have been a fluke or, even more likely, he could have gotten caught in his own mischief.

David thought back to the anonymous warning they'd received yesterday morning. Haynes had seemed dismissive when he'd told him about it, but considering the tools found in the man's pockets when he died, sabotage was starting to sound more plausible.

David had investigated enough murder cases to know a suspicious death when he saw one. He was dealing with a murder;

he was certain of that, even though he wasn't planning to make it known yet.

He wondered what Harlow's gut told her. He was pretty sure she would be on the same page; she'd seen too much to think anything else.

David pinched the bridge of his nose and sighed. At some point he had started thinking of her as 'Harlow' and it had stuck almost immediately. He did his best to address her more formally to her face and add 'Miss', but he slipped up a few times, and he knew it.

He checked the time; it was almost 7:30. He'd gotten up around sunrise and gone for a run. He sometimes did that before work, but not usually when he was first starting a case. He tended to save his energy until he had a handle on things.

In this instance, he needed to clear his head, mainly because he'd dreamed that Harlow had dragged him into the backseat of his car and asked him to show her how his handcuffs worked.

You've got problems, David. He smirked at himself. *One of them is that you wake up too soon.*

He considered Doc Jenkins' question from last night—*Have you asked her out yet?* There was no 'have you thought about' or 'should you maybe consider'. *Yet.* It was a foregone conclusion.

The pressure was starting to build, and that gave him pause. They'd met last month and hadn't spent that much time together; it wasn't as if they knew each other. But the chemistry had been instant, and it was intense. That had never happened to him before, and it scared him.

He was close to being out of his depth, but he knew himself and he knew how easily he could get carried away with someone like her; he needed to keep a tight grip on the reins.

"Settle down, McAlister," he muttered into his coffee. "You'll see her today and you need to be able to look her in the eye. Murder case; try thinking about that."

Maiden sat behind the front desk and patted back a yawn. She was still tired and full from last night, so she'd opted to have an extra cup of coffee and skip breakfast.

It had been a long evening thanks to another corpse, a late dinner and an embarrassing amount of conjecture from Gloria and Vonny about her non-existent love life.

In the end, Maiden had laid her head down on the table and dozed off while the other women speculated on whether Captain McAlister would go so far as to arrest Alfie as an excuse to see Maiden again.

Added to that inane twaddle was the impromptu tasting of some surprisingly mediocre pies. She had been diplomatic, and Vonny had been less blunt than usual, but she'd expected far better. She now wondered if growing up with a southern mom who loved to cook had led her to just assume the lady was great at making everything.

By the time she had forced down a bite of the fourth over-ly-sweet pie with its hard, crumbly crust, she was ready to suggest that Gloria stick with mashed potatoes and fried chicken. But cowardice won the battle, so she said she was exhausted and went to bed.

Now, in broad daylight, with a somewhat restless night since the discovery of Keith's body and her last encounter with McAlister, Maiden was wary and alert.

Her nerves were further tested when she glanced over and saw Kylie meekly approaching. She was carrying a tray with a steaming cup and a plate of something. As she drew closer, Maiden's heart sank and dread unfurled within her; it was a piece of pie.

"Good morning," Kylie said with a shy smile as she set the tray on the desk. "I was wondering if I could offer you a little snack?"

"Wow, thanks Kylie." Maiden eyed the plate as if it might explode. "It looks great...but I'm pretty full at the moment."

"Oh." Kylie's smile faded; she looked so small and disappointed. "I see. It's just that I was hoping you could give me your honest opinion, that's all. I don't want to ask Gloria yet; I doubt she'd tell me if she liked something that I made. But I really do need impartial feedback."

Maiden met her earnest gaze and felt herself weaken. Kylie was so nice and so hesitant to ask for anything. She didn't have the heart to turn her down. She glanced at the beautifully presented dessert and only hoped she had the stomach to humor her.

"I also brought you some coffee," Kylie said more brightly as she set a steaming cappuccino beside the plate.

"You're sweet." Maiden smiled weakly and picked up the fork, staring resignedly down at the pie. *So disgustingly sickly sweet.*

The pie was neatly plated; the crust looked tender, and the filling was firmly set. It looked like the work of a pro and, frankly, far better than any of Gloria's efforts. Maiden took a tiny nibble and suddenly felt hungrier. She sat a little straighter and smiled at the watchful chef.

"This is great!" she said and took another bite. "What is it?"

"It's my take on Cheese Danish." Kylie smiled modestly. "In pie form."

"I love it," Maiden said sincerely, but then her eyes flew to Kylie's. "Do *not* tell Mom I said that!"

Kylie beamed, by her standards at least. She squared her shoulders and clasped her hands in front of her. Her smile was quietly pleased and perhaps a tad smug.

"I'd never cause trouble in the family, Maiden," she assured her, although her expression held a watchful, pitiless calm. "But I am a little concerned about this collaboration that your father's orchestrated. Quite frankly, Gloria's techniques aren't very refined. I'm not being mean, it's simply the truth. And I don't particularly want my name put on that sort of effort."

"Mm," was the closest Maiden was willing to come to agreeing with her, but she definitely saw her point. "I'd say you and Mom both have very different approaches to...pie and things."

"Yes." She nodded and held her gaze for a long, intense moment. "I'm not sure what to do about it. It needs to be sorted out, but kindly and sensitively. It's tricky, isn't it, Maiden?"

Maiden stared at her, but then looked away with a sigh as the real purpose of Kylie's visit became clear. On top of her mother's unquestioning confidence that she could keep Alfie out of trouble, she was now expected to sort out the pie battle as well.

"I'll give it some thought," she said as she pulled the plate and the coffee a bit closer.

"Thank you." Kylie smiled serenely. "I know you'll be fair and do what's best for Harlow House. This is about the greater good, isn't it?"

That seemed to be an ominous overstatement, but Maiden didn't want to encourage more discussion by mentioning it.

Kylie silently reclaimed her tray and slunk back to her kitchen lair with needless stealth.

Maiden shook her head and propped her chin in her hand. She heard the shuffling of papers in the next room and glanced over at the slightly open door to the office. Alfie was in there whiling away the time with some paperwork as they waited for the police to turn up and question him.

Maiden had taken him aside as soon as he left his bedroom that morning and told him about what had happened. Alfie wasn't terribly concerned, apart from the annoyance of having to wait before opening his market stall for the day. She could only hope he'd show a little more sensitivity when speaking to the police.

Time dragged on with no word from McAlister. She had been sure he'd come early, but it was already almost 10 am and he hadn't turned up. Maiden was running out of odd jobs to keep herself distracted.

She assured herself that no one would really suspect her father of anything sinister. He was harmless; everyone knew that. She chewed at her lip and finally turned to her last resort; she opened the drawer to her left and pulled out her never-ending library book.

She'd barely plowed through half a page when the front door opened and a familiar, deeply masculine voice raised goosebumps on her arms.

"Are you *still* reading that?"

She glanced up sharply as McAlister strolled to the desk with a smile. He looked steady and confident as usual; his dark hair was neatly combed back, but an errant lock had fallen rather attractively across his forehead.

Maiden pulled a face and stared dejectedly down at the hated book. She'd been chipping away at it for weeks, had renewed it twice at the library, and had been reduced to hoping the protagonists would choke each other to death so it could end.

It was a historical novel filled with ballgowns, flowing locks of auburn hair, and preposterously heaving bosoms. The insipid plot revolved around a young urchin who seemed to spend half her life being berated by the 'dashing' hero and the other half apologizing for driving him to it.

"You must really like that stuff," McAlister said as he craned his neck to see the cover.

"No I don't, I hate it!" Maiden shut the book and scowled down at it. "I hate it so much."

"'*Hero of the Heather*'," he read the title and slid her a questioning look. "Seriously?"

"I know. It's awful," she groaned and rubbed her face with her hands. "Ms. Adams recommended it so strongly that I felt bad not borrowing it. And now I can't go near the library, or her, until I've finished it."

"Who's Ms. Adams?" he asked as he scanned the back cover. "Apart from a lover of burly Scottish men?"

"She's the head librarian. I've known her since I was five." She blew a few strands of dark hair out of her face. "And if that book is anything to go by, Scottish men are total jerks."

"You know my name's 'McAlister', right?" He gave her a speaking look.

"I haven't forgotten, Captain," she said mildly.

He chuckled and set the book in front of her again. "So just skip to the end and throw it back to her."

"I can't, that's cheating." She pushed it away with a miserable sigh.

"Suit yourself, Miss Harlow," he said with a lingering smirk.

"Can I help you with something?" she inquired tolerantly.

"You know I'm here because I need to speak with your father," he said.

"Yes, I do." She felt her shoulders droop a little and gave him a mildly pleading look. "You can't really suspect that my dad was involved?"

"I can't?" He matched her earnest expression, but quickly relented. "Firstly, we don't know if an actual crime has taken place. Secondly, if I'm honest, I don't really see Alfie as menacing. But I still have to question him since that birdhouse was found at the scene."

"So, if Mr. Haynes had been clutching a corn dog, you'd be chasing down the teenager that sold it to him?" she asked dryly.

"You should be a cop, Miss Harlow. Your depth of investigative knowledge is remarkable," he replied.

"Typical rude Scotsman." She looked him over with a wry smile and then glanced back at the partly open office door. "Dad! Captain McAlister is here to see you."

A fair bit of distracted grumbling heralded Alfie's approach. Her father wasn't a tall man, maybe an inch or so shorter than her. He wore a smart pair of slacks and a dark blue polo shirt with a couple of hand-turned wooden pens clipped to the collar.

That wasn't too bad unto itself, but combined with another three hanging out of his pocket and a sixth tucked behind his right ear, left him looking just shy of completely lucid. It didn't help that the collection of writing implements made him clatter gently as he walked.

He stepped out of the office and removed his reading glasses so he could look McAlister over critically. Somehow the pen behind his ear stayed in place; Maiden silently hoped he hadn't accidentally glued it to himself. Again.

"Can I help you with something, young man?" he asked soberly.

"Yes, Mr. Harlow." McAlister kept his tone polite. "There was an incident at the Spencer and Spencer carnival yesterday involving Keith Haynes. I need to speak with you to clarify a few things. Perhaps we could talk privately?"

McAlister glanced at Maiden and gave her a speaking look. Alfie noticed and misunderstood it completely; he scowled and arched a graying brow.

"I'll thank you to stop leering at my daughter!" he said sharply.

Maiden and McAlister were both startled at that stern command. Maiden looked up at the captain very briefly before grabbing her book and taking refuge inside it. McAlister was in no position to complain about her cowardly retreat; from the corner of her eye she saw him smile patiently at Alfie.

"I wasn't leering, Mr. Harlow." He managed to sound dignified. "But, out of regard for your privacy, I thought you might prefer to speak away from others."

"Are you talking about Maiden?" Alfie scoffed as he came and stood beside her. "Not at all, smart as a whip, my little girl here. Not like her sister; Vonny's a spitfire but about as observant as a drowsy teenager."

"Dad, come on, that's not true," Maiden sighed and shook her head at him. "In any case, Captain McAlister is here to talk to you about the suspicious death."

"Yes, precious, I realize that." He smiled indulgently at her as he patted her shoulder and glanced back at the captain. "Which one are you worried about, young man?"

"How many do you know of?" McAlister asked carefully.

"Well, we had those two here not even a month ago." Alfie shrugged. "And now the idiot who tried to steal that birdhouse. Take your pick."

"Let's stick to the birdhouse idiot," McAlister murmured. "Had you met Mr. Haynes before the day of the murder?"

"No, I certainly hadn't," Alfie sniffed. "And I'm glad of it; he was a pig of a man."

"Dad," Maiden whispered, and gave him an uneasy look. "The guy's dead."

"How does that make him any better when he was alive?" Alfie asked stoically. "Is a rat less of a rat because it's been caught in a trap? Oh, caught in a trap...he was crushed, wasn't he?...Ironic. Do you have any objections to rat traps, young man?"

"It depends on the size of the rat, sir," McAlister replied with a noncommittal shrug. "You said Mr. Haynes tried to steal that birdhouse? Did you argue with him about it before he died?"

"Yes I did," Alfie said without compunction. "The man stormed into my stall and demanded to buy the gold and pink birdhouse that little blonde girl loved so much. He should've just bought it for her when he had the chance, I mean who *demands* a birdhouse? Anyway, I told him it was already sold and he flew off the handle! What a nut."

Maiden's eyes snapped to McAlister's, and she held up a warning finger. She was fully aware of the irony, but no one called her dad a nut. One glimpse at her stern face had McAlister grinning at her.

Alfie hadn't missed the silent exchange; he tut-tutted and shook his head. McAlister quickly sobered his expression and pressed on.

"Who did buy the birdhouse?" He pulled his notebook from his pocket and flicked it open.

"Not sure." Alfie shrugged. "Some young guy that was covered in tattoos. He was polite, though."

"Did you get his name?" McAlister glanced up.

"Any reason why I should've asked for his name?" Alfie replied patiently.

"Was it on his shirt?" McAlister smiled a little at the older man's dry tone.

"Might've been." Alfie shrugged.

"Well, can you describe him?" he tried again.

"Yeah," Alfie sighed loudly. "Young guy—"

"Covered in tattoos," Maiden whispered along with him, "polite."

"Are you *sure* you don't want to wait in the other room?" McAlister eyed her wryly.

"Do you think that's going to help the situation?" she replied. "*I'm* the source of your problems? Really?"

The captain grinned down at his notebook, although he was clearly fighting it. Alfie glanced from him to Maiden and back again; she braced herself.

"Are you here to see me or my daughter, Captain?" he grumbled a tad sarcastically. "You seem to keep drifting back to her for some reason."

"Coincidence, sir." McAlister cleared his throat and faced him again.

"Yeah right. She's looked like that since she was fifteen." Alfie pointed at his daughter and gave a long-suffering shake of his head. "The number of overheated young men her mother and I had to put up with was ridiculous!"

"I can only imagine, Mr. Harlow." McAlister's tone was polite.

"I almost wish someone would club *me* to death with a birdhouse right about now." Maiden rubbed her eyes as embarrassment washed over her.

"Haynes didn't die from a birdhouse clubbing," he pointed out.

"He could've though!" Alfie declared with a hint of triumph. "Built to last, my birdhouses. Every last one of them is made with pride, love...and half a bottle of glue."

"How well-ventilated is your workspace, Mr. Harlow?" McAlister shook his head at himself the instant the teasing remark slipped out.

Maiden barely noticed as she buried her face in her book in an attempt to laugh silently.

"What?" Alfie frowned at him, but then his expression brightened. "Oh! Do you want to see my workshop? I suppose I can delay opening the stall for a bit longer. All right, come along detective, you can chat to my Maiden later. Hurry up."

"Great, thanks." McAlister smiled benignly as the older man slipped out through the office door.

Maiden was smirking at him, quite enjoying the corner he'd painted himself into. She set her book back on the desk and rested her chin rather daintily in her hand as she pretended to start reading again. She could feel him watching her as he slowly stepped around the desk. McAlister leaned closer to her as he walked past.

"Enjoy your trashy book, Harlow," he whispered mischievously.

"Go squeeze a bagpipe, McAlister," she retorted without looking up. She was sure she heard his badly suppressed amusement as he stepped through the office door after Alfie.

Chapter Seven

The morning finished peacefully enough, considering it had included a visit from a homicide detective. Maiden didn't see McAlister leave, but she certainly didn't expect him to pop in and say goodbye, despite her mother's winks and nudges when she found out he'd been there. She made better use of her time by calling the council offices and booking a clandestine appointment.

Early that same afternoon Maiden went to City Hall to meet with Sam Chalmers. The official reason was to inquire about the pie competition, but if he felt like talking about his fight with Keith Haynes, she wouldn't refuse to hear his side of the story.

She had slipped on a fitted pair of black pants and a silky green shirt that accentuated her eyes; black high heels completed the look. She didn't often resort to dressing up to try to gain favor, but Gloria and Kylie's feud had left her desperate enough to take every advantage she could get.

The sun was shining brightly as she arrived at the handsome building. It was an old and stodgy slice of respectability set in the heart of downtown Golden Glen. She looked up admiringly at the leaded windows and antique chimney stacks before composing her features and climbing the long flight of stone steps.

It only took a moment to check the directory in the foyer and make her way down the correct hallway. After a few turns, she was rewarded by the sight of *Samuel Chalmers* written on a door at the end of the hall. She ran a hand over her hair, squared her shoulders and stepped inside.

She found herself in a very placid and dull waiting room; her eyes shifted to the receptionist's desk, which sat on the side wall. There was a youngish woman with frizzy red curls and a smattering of freckles on her button nose, sitting and opening a small pile of letters. Maiden smiled when the lady glanced up at her.

"Hi, I'm Maiden Harlow," she said politely. "I have an appointment with Mr. Chalmers."

"Ah yes. Hello, Miss Harlow." The young woman gestured towards the empty chairs in the middle of the room. "Mr. Chalmers is just finishing up a meeting, he won't be long."

Maiden nodded and glanced around at the generic gray and beige furnishings as she took a seat. The waiting area was quite basic and sterile, but fit for purpose. She thought idly that a few potted plants and some better pictures than the motel-style abstracts hanging on the walls would've gone a long way to making the area nicer.

After another ten minutes, the door to Chalmers' office opened, and the man himself stepped through it. Chalmers was an unremarkable-looking guy, probably in his late forties, with dark, thinning hair and thick glasses. He wasn't tall or especially fat, just a bit soft around the middle, and he had a bushy mustache that was threaded with strands of gray.

All of those observations faded away when Captain McAlister walked out behind him. Chalmers had stopped and stood slightly off to the side to allow the much taller man to step past. McAlister's richly brown eyes locked onto Maiden and narrowed uncertainly.

Uh-oh, just act cool and natural. She held her breath for an instant before forcing herself to relax. *You're not in trouble; you haven't done anything. You haven't had the chance yet.*

She glanced up at him and blinked her eyes ingenuously. McAlister stilled and frowned at her; she could only imagine what he must've been thinking.

"What are you doing here, Miss Harlow?" he asked carefully.

"I have an appointment with Mr. Chalmers," she replied calmly and without apology. She had every right to be there.

"Yes, I'm actually running a bit late." Chalmers glanced at his watch and then smiled at her. "Sorry to keep you waiting, Miss Harlow. Please come straight in."

Maiden stood and headed towards the door, but McAlister stepped to the side to block her path. Maiden was taken aback, but her temper stirred enough to help her raise her chin to a confident, almost defiant, angle.

Chalmers clearly noticed the tension but didn't mention it as he exchanged a shrug with his equally confused secretary and watched the flinty pair.

"What's up, Miss Harlow?" McAlister asked.

"Some weird guy's is physically stopping me from entering an office for a legitimately arranged meeting," she replied. "Do you have any advice on how to make him behave himself?"

"Look, if you're trying to poke your nose in—"

"To a pie?" she cut in coolly as she draped her hands on her hips and arched a dark brow.

"A pie?" He gave her a confused look and folded his arms across his chest.

"Yeah." She started tapping her foot. "Mr. Chalmers is coordinating the annual baking contests at Summerfest, a competition that my business has entered. Feel free to ask the receptionist for the entrant's list if you think I'm lying."

"It's true, officer," the little redhead volunteered in a nervous voice. "I swear."

"Oh," McAlister murmured. "Right."

"If you'll excuse me," she said loudly and gestured to the doorway he was still blocking.

He obligingly stepped aside again. Maiden refused to meet his eye as she breezed past. Chalmers slipped back into his office and smiled politely as he pointed her towards a set of chairs in the corner. He gave McAlister a quiet, uneasy look as he shut the door.

Maiden forced herself to shrug off her lingering irritation and smiled pleasantly at Mr. Chalmers. She was there to ask a favor and hadn't really needed that awkward start to the conversation. She walked over to the chairs and sat in the closest one.

"Goodness," Chalmers said in a carefully lowered tone as he took up the seat next to hers, "that was a bit different. I didn't realize that you knew each other that well."

"We don't," she replied as mildly as she could.

"Oh?" He looked dubious. "Well, in any case, I apologize for the strange greeting, Miss Harlow. I can't imagine what got into the man."

"It's quite all right, Mr. Chalmers." She tried not to sound as irritated as she felt. "I'm here on more pressing business."

"Ah yes, the contest," he said. "How can I help you?"

"As you may or may not know, Harlow House has been entered in the Best Pie category." She stacked her hands neatly in her lap. "Specifically under the names of Gloria Harlow and Kylie Abrams. I've come to ask if it would be possible for them to compete separately."

"That's...an unexpected request." His mustache twisted as he considered it. "Any particular reason for it?"

"Yes. They don't get along and the rest of us are sick of the fighting," she said candidly.

"I see," he chortled. "It's amazing how hotted up people get over baked goods. But I suppose reputation and pride are at stake. The only potential problem I can think of, Miss Harlow, is if the other entrants feel that it's giving your business an unfair advantage. Two chances instead of one, if you see what I mean."

"I do understand that, Mr. Chalmers. But there are a few points I'd like you to take into consideration," Maiden said firmly but politely. She'd done her research before coming. "The rules don't state how many times an individual may enter the same category. There are also precedents in two of the past four years."

"Are there?" Chalmers looked intrigued.

"Four years ago, Agnes Rainey submitted both Strawberry-Rhubarb and Chocolate Silk." Maiden's tone was all business. "And two years ago Dan Llewellyn entered a Cherry Upside-down pie and Lemon Meringue. He won first and second place."

"Oh, that's right. I remember the fallout from that decision." He fingered his bushy mustache. "It caused quite a stir."

"Which certainly didn't hurt the festival at all, considering the extra exposure it got," she pointed out smoothly. "And in this case, at least the cooks would be different, they just happen represent the same business establishment."

"That's true..." His small, close-set gray eyes looked shrewd. "I suppose any hint of controversy would draw more attention to the fair. And anything we can do to downplay that fool Haynes' death would be welcomed. All right, Miss Harlow. I'll see to it that both ladies are entered on their own."

"Thank you, Mr. Chalmers." She resisted the urge to wring her hands like a cartoon villain; her plan was working perfectly.

"But what was that about Mr. Haynes' death? It won't shut the fair down, will it? It's only just started."

"So far we seem to be safe." He scowled. "But Captain McAlister didn't promise anything. He wasn't terribly reassuring either, to be honest."

"I suppose he couldn't be." She gave a commiserating sigh. "But surely Keith Haynes death doesn't mean the entire carnival, or Summerfest itself, can't keep going? I understand closing the mirror maze but..."

"Well, that's the issue!" He warmed to the topic quickly. "If the maze wasn't safe, what does that suggest about the rest of that travelling menagerie? Ferris Wheels throwing people up into the air, or spinning them around in carousels on the verge of collapse? That whole place is a potential death trap!"

"Everything seemed pretty sound when I was there yesterday." Maiden tried to come across as impartial while still keeping him talking. He certainly seemed to hate the carnival, despite its being a primary tourist draw.

"Sure, until that moron got clocked on the head by one of the least insidious props in the whole place!" Chalmers scoffed. "How anyone could get themselves clobbered like that is beyond me. What a fool."

"You seem well-acquainted with Mr. Haynes," she said tactfully. "I never spoke to the man myself, but I saw him a few times. He did come across as...grumpy."

"He was an argumentative buffoon!" Chalmers replied irately. "An overconfident two-bit salesman that acted like he knew it all. His job, yours and everybody else's! He was nothing but trouble and complaints since that mess of a carnival hit town."

"You must've found him very hard to deal with." She shook her head sympathetically.

"To put it mildly." He rolled his eyes but then visibly remembered himself. "Of course I'm terribly sorry that he's dead. I never meant to sound unfeeling about that, but he wasn't a nice man."

"Mm. Had you met him before?" she asked. "Last year when the carnival came through, I mean."

"No, I wasn't assigned to oversee Summerfest last year," he murmured, rubbing his chin thoughtfully. "It's funny, Captain McAlister asked me the same thing."

"Did he?" She looked appropriately surprised. "I suppose he's trying to learn more about Mr. Haynes. The opinions of the other carnival workers could be biased. I'm sure the police don't suspect you of anything, Mr. Chalmers."

"Suspect *me*?" His eyes widened and he sat a little straighter. "That's ridiculous! I barely knew the man!"

"That's right." Maiden nodded supportively. "You're only trying to do a difficult and stressful job, you mustn't let this worry you."

"Why would it worry me?" His laugh sounded hollow and nervous. "It was an accident after all."

"Oh, was it?" she asked innocently. "Is that what the captain said? What a relief! I guess I assumed that since he's questioning people there might be some doubt."

"Well, he didn't actually say if it was an accident or not," Chalmers admitted. He looked uncomfortable now. "But it had to have been. Just a dumb fluke."

"Like I said, Mr. Chalmers, don't let it get to you." She waved it away. "It's not like he was checking for an alibi or anything, right?"

"No," he said quietly. "Certainly not."

"Good, nothing to be concerned about then." She smiled and gave a satisfied nod as she pushed to her feet. "And you won't forget to change the entries for Mom and Kylie?"

"Hm?" He frowned up at her vacantly, but then quickly recalled the point of her visit and stood. "Yes, yes of course. I'll see to it today, I promise."

"Thank you very much, Mr. Chalmers."

CHAPTER EIGHT

Maiden was feeling quite pleased with what she'd achieved. She smiled to herself as she stepped outside and into a soft afternoon breeze. The weather had been mild for summer; it made the prospect of returning to the carnival even more inviting.

She wasn't really trying to keep getting involved, but a few things were nagging at her and she was genuinely worried about her dad. Between the fight with Keith and the birdhouse at the crime scene, he probably couldn't be excluded as a suspect yet, no matter how preposterous the idea might seem.

She descended the stairs gracefully, her thoughts lingering on Alfie. While McAlister hadn't seemed especially interested in him, he couldn't ignore the unexplained connection there. If Keith wasn't the one who bought the birdhouse, how and why had it ended up next to his body? This question was whirling through her thoughts when she heard a short, sharp honk.

She glanced over and held her breath for an instant when she saw McAlister sitting in his car. The driver's door was open, and he was leaning quite casually back into the seat with one foot still on the ground. She folded her arms and strolled towards him with slow and deliberate steps.

She knew he would be after a fuller explanation for why she was there, and she was determined to make him work for it. As she drew closer, she refused to dwell on how long his legs were or how the position he was in caused the fabric of his trousers to mold to the shape of his lean muscles.

"Hey, Harlow." He smiled faintly.

His expression was warm as his eyes flitted over her subtly. She noticed that he sometimes called her 'Harlow' when no one else was around. It was no doubt a foolish and risky assumption, but it felt almost like a pet name. She liked it, and there was no need to admit that. Ever.

And at the moment, he was after information that she was not inclined to share. It was time to be uncooperative. She stood in front of the open door and gave him an expressionless stare. But he didn't unnerve easily, and his slight smile never faltered.

"How'd you go?" he asked.

"Good," she allowed. "You?"

"All under control," he said confidently. "So what did Mr. Pie-man have to say for himself?"

"He granted my request, but I didn't leave him much room to refuse me," she said with a small, pleased smile.

"And that request was?"

"Confidential pie business, I'm afraid." Her eyes narrowed a fraction. "Do you have a warrant, Captain?"

"Not on me, no." He patted down his pockets.

"Too bad for you, then," she said sweetly. "How was your chat with Dad?"

"Extensive." McAlister pulled a face at her obvious amusement. "We spoke for half an hour and established precisely nothing."

"That's fairly standard for Dad," she acknowledged. "But how were the birdhouses?"

"Really cool. He gave me one," he conceded with a faint smile and let his eyes wander over her again. "You look nice today."

"Thanks."

"Are you up to something?" He held her gaze steadily, as if willing her to tell him everything.

"Just heading home, officer." She twirled a lock of her dark hair around her finger innocently.

"C'mon," he sounded far more reasonable now, almost coaxing. "I apologized for coming out swinging back there."

She draped her hands on her hips. "No, you didn't."

"I implied it by backing off." The dimple in his left cheek flashed into view.

"You got the door closed in your face, Galahad." She started to smirk but brutally subdued it. She refused to be teased out of justified offense, or to fall for a transparent attempt to get information. "That hardly makes you a gentleman. Not to *me* anyway. Incidentally, how is Janet today?"

"She's not my type, Harlow. You don't have to worry about her." He grinned wider.

"Way to lead her on, Captain," she tsked and took a step back.

She hadn't gotten far when a car tore past. As it went, a young man leaned out of the passenger window and let out a loud wolf whistle.

"*I love you, gorgeous! Will you marry me?*" he shouted while his friends laughed and tried to drag him back inside.

Maiden arched a fine black brow and watched the car disappear from the corner of her eye. She wasn't sure whether to be mortified, angry or flattered, but she was certain she could've done without being cat-called in front of McAlister.

She flicked him a glance to find him sort of frowning while also trying not to laugh. She rolled her shoulders back and strove to look dignified and aloof despite the warmth she felt in her cheeks.

"Where was I?" she asked. "Ah yes, get lost."

"Yeah, I'll do that." He nodded and then smiled. "Do you want me to walk you to your car first?"

"No, it'd cramp my style." She shrugged. "By the way, were those idiots speeding?"

"Looked like it."

"Thanks," she said tightly and stalked away.

Maiden walked back into the inn and looked around the foyer. She didn't see any sign of anyone, so she headed into the dining room. She could at least duck into the kitchen and give Kylie the good news.

As soon as she swept her gaze over the room, however, she spotted Kylie and Gloria sitting opposite each other at one of the tables. Their gazes were locked in some kind of unspoken combat; they were scowling across a sea of half-eaten pies.

Maiden froze at the intimidating sight and considered slipping out again when the grim pair slowly turned their heads to stare at her. Despite being completely creeped out, Maiden dredged up a smile and edged closer.

"Hey, how's it going?" she asked in a feeble attempt to sound casual.

"Fine," Kylie muttered.

"Absolutely dandy," Gloria added acidly.

"Great. That's really...really great. Hey, I hope you two won't mind," she cleared her throat and clasped her hands behind her back, "but I was talking to one of the event coordinators today and we sort of agreed that it might be a good idea if you two competed separately in the pie competition."

Kylie came the closest to grinning that Maiden had ever seen; she actually showed a brief glimpse of teeth. Gloria was also deeply pleased; she glanced at her rival and sat straighter.

"You mean, we each enter our own pie?" Gloria asked hopefully.

"Yeah." Maiden kept her tone light. "Hopefully you won't mind being in direct competition rather than...allies, sort of. Almost were."

Kylie and Gloria both rose to their feet. They exchanged a look of quiet satisfaction and then turned and crept menacingly back to their respective kitchens. It was oddly terrifying; Maiden watched both doors nervously as she approached the table.

Maiden ran a dubious eye over the assembled pies. Half were over-cooked to the point of looking burnt, and the other half were pristine and fussy. Acknowledging how close the two women would have been driven to beating each other to death with rolling pins, Maiden hurried to the stairs and up to the family apartment.

She tiptoed through the kitchen past Gloria. Her mother was singing and shimmying her ample bottom as she rattled pots and pie plates around. Maiden avoided eye contact and dashed to her room.

She quickly changed out of the more formal, businesslike attire and into jeans and a snug, royal blue t-shirt. She wanted to get back to the carnival to see what was happening and needed to try to blend in with the tourists.

Gloria was happily slicing apples as Maiden snuck past and headed downstairs. She dodged Vonny, who had just stepped into the office, and slipped outside to her waiting car.

The drive downtown was a bit surreal. The sun was still shining; the roads were full of traffic, and everyone she saw walking around appeared cheerful and relaxed. She found a parking space on a bustling side street and walked the rest of the way.

Maiden wove through the numerous market stalls and headed into the carnival. She stopped for a moment near the entrance and frowned a little as she looked around. Everything seemed completely normal.

She wasn't sure what she had been expecting, but nothing was different. The same bright balloons floated on the breeze along with the banners and ribbons that decorated the entrance to the carnival.

There were families and children everywhere, running, smiling, and laughing. If one didn't know better, they'd never imagine that someone had died there—in suspicious circumstances—only the night before.

And it wasn't just the fair-goers; the staff seemed to be going about their business as usual. She found it strange that the people Keith Haynes had evidently lived and worked with for two years were carrying on as normal less than a day after he died.

Maybe it was due to a lack of choice; if the carnival didn't make money, presumably none of them did either. Or it could be that they weren't sorry to see him gone. Janet had said he was harsh with his workers, and his conduct yesterday hadn't done much to suggest she'd exaggerated.

Maiden shook her head in wonder and pressed forward, looking for her true quarry; her first stop was the food trucks.

She noticed the lines were long, and that same man was again scrambling to do everything on his own. But under the circumstances, it was hardly surprising that Janet wasn't at her post.

Maiden glanced over towards the funhouse and saw the purple-haired lady leaned casually against the ticket booth, filing her short, black nails. The woman was throwing an occasional glance at the lines in front of the food trucks. They all looked understaffed, and the customers were growing impatient as they stood in the warm sun.

More than a few people gave up on any hope of ice cream or funnel cakes and walked away irately. Maiden saw the purple-haired woman give an exasperated shake of her head. She quietly approached her.

"Pretty busy today," Maiden said and nodded towards the concession trucks. "They must be short-staffed."

"No, sweetie," she muttered. "They're just badly managed."

"Oh, you think that's the problem?" Maiden blinked at her. "You'd certainly know more about it than I do."

"I know more about it than most people." She rolled her eyes and tugged at the cuffs of her tie-dyed tunic, which she wore over a thick pair of dark red tights. "I used to run it."

"Really?" Maiden looked at her in quickly hidden surprise; she didn't honestly look like management material. "No offense, but it kind of looks as if no one's running it now."

"That's because the person who swooped in and stole that job can't be bothered to do any work," she said with more than a hint of bitterness. "She took whatever she could get and then let it all go downhill. The job, the man that was dumb enough to give it to her, *everything*."

Maiden suspected that they were discussing Janet, which made the lady's poorly timed absence from the concession trucks even more telling. Working there was one thing, but running the place was quite another, and Janet didn't appear to be too interested in either prospect.

"I saw you last night." Maiden decided to alter the subject in hopes of keeping the conversation going. "You were there when Oliver Armstrong was found, right?"

"Yeah, I was around." She shrugged and gave her a questioning look. "Why were you there?"

"I was talking to the police," Maiden sighed and watched her a little more closely as she continued. "I found Keith Hayne's body."

The lady's reaction was immediate; she wet her lips and her expression became very guarded. She stopped filing her nails and shifted her dark eyes to some point in the distance.

"That must have been difficult," she said quietly.

"It wasn't very nice," Maiden conceded, causing the other woman to give a humorless laugh.

"I'm Daisy." She turned back to her.

"Maiden," she replied.

"Cool name." Daisy smiled briefly, but then cleared her throat and rubbed her arms. "How, um...how did Keith die?"

"I don't think I can say yet. Sorry." Maiden pulled a face and shrugged. "The police haven't officially decided if it was an accident or murder. Did you know him well?"

"Yeah, you could put it that way," Daisy murmured. "But that was a lifetime ago. I'd better go back to work."

Maiden watched her wander back into the ticket booth. It was an obvious ploy to end the conversation; there weren't throngs of people clamoring to get into the funhouse. She let it go, doubting she'd get anywhere if she were too pushy.

Maiden stepped away and continued deeper into the carnival. She passed a souvenir stand and then a tent filled with caramel apples, glossy lollipops, and bags of rainbow-colored cotton candy.

As she approached the office, she heard hushed voices. She recognized at least one of them and suppressed a pleased smile.

She followed the voices around the side of the old trailer and found Janet talking with Gabby. Gabby looked drained.

She wore a pair of faded yellow Bermuda shorts with a baggy gray t-shirt over top, while Janet almost glowed in a spandex tiger-print bodysuit and black high heels.

Maiden noticed that Janet was looking quite determined; she slapped her fist against her palm for emphasis a few times. Gabby, on the other hand, was very guarded.

Maiden stepped closer and cleared her throat. The women both tensed when they looked over and saw her standing nearby. Gabby frowned a little, but Janet soon recovered and smiled gently.

"Oh, hello again," she said nicely.

"Sorry if I'm interrupting," Maiden said with a kind smile as she stepped closer.

"No, not at all, beautiful." Janet pulled an apologetic face. "I don't know your name. Sorry, honey, that seems ridiculous at this point."

"I'm Maiden," she chuckled. "Maiden Harlow."

"What a sexy name!" Janet purred and gave her a teasing wink. "I love it!"

"Thanks." Maiden smiled faintly. She wasn't used to people responding so favorably to her unusual name; trust carnies to keep an open mind. "Like I said, I didn't mean to interrupt, I wanted to see how you two are doing."

"Okay I guess." Gabby slid a less certain gaze to Janet. "As well as we can be."

"We're doing our best," the lady sighed down at her feet. "It's so unreal, it still feels like a horrible dream. I keep thinking I'll wake up and find Keith working away at his desk."

"Understandable, it hasn't been very long," Maiden conceded. "Do you know what you're going to do? As a business, I mean."

"Soldier on. We have to." Janet's eyes were filled with purpose as they snapped back to hers. "The place can't fall apart just because Keith is...we can't let everybody down. No one works here because they're rich, or have the luxury of options. We have to keep things going."

"Yes, of course." Maiden nodded. "I guess the corporate office will hire a new manager or something?"

"Yeah, they'll do something." Gabby let her gaze drift to the ground. "They sometimes promote from within."

"Exactly," Janet said more emphatically as she pounded the bottom of her fist against her palm again. "And that's what we're anticipating. We'll pull together and pick up where Keith left off. This place meant a lot to him, I won't let it collapse, I *won't*."

Maiden noticed Janet had gone from 'we' to 'I' in a heartbeat. If the state of the concession stands was anything to go by, she doubted Janet had the skills for the job. She slid her gaze to Gabby; she looked tired. That was understandable, but Maiden also detected a hint of something darker and angrier in her eyes.

She wanted to ask her a few questions but was starting to see that Janet's presence inhibited her; she'd have to wait until she found her alone. She shifted tactics.

"How's Mr. Armstrong, by the way?" Maiden kept her eyes wide and filled with ingenuous worry. "I saw him lying on the ground last night as I was leaving, I hope he's okay."

"Yeah, that was so strange." Janet hugged herself. "When Gabby went to find him, he was passed out behind the ice cream truck. He says he can't remember anything about it and no one knows how long he'd been there."

"That's...weird," Maiden said slowly. "Was he knocked out or something?"

"We don't know what happened yet," Gabby admitted and glanced away. "The paramedics took him to the hospital for tests, he's supposed to be released this afternoon."

"We're here waiting for him actually," Janet volunteered. "Hopefully he'll be well enough to get back to work soon, we can't afford to have too many people out of action."

Gabby stiffened and failed to catch a gasp. Janet gave her a look, but then seemed to realize how callous she sounded.

"Oh, I didn't mean it like that," she cried, burying her face in her hands. "I just want everyone to be all right!"

"Forget it, Janet." Gabby patted her shoulder. "I'm a little on edge; everything is so weird today. I'm sorry."

"It's okay, excuse me," Janet said in a trembling voice and hurried away.

Maiden watched her go until she disappeared around a corner. She glanced back at Gabby and noticed the woman was reluctant to meet her gaze. She decided to try and forge some common ground.

"I don't think you did anything that you needed to apologize for, to be honest," she offered with a shrug.

"Oh, thanks." Gabby almost smiled and shifted her weight from one foot to the other. "Janet's sensitive, I have to be really careful around her. Sometimes I react before I think it through."

"We all do that. And you've been through a lot too," Maiden reassured her. "It's not easy being the one behind the scenes. Keeping everything running smoothly, even though most people have no idea we exist."

"You sound like you know something about that." She considered her curiously.

"Oh, I've worked in the family's inn since I was a kid." Maiden hooked her thumbs in her belt loops. "As I got older the workload increased. I don't mind it, but there are those times when I'm up for hours balancing the books or ordering supplies that someone else forgot while the rest of the family's asleep in bed. It can feel thankless but, well, it's a job that has to be done."

"I'm *quite* familiar with those sorts of jobs," Gabby said with a humorless laugh.

"I can tell." She smiled. "You probably know more about this place than anyone. That's what happens when you run the office, you know the way things really work."

"Yeah...I guess I do," she conceded.

"So, will you run everything until an official replacement is chosen?" Maiden lifted her dark brows.

"I, um, can't really say what'll happen there, It isn't my call." Gabby pressed her lips together. "A few people are floating some ideas around."

"Oh!" Maiden affected a look of startled understanding. "Is that what Janet meant? But she couldn't actually take over? Could she? She told me she's only been with the company for six months."

"And that's true," Gabby rolled her eyes. "But it's been an eventful six months."

"I was talking to a lady named Daisy, she seemed to feel that Janet couldn't even run the concession area," Maiden said in a secretive whisper. "How could she hope to run the whole operation?"

"Yeah well, she's got me, doesn't she?" A note of resentment crept into Gabby's voice. "Just like Keith did. People think he ran the show, well let me tell you, he only checked the profits and argued with the local officials when they got to be a problem. I do everything else!"

"And yet he got all the credit? That's typical, isn't it?" She frowned and shook her head. "So, what Daisy said is true?"

"That's a touchy area," Gabby said uncomfortably. "She's not impartial, but she's not exactly wrong either."

Maiden gave a confused shake of her head and waited for her to elaborate. Gabby glanced around to ensure they were alone before stepping closer.

"Daisy had that job for a couple of years...until Janet came along," she confided. "Next thing we all knew, Keith gave the job to her and Daisy was stuck in one of the ticket booths."

"Oh." Maiden's eyes widened in understanding as a few more details clicked into place. "Was Daisy not doing a good enough job?"

"No it wasn't that. Look, it was complicated," Gabby sighed resignedly. "But Janet isn't the most organized person and it's caused a few...problems."

"That's tricky." Maiden rubbed her chin in a thoughtful manner. "Is there anything you can do about it?"

"Oh no, no!" Gabby caught herself and instantly cleared her expression. "I'm not complaining, no one is, not really. I shouldn't have mentioned it at all, sorry."

"There's nothing to apologize for." Maiden waved it away, hoping to keep Gabby feeling comfortable so she wouldn't clam up completely. "You're overworked, stressed and grieving. Don't let a few words worry you."

"Thanks, Maiden. That's nice of you." She peered around. "But do me a favor and don't say anything to Janet about it, okay? Please?"

"You got it." Maiden gave her a conspiratorial wink.

"Hey, Gabs."

They both glanced over to see Oliver Armstrong heading towards them. His hair was mussed, and he had his overshirt tied around his waist. The sweat-stained singlet he wore underneath exposed his huge shoulders to the warm sunshine.

"Oliver!" Gabby finally found a genuine smile and waddled over to hug him. "Thank goodness you're all right!"

"Yeah, not the best night's sleep in recent memory, but I'm fine." He smiled and patted her shoulder as she let go and stood back a bit. His eyes flitted over Maiden. "I know I've met *you* before."

"Yesterday, right after your fight with Keith Haynes." She smiled faintly. "The name's Maiden."

"Ah yes, the fair and lovely Maiden." He snapped his fingers as though it had all come rushing back to him. "I heard about Keith too, I guess it makes me seem pretty suspicious."

"No it doesn't, you were passed out," Gabby assured him.

"Yeah, but for how long? And starting from when?" He gave her a wry look. "I can't claim to have an alibi if I can't remember what happened."

"You don't sound terribly worried about it," Maiden pointed out.

"I know I didn't do it." He shrugged.

"You also seem to think it was murder," Maiden said as she took a step towards him. "Have the police officially decided that it wasn't an accident?"

"It was no accident," Oliver said with complete certainty. "I assembled those panels myself, and anything I don't personally put in, I inspect. My name's on it, after all. The mirror maze was perfectly sound. Besides, the panels are too heavy at the base to topple over for no reason. Someone helped it along."

Maiden considered that as she studied his guileless expression. He looked absolutely unruffled and convinced of what he was saying. She supposed it could be an act, but she'd seen him respond to Keith's accusations with the same placid calm.

"Any idea who would've done that?" she asked.

"Everyone who'd met him," he replied easily. "He was awful, Maiden. Anyone he couldn't threaten, he bribed, anyone he couldn't bribe, he tried to blackmail. He liked to get his own way and you can only push that hard for so long before someone pushes back harder."

"He sounds like a real prince," she said with a hollow laugh. "Well, maybe you two could help me with something. When he and Janet came to my dad's market stall yesterday, she fell in love with one of the birdhouses he made. Keith acted like he couldn't care less."

"Mm, I remember that," Oliver grumbled disdainfully. "That was typical of Keith, if it wasn't for him, it wasn't important."

"Sure, okay. But when I found his body—" She waved away their startled looks. "Yes, I found the body. The birdhouse was sitting next to him."

Oliver and Gabby were staring at her with confused scowls. She said nothing, just waited for one of them to venture a comment. They turned to each other and then back to her.

"What?" Gabby shook her head. "Why would he have a birdhouse?"

"That was essentially my question to you," she reminded her.

"I have no idea." Oliver ran a hand over his long beard. "Did he go back later and buy it for Janet maybe?"

"No." Maiden folded her arms. "Dad said that he did go back and try to buy it, but it was already sold."

"Well, could Janet have bought it?" Gabby suggested with a shrug.

"Dad didn't get a name, they paid cash," she sighed. "But he said it was a youngish guy with a lot of tattoos."

"That doesn't narrow it down around here," Oliver said dryly.

"No, not a lot," she agreed. "So, any ideas? Any at all?"

They both shook their heads unhelpfully. She couldn't be sure, but something told her they both knew, or at least suspected, more than they were willing to share.

Chapter Nine

Oliver excused himself soon after and headed for his trailer, which evidently doubled as his workshop, and Gabby retreated to the office. With no one inclined to tell her much of anything, Maiden wandered back the way she'd come and tried to think the situation over.

She passed the concession stands again but still saw no sign of Janet there. The determined woman was probably hidden away somewhere, dreaming of saving the day, carrying on courageously in Keith's place. Maiden wondered if the grief was fueling her plans or if she was afraid of losing her job there without Keith to protect it.

Maiden shook her head at Janet's ambition. Unless she had a background in management that she'd never mentioned to anyone, she couldn't hope to know how to run a traveling carnival. It didn't strike her as the sort of job that a person could bluff their way through.

Of course, if you had an experienced office manager to do all the hard work for you, that might make the prospect seem more achievable. Maiden wondered if Gabby was perhaps harboring some secret ambitions too; she had to be a far more likely candidate than Janet to take over Keith's role. Surely.

Her eyes stole over to the funhouse, which reminded her of Daisy. If Keith had really snatched away her job and handed it over to Janet, what did his death mean for Daisy's prospects?

She looked over at the ticket booth but didn't see her at her post either. The staff seemed a bit casual about their roles, maybe because Keith wasn't there to keep them in line anymore.

Maiden walked on past the carousel and spotted Timmy Gibson. He was hiding behind a large sign advertising the ride. He swayed slightly as he sat on an old wooden crate tucked in the shadows. She debated the wisdom of approaching him, but it was broad daylight and there were a lot of people around.

She stepped closer and looked him over critically. His eyes were bloodshot and his hair was even greasier today; he didn't seem fussed about personal hygiene. Maiden spied several crushed cigarette butts lying at his feet and guessed that he'd been tucked away there for a while.

"Hey Timmy," she said. "What are you hiding back here for?"

"What?" He squinted up at her uncertainly, but then managed a smile. "Oh, hey. Didn't expect to see you again."

"You mean after what happened in the mirror maze?" she asked.

"Were you there?" He scratched his head. "Oh yeah, I took your tickets. Yeah, I remember."

"Just before Mr. Haynes was found dead," she supplied when his gaze started glazing over.

He jumped at the stark reminder, and a scowl darkened his entire countenance. He rubbed at the stubble on his face and mumbled under his breath.

"What was that?" Maiden asked a little louder.

"Life ain't fair," he muttered.

"That's not really a novel observation," she replied, meeting his confused look. "But please go on."

"I grew up in a bad neighborhood with a family that didn't like each other." He lit another cigarette and took a few puffs.

"I never even met my dad, and I was about twelve when my big brother went to jail. Mom was always drunk..."

Timmy was clearly drunk himself; he swayed again and nearly missed his mouth with the cigarette. Beginning to regret her decision to come and talk to him, Maiden looked around for a tactful means of excusing herself. He continued before she could speak up.

"This place," he gestured to indicate the entire carnival, "this stupid, noisy, grubby place, is the only home I got. If this gets shut down, there's nowhere else to go. And I ain't the only one."

"What makes you think the carnival will shut down?" she asked curiously. "It's still busy, even after what happened last night."

"Because Keith was the only one that kept this place running," Timmy muttered. "He was the only one that knew the right people to talk to, how to make the best deals and get the most money."

"Who told you that?" she asked with a quirk of her left eyebrow.

"He did of course!" He rolled his eyes as though it were a ridiculous question. "And now he's gone and all our necks are on the line."

"I'm sure Gabby and Janet will keep things going until they hire a new manager." Maiden deliberately said Janet's name a bit louder and watched to see his reaction.

"Janet?" he spat furiously. "That fire-breathing tramp?! Are you serious?"

"Well, what's wrong with her?" Maiden shrugged.

"She breezed in one day out of nowhere and was all over Keith! That's what! And just like *that* she gets the best of everything!" He snapped his fingers, but it was the hand he was holding his cigarette in; it burst into pieces all over his grungy jeans. He barely noticed. "The cushiest jobs, her own private trailer and more money than the rest of us. Even the ones that've been with the troupe for years!"

"Ouch, that would be tough." She shook her head. "How did you find out about all of that?"

"Word gets around," he said with a knowing look. "She wasn't even serious about him. Janet was always hanging around Oliver or any other decent-looking guy that paid her any attention. Yeah, old Keith was getting pretty tired of it too."

"You mean he thought she was cheating on him?" She gave a tiny, scandalized gasp.

"She *was* cheating! Every chance she got!" He lowered his voice and leaned closer; his breath reeked of beer. "And she used to snoop through his papers when he wasn't around. I caught her once trying to get into the safe in his office."

"Really?" She stared at him. "How'd she explain that?"

"She didn't." He smirked. "She gave me fifty bucks and said if I ever told Keith she'd deny it."

"So, you never told him?"

"Nah, he wouldn't have believed me." He shrugged. "And I didn't like Keith enough to start that kind of trouble just to warn him."

"What about Oliver then?" she offered as though she couldn't imagine a bad word to say about the burly man.

"He's smart, smarter than a lot of people think," Timmy said seriously. "But Janet's got her hooks in him too, so it wouldn't make any difference. But that's the least of my problems right now. This show has to keep going, that means we have to survive this town and get moving on before it's too late."

"Too late for what exactly?" She watched him pull a flask from his pocket and take a swig; apparently beer wasn't doing the job anymore.

"The weak link. There's always a weak link in the chain, that's what old Keith taught me." He smiled and took another drink. "But this town's different, the chain wasn't weak enough. Greedy politicians, busted equipment, big mess, big problems and Keith ain't here to solve 'em. We got big problems, honey."

"Sorry to hear that." Maiden decided it was time to get moving, but she pulled out her phone and subtly snapped a picture of him as she stepped back. "Take care."

"Oh, I will...I'll take care of it," he mumbled even as she walked away. "I just need to sit down for a while first."

Maiden thought about Timmy's garbled chatter as she headed towards the markets. Her phone buzzed in her pocket; she pulled it back out and saw a message from Vonny.

Vonny

> *Are you working today or what?*

Maiden

> *Yes and no. I worked this morning and now I'm busy.*

Maiden inserted a smug-faced emoji.

Vonny

> *Thanks a lot. Mom and Kylie keep forcing me to taste their pies...I'm scared.*

Maiden grinned down at the screen. She didn't blame Von for wanting reinforcements, but she had bigger fish to fry. She also had a suggestion that might appease her sister.

Maiden

> *See if Tony's nearby. Maybe he can stop by and help you.*

Good idea! See you later, detective. And don't forget to give Captain Sexy-pants a big smooch when you see him.

"You're such a twit," Maiden said under her breath.

She made her way along a now-familiar route and soon walked into her father's tent. She glanced around; he didn't have any customers at the moment, which meant they could have a discreet word.

"Hey, Dad." She smiled when she spotted Alfie sitting at his makeshift desk behind a table full of pens and cutting boards.

"Hello, sweetheart." He returned the greeting and glanced over, arching a bushy brow. "Is that boy still hovering around you?"

"Are you referring to the head of the local police department?" She gave him a patient look.

"Yes, that's the one." He nodded.

"No, I think he must be off chasing burglars or something." She smiled. Alfie never teased her, so she never found his assumptions as offensive as Vonny's or Gloria's.

"'Or something' is right," he grumbled as he shifted whatever he was holding; she couldn't see what it was from where she was standing. "Just keep your wits about you there, sweetie."

"Oh Dad, not you too," she sighed. "You're starting to sound like Mom."

"I doubt your mother ever advised much caution," he pointed out dryly.

"That's true." She had to laugh.

"Look, I'm not complaining. I don't mind him," Alfie said tolerantly. "He was very polite this morning despite my prattling. I laid it on pretty thick too, it's surprisingly fun being old."

"I love you, Dad," she said fondly. She knew he played up the eccentric older guy role a bit, but it came more naturally to him than he realized. He wasn't all that old, but he was a tad eccentric.

She walked a bit closer and frowned when she realized that he had an ice pack on his hand.

"What happened?" she asked as she came and stood next to him.

"Nothing much, just a bit of a dust up," he mumbled and flexed his hand before tucking it under the ice pack again. "I'm out of practice...not that I ever practiced that sort of thing."

"What do you mean 'that sort of thing'?" she asked seriously. His skin looked bruised. "What happened?"

"Don't worry about it, it's fine," he grumbled stubbornly. "What have you been up to?"

"Looking around a bit and talking to a few people. I'm trying to find out who bought that birdhouse yesterday." She still eyed him suspiciously but left his discolored knuckles alone for the moment. "Here have a look at this, see if you recognize this guy."

She pulled up the photo she'd taken of Timmy and showed him the screen. Alfie scowled at the picture for a few seconds and then shook his head a little.

"Could be the one," he said dubiously. "But these tattooed biker boys all look the same to me."

"He's a carnie not a biker," she pointed out. "If you're going to pigeonhole people you could at least try to be more attentive to detail."

"Some of us are too busy to go around digging into motives and such, smarty-pants," he said with a smile. "So how's it going overall?"

"I've learned a bit." She shrugged. "No one really seemed to like Keith, and I don't think too many people like Janet either."

"Is that the girlfriend who was dressed up like a cat?" He furrowed his brow.

"Yes, Dad," Maiden said mildly.

"She's a pretty little tomata." He shook his head. "But don't tell Gloria I noticed. So why don't people like her?"

"Depends who you believe." She tucked her phone into her back pocket and folded her arms loosely. "She might be a heartless opportunist or an ambitious woman that came from nothing and found a measure of success."

"Could be both," he pointed out. "Or neither."

"That's helpful," she laughed. "But, speaking of being helpful, I arranged for Mom and Kylie to be entered separately in the bake off."

"Oh no!" he said with a look of horrified disappointment. "You spoiled all the fun!"

"It wasn't fun, Dad." She frowned sternly and draped a hand over her hip.

"It was funny! Gloria's spent days prowling through cookbooks she forgot she had and little Kylie finally found a backbone," he protested. "I was trying to force them to work together so they could get to know each other and become friends!"

"Yeah sure, and you conveniently did it at a time when you wouldn't be home to have to deal with it," she retorted.

"I'm not stupid," he chuckled shamelessly.

Maiden smiled wryly and shook her head at him. A moment later, they were both distracted when they heard someone enter the tent. Maiden glanced over and saw Officer Jeff Briggs standing in the doorway, watching them cautiously.

She had first met the quiet policeman a month ago when he came to investigate her report of a dead body at the inn, but she'd barely spoken to him then or since.

He seemed like a nice enough guy, and he wasn't hard to look at. Reasonably tall and fit, with white-blonde hair and lean, angular features. But despite betraying an indiscreetly obvious attraction to her on more than one occasion, he was stiflingly shy. Which was just as well; she wasn't interested and did not want to have to tell him that.

"Good afternoon," Briggs said as he took another step inside. "Hello again, Miss Harlow."

"Hi, Officer Briggs." She nodded, ignoring the way his gaze wandered down the front of her shirt. "Can we help you with something?"

"Um, I have to follow up on a reported assault," he said uncomfortably and shifted his eyes to Alfie. "A Mr. Sam Chalmers claims you attacked him, Mr. Harlow."

"*What?*" Maiden looked from Briggs' unreadable expression to her remarkably calm father. "Dad...did you get into a fight with Mr. Chalmers?!"

"Not really." Alfie smirked. "That turkey's too slow and doughy to engage in anything resembling a fight."

From the corner of her eye, she saw Briggs subtly pull a notebook from his pocket. She felt a queasy fear slither through her as she knelt beside her father.

"Dad," she said quietly and nodded significantly towards the stoic officer, "be *very* careful what you say. Now tell me what happened."

"Fine. Chalmers was sniffing around in here a little while ago. He just picked stuff up and set it down again for a few minutes. Then he sauntered over and started talking about how successful my stall seemed to be this year, how many items I'd sold and so on." Alfie frowned and took another peek at his knuckles. "I asked what he was getting at. He said something about fees going up and fines for not updating 'permits and so forth'. It was baloney and I saw through it in a second. I did all the required paperwork, I check that every year. So I told him that if there was any *real* problem I would wait to hear from the proper authorities."

"Okay." Maiden nodded; she noticed that Briggs had moved closer. "How did that turn into a fight?"

"Chalmers started talking about making things easier and 'cutting through the red tape'." Alfie gave a couple of exaggerated winks. "I told him he was a crook and he could cram it; he got mad."

"Mr. Harlow," Briggs interjected, "Mr. Chalmers said you punched him in the face. Is that true, sir?"

Maiden's eyes widened incredulously, but she had to quickly suppress a laugh at the ridiculous image that gave rise to. Her father stirred and fisted his uninjured hand on the desk.

"Chalmers started an argument, and then he got angry and violent!" Alfie scowled indignantly. "He lunged at me with a clenched fist! He's too fat and useless to back up that sort of temper. Yes, I did hit him, but only after he attacked me!"

Maiden pushed to her feet and turned to Briggs with widened eyes. He met her gaze and then glanced at her parted lips and cleared his throat.

"So," she gave him a prompting nod when he kept quiet, "it's self-defense, right?"

"The problem is proving that," he said as he looked away. "Mr. Chalmers has evidence of injury and Mr. Harlow's admitted to striking him. No one else witnessed the actual fight."

"Dad only admitted to defending himself," she clarified firmly, and even took a step closer. "So what do we do, accuse Chalmers of attacking him?"

Briggs pulled a face; he clearly didn't want to be dealing with any of this. Maiden wasn't concerned with the man's comfort at the moment; she folded her arms and waited.

"Officer Briggs?" she prompted again, a little louder this time.

"Look, I'm going to report all of it and then we'll see how it goes." He slid his notebook back into his pocket and edged towards the door. "I'll put it on the record that Mr. Harlow alleges that he was the one that was attacked...I'll go and do it now."

"Great." Maiden shut her eyes and shook her head wearily. "Let me walk you out."

Briggs nodded and ducked out through the doorway. She was frowning uneasily as she followed.

"I'm really sorry for any distress, Miss Harlow. I didn't know you'd be here," he apologized when they were both outside and discreetly away from Alfie.

"Does it make a difference?" she asked.

"No, I guess not." He shrugged and glanced down at his feet. "It's just not very nice for you; he's your dad."

"I wouldn't feel too badly, Officer Briggs," she said. "I'm glad I was here."

"Yeah. So...you didn't know anything about the incident before I came here?" he asked carefully.

"Of course not." She shook her head. "You think I'd have done nothing if I knew about it?"

"No, I suppose not." He cleared his throat again. "But the captain will probably ask me about it."

"Yeah." She rolled her eyes. "He probably will."

"Well, I'd better go." Briggs risked another glance at her, he even smiled a little. "I might see you around sometime. Have a really nice evening, Miss Harlow."

Maiden watched him walk away for a moment before shutting her eyes and exhaling slowly; life was getting far too complicated.

"Dad!" she called out as she slipped back into the tent. "You're closing early today. We need to go home and call your lawyer."

CHAPTER TEN

David was at his desk reading through the statement Oliver Armstrong had just given. The massive man sat in a chair across from him, looking completely unperturbed.

Oliver's account had been sparse, but in his defense, he'd been unconscious for hours. The tricky bit was figuring out exactly when he had been knocked out and who was responsible.

"You have absolutely no idea who might've drugged you?" David asked, not for the first time.

"As I said, Captain McAlister," Oliver sighed and shrugged a large shoulder, "it could've been anyone. And I can't think what anybody gained by taking me out of commission like that. I checked my workshop, nothing was missing, I woke up with my wallet too."

"I'm more concerned about the timing in relation to Keith Hayne's death," David pointed out.

Oliver gave a conceding nod, but still looked remarkably tranquil. David studied him with a quirked brow.

"Did you get along well with Keith Haynes?" he asked after a deliberate pause.

"No, I didn't," Oliver said. "He wasn't a nice man and I never liked how he treated others."

"What about Miss Lee?" he murmured. "How did he treat her?"

"Badly." Oliver shrugged again. "From what little I saw and what she claimed, at least."

"Did that bother you?"

"It did at first," he admitted. "But she chose to stay with him."

David stilled and considered him pensively. Oliver presented himself as a mellow and perhaps kind man; that last statement didn't fit.

"Really?" David asked. "A lot of women in bad situations don't believe they have options." It was true; he'd seen it way too many times, and it always left him feeling unsettled.

"I'm aware of that, Captain," Oliver acknowledged. "Not every situation is the same though."

"Did you and Haynes argue much?" he continued, putting the focus back on Oliver.

"We disagreed regularly. Keith got angry a lot, but I don't argue with anyone. I don't like fighting and it rarely does enough good to make it worth dealing with." Oliver smoothed his beard.

"What did you disagree about?"

"Maintenance," Oliver answered dryly. "Keith was a total hypocrite. He was constantly after me to cut costs and take shortcuts and then he turned around and started whining that he didn't think the place was safe."

"Was it safe?" David asked and noted the first stirrings of temper in the larger man.

"Yes, Captain. *Everything* was safe," he said with a hint of irritation. "I never compromised in my duties and I never will."

"Admirable." David kept his own tone serene. "Any fresh ideas about who might have phoned in that tipoff about potential sabotage?"

"No." Oliver folded his arms, clearly done with the conversation.

David didn't want to press him too much yet. The man was obviously not in a frame of mind to be helpful, but he'd unsettled him. That was a good start.

"All right, Mr. Armstrong." He sat back and tapped his fingertips on the arm of his chair. "That's all for now."

Oliver released a slow breath and nodded once as he pushed to his feet and walked out. He was an interesting person, Oliver Armstrong. David had ordered a background check on him, along with everyone else closely linked to Keith Haynes; the results in Mr. Armstrong's case were surprising. He had no criminal record whatsoever, but he was actually a mechanical engineer by trade. He had left a rather lucrative career to become a maintenance man in a travelling carnival.

David glanced at the doorway and shut his eyes briefly when he saw Briggs standing there. He'd sent the young officer to talk to Alfie Harlow about Chalmers' assault allegations. It was an unwelcome distraction and a potentially awkward conflict that he really didn't need dropped on him right now.

"Hey, Briggs. How'd the talk with Mr. Harlow go?" David asked cautiously.

"Um, fine, sir." He sounded subdued and stared off at a potted plant in the corner. "Mostly...Miss Harlow was there too."

"Maiden?" he clarified, somehow not at all surprised that she'd turn up at the worst possible time.

"Yeah," Briggs said with a wisp of a sigh.

"How was she?"

"Pretty," Briggs said without thinking but quickly recovered. "Upset. She was pretty upset, understandable under the circumstances...She was still nice though."

"Did she know about the incident already?" David mercifully ignored Briggs' obvious infatuation with the gorgeous brunette.

"No, sir," he said. "I made a point of asking her that."

"Right." He wasn't as confident as he'd like to be that Briggs would report anything negative about Maiden Harlow. "What did Alfie have to say for himself?"

"That Sam Chalmers was soliciting bribes and then attacked him." Briggs shrugged.

"Are you serious?" David's eyes widened at that unexpected reply.

"Yeah." He nodded and apparently saw no need to elaborate.

"Did Miss Harlow hear that part as well?" he asked as he rubbed his temples; he could feel a sudden headache coming on.

"She did, yes sir." Briggs almost smiled, but it never fully emerged.

"Great," David sighed, knowing with sickening certainty that Harlow would never leave this for anyone else to sort out. "That's exactly what I needed right now."

Maiden had called her mother as she walked back to her car and told her what she knew of Chalmers' allegations. As a result, Gloria, Vonny and Billie had banded together in the foyer and descended on Alfie as soon as he and Maiden stepped inside.

Maiden didn't join the fray but listened as Alfie was first scolded for fighting and then fussed over for being attacked. Alfie didn't argue with any of it, but he wasn't too bothered by the dramatics either. Within moments he'd been escorted upstairs and given a fresh ice pack. Vonny and Billie, the hottest heads present, loudly declared Sam Chalmers to be the absolute worst man in the entire history of the town.

Alfie called his lawyer, who suggested that they first wait and see if Chalmers would cool off and drop the matter. If he didn't, then they'd mobilize and fight any charge he tried to press. That simple plan seemed to mollify Alfie and Gloria completely; they went back to discussing the pie contest and whether Alfie would run out of birdhouses to sell before the end of the week.

Maiden found it much harder to dismiss the looming threat to her father. The frivolous conversation at dinner seemed odd and overly optimistic; she couldn't relax enough to join in. Ultimately, it had to be Chalmers' word against Alfie's. But, as Officer Briggs had pointed out, Chalmers had a black eye, and Alfie had no witnesses to dispute why he gave it to him.

After an evening that didn't last as long as it felt like it did, Maiden crawled into bed. She was tired, but she was even more worried, not only about her father but also about the death of Keith Haynes. It made for a very restless night.

The following morning brought bright sunshine that almost mocked Maiden's worried mood. She covered the desk for a few hours. From her post, she watched uneasily as Alfie waved and left for the markets, whistling happily. She didn't know how both her parents could be so convinced that everything would work out and just carry on as normal; she wished she had inherited that unsinkable confidence.

She realized that worrying about what Chalmers might or might not do was only wasting energy. Punching was bad enough, but she'd be better off trying to prove that Alfie didn't kill anyone. Momentarily struck by the amount of trouble her father had somehow landed himself in, Maiden checked the clock. It was almost 10:30.

She had been at work for about two and a half hours; that was probably plenty. She turned to the office and started tiptoeing towards it when Gloria appeared at the far end of the front desk.

"Angel!" she called happily, causing Maiden to trip and nearly land on her face.

"Could you not start the conversation with shouting at me, please?" she asked as she gave her mother a patient look.

"Hmm?" Gloria smiled as she made the inquiring noise, but continued on before Maiden could answer. "I baked more pies, I need a beta tester!"

"But I need to—" she barely got the words out before Gloria swatted them away.

"That'll keep for twenty minutes," Gloria assured her, despite not knowing what she was going to say. "Come and help your mama!"

"Oh good." Kylie spoke from the doorway of the dining room as her cool gaze rested on her sworn rival. "I was about to come and ask for Maiden's input too. She can test for both of us."

"Do you have to steal my daughter on top of insultin' my crust?" Gloria rolled her eyes ungenerously.

"The one has nothing to do with the other," Kylie replied, clasping her hands in front of her. "If you'd like to bring your specimens downstairs, we can get this over with."

"Um, actually," Maiden raised a finger in a desperate attempt at self-preservation, "I think I might be allergic to pie. I'm still feeling the effects of the last round."

"I have antihistamines in my purse," Kylie said without pity. "This is important, Maiden. The bake-off is next week and I need to narrow down my recipes."

Maiden sighed in defeat and followed her into the dining room as Gloria hurried upstairs, grumbling all the way.

As it turned out, her sacrifice was pointless. The entire ordeal was uncomfortable and needlessly tense. Maiden wasn't good at taking sides or trying to give honest feedback to someone that only wanted to accept praise. Any comment she offered that might've been construed as constructive incited a cranky look from the baker and smug satisfaction from her competitor.

Maiden adopted the most cowardly strategy she could think of. She took a tiny bite of eight different pies and swore that she loved each of them.

Her lackluster performance quickly frustrated Gloria and Kylie, and she was tersely excused. Maiden didn't complain or question; she threw her napkin onto the table and nearly ran out of the room.

It was almost lunchtime when Maiden headed back to Summerfest, hoping to pick up where she'd been forced to leave off yesterday thanks to Sam Chalmers' mischief. Vonny, who'd been hiding in the office, had complained about Maiden going without her again, but the promise of a caramel apple placated her.

As Maiden drove towards the fair, she planned out her next move. She needed to talk to Janet about that birdhouse. It was safe to assume that McAlister had already asked her about it, but he'd hardly share that information around. She also wanted to ask her about Daisy; she wasn't so sure that McAlister knew about *her* yet.

Downtown was bustling with happy tourists, and she was forced to park a little further out. She'd found a space a few streets away, but the sky was blue with no chance of rain, so she didn't mind a bit of a walk.

She trekked ever closer and looked over at one of the small seating areas set up on a nearby sidewalk. The local restaurants were trying to claw back some business from the markets and concession stands by offering alfresco dining right outside their front doors.

As she looked over the patrons, her attention was caught by one of the intimate corner tables outside the Jazz House Café. Mellow music drifted from the outdoor speakers, and several couples sat sipping coffee and eating sandwiches. But the only pair that interested her was Gabby Lopez and Sam Chalmers.

Maiden tried not to stare but slowed her pace considerably as she walked towards them. She could see them both side-on and could only hope they wouldn't spot her. They were talking quietly, but neither appeared to be enjoying the other's company.

Chalmers looked far more weaselly than she'd ever noticed before. His jaw was stubbornly set. and his beady little eyes were selfish and calculating. The thought of this guy taking a swing at her father was infuriating. She knew she was looking for faults, but the smile he kept flashing at Gabby was absolutely devious.

Gabby appeared confident and unfazed; however. It was the first real display of strength that Maiden had ever seen in her. Each time Chalmers held up a finger and sneered as if he'd won, Gabby would produce a page from the stack of papers that she had tucked in a folder on her lap.

Chalmers looked annoyed, but Gabby's expression was stern. Whatever they were talking about, the unexpectedly feisty woman was sticking to her guns.

Maiden stopped under the shade of a maple tree that was planted in front of one of the more eclectic shoe stores in town.

The Shoe Tree lived up to its name; the hapless maple dripped with a collection of old, weather-beaten shoes.

She narrowly avoided being hit in the head by a sneaker that had been painted bright yellow and pretended to be looking at her phone as she kept observing the pair across the street.

Gabby gave an adamant shake of her head and even held a hand up between them. She said something that had a noticeable impact on Chalmers. He sat back in his wrought-iron chair and stared at her. After a few more words from her, he inclined his head meekly.

Gabby looked smugly pleased as she gathered up her papers. She hugged the stack to her chest and turned her nose up at him before walking off toward the carnival.

Chalmers sat for a moment with his chin in his hand and then shook his head and sighed. He drained the last of his coffee and stood. As he turned to pick up the briefcase he'd set next to his chair, Maiden couldn't help seeing his rather impressive black eye.

She hid a rueful smirk and stepped smoothly behind the tree. She edged around and pretended to be looking at a pair of red high heels in the shop window as Chalmers walked past.

Once the loathsome weasel had turned a corner and disappeared from sight, Maiden resumed her journey into the market. She found herself deeply curious about the encounter she'd just observed.

She wondered if it had anything to do with the argument she had seen between Chalmers and Keith the day of the murder. She faltered, even she was calling it murder now, but that had been a niggling suspicion from the start.

With Keith Haynes gone, Chalmers had turned to Gabby with whatever his problem was, not to Janet or anyone else. It was becoming more and more obvious that Gabby was the one who was really running the carnival, just as she had started to admit before. It was also obvious that she wasn't happy about being pushed into the background while bigger personalities scrambled for the glory.

That raised the question of where Janet fit in. If Keith had been the burly frontman who issued threats when needed and closed the deals that Gabby likely orchestrated, then he was expendable. Or at least replaceable from a business perspective.

But if Janet, as his unmotivated girlfriend, did little more than soak up the fringe benefits of dating the boss, then she was a liability. A money pit with little to offer the business in return. Did that put her at risk of being next?

Be careful, Maiden thought to herself. *Keith may have been killed out of personal dislike or some sort of grudge. Don't jump to the conclusion that there's more to it than that.*

She needed more information before anything could make sense. She needed to know what Janet's angle was, who bought the pink birdhouse and why it was sitting by Keith's body.

She also wanted to find out more about what happened to Oliver. He didn't mention being hit over the head and, despite what the movies led one to believe, that probably wouldn't have left him unconscious for hours. If the blow had been that severe, he'd be dead or still in hospital.

What did that leave? Was he lying? Had he faked being unconscious to avoid suspicion? Or had he been drugged? The last possibility was the most intriguing and, in her opinion, was also emerging as the most likely. She'd have to speak to Oliver to see if she could get him talking.

But once again, there was the complication of Janet. According to Timmy Gibson, she was involved with Oliver and possibly others as well. If Oliver felt loyalty to Janet, she would have to be incredibly careful if she got the opportunity to question him.

CHAPTER ELEVEN

Maiden walked under Spencer and Spencer's welcoming banner and started looking around for Janet.

She wasn't surprised that the lady was absent from her post in the concession trucks again; Janet was clearly eyeing off greener pastures now. The lines were long, and the lone attendant serving up the ice cream didn't look like he was loving his life at the moment.

Maiden went deeper, knowing the layout a bit better now. She slipped off between the Ferris wheel and the popcorn wagon and headed for Gabby's office from a different, and hopefully less-used, direction. The last thing she wanted was for anyone to spot her loitering around.

She approached the dinged-up trailer and peeked in the nearest window. She saw only Gabby, poised attentively at her desk. The lady hummed cheerfully to herself, no doubt still basking in her victory over Chalmers, as she signed a few papers and then turned to her computer and started clicking away at her keyboard.

Maiden watched her for a moment, but she barely moved again. She pulled a face and was about to keep walking when she saw someone else approaching. It was Daisy; she was dressed in green velvet shorts and a brown leather bustier complete with metal studs crisscrossing over each breast.

She was an interesting sight; her fluorescent purple hair was in two curly pigtails today and her clothes were quite snug on her tall, robust frame. Her skillful flair for the eccentric made her mesmerizing to behold. Like some sort of medieval lava lamp.

Despite feeling a tiny stab of guilt for being sneaky, Maiden ducked into the shadows and listened as Daisy walked up the creaky steps to the office and rapped loudly on the open door.

"Hey Daisy, how are you?" Gabby greeted her in a placid tone.

"Fantastic, how else would I be?" Daisy's reply was caustic. "I need to talk to you."

"What about?" she sighed.

"Keith's disaster of a playmate," Daisy said flatly. "You realize she's just about ruined the concession stands, right?"

"I haven't taken a close look at them yet," Gabby told her. "There've been a few more pressing problems of late."

"How close do you need to look? You can see it from here!" she huffed. "We both know perfectly well why Keith gave her that job. We also know that she can't do it. She doesn't order supplies, she doesn't order more food, they're out of almost everything and there's only one person working during the busiest shifts! How much money does this place have to lose before someone has the guts to stand up to that cow?!"

"I understand that this is difficult for you," Gabby said. "I'm taking care of things, but some problems are more urgent than others."

"A huge chunk of the carnival's revenue is going up in smoke!" She didn't relent for a moment. "How is that not important?"

"I never said it wasn't." Gabby's tone grew crisp and firm. "Frankly, I don't need *more* people telling me what to do right now! I know how to run this place and that's what I'm doing. I will deal with Janet at the appropriate time. If it bothers you, go and do an inventory and I'll order what we need for the short term."

"I am *not* doing all the work to make that trashy chick look good!" Daisy spat indignantly. "If you hand that job back to me I'll whip it into shape and get it running like clockwork. Just like I *always* did! Until then, that woman stands or falls all by her lonesome."

"Don't be petty, Daisy," she said. "That won't get you your job back."

"We'll see if I don't get my job back," Daisy muttered. "I'll sort this out myself since you're too weak to do anything."

Maiden's eyes widened and she ducked around a corner when she heard Daisy's sudden and angry departure. She watched as the woman stalked away with her hands fisted at her sides.

Maiden stared at her until she was out of sight; she then eased back enough to risk another peek at Gabby. She saw her take a deep breath and then resume her typing, but her sharp, jerky movements revealed her lingering irritation.

The angry discussion was curious, and she suspected that Daisy's disgust with Janet was a common sentiment among the crew. It raised an important question: with Keith out of the picture, why hadn't Gabby fired her yet?

It was possible that Gabby was too kind-hearted to throw Janet out right after her boyfriend had been murdered. But it was interesting that Daisy mentioned no one having the guts to deal with the woman; it seemed odd with the protection of Keith gone. What other clout was Janet likely to have?

Maiden snuck away before Gabby could catch her eaves-dropping. As she walked further in, she did her best to blend in like a tourist, pretending to admire the rides and taking pictures on her phone of the Ferris wheel and a scary-looking pendulum ride in the distance.

There were a handful of other patrons wandering about, but it was still close to lunchtime and most of the fair-goers were packing the overwhelmed concession areas. That suited Maiden just fine; it meant fewer people to either see her prowling the area or obscure her target.

Janet had to be around somewhere; even the most irresponsible of employees had to turn up once in a while to keep their toe in the water. Her efforts eventually paid off when she rounded a corner and spied Janet's platinum hair in the shaded alleyway formed between a massive jumping castle and the shooting gallery.

The satisfaction of victory turned to horror when Maiden saw that the lady wasn't alone. A man with a bandana covering the lower half of his face had his arm locked around her throat. Janet's face was contorted with fear and her struggle to keep breathing even as she thrashed at the man's legs with her stiletto heels. He shifted out of the way and pulled his arm tighter.

"Hey!" Maiden shouted and started towards them. "Get away from her! *Help!*"

The man looked up, and his pale eyes widened. He let go abruptly and took off running in the other direction. Janet dropped to the ground and grasped at her throat as she tried to pull in a few breaths. Maiden was beside her a moment later.

"Are you all right?" she asked as she glanced around for any sign of lingering danger.

"Yes, thank you." Janet wheezed and coughed a few times. "I'm glad you came along."

"Yeah, so am I." Maiden shook her head anxiously and pulled out her phone. "Keep an eye out in case he comes back, I'll call the police."

"No!" She winced as the effort to speak came at a painful price. "No, don't do that, it's okay. Just a mix up, that's all."

"A mix up?" Maiden gaped at her. "You think that creep mistook your head for a bottlecap? I'm calling the cops."

"Please leave it!" Janet said urgently, grasping her arm. "I don't want to make a big deal out of this; it's just one of the boys, he's a bit drunk."

"You know who it was, don't you?" Maiden watched her with burgeoning suspicion.

"Of course not, but he looked like a member of the crew." She waved it away.

"And you're okay with employees of this carnival getting drunk and randomly choking people?" she demanded, hardly believing what she was hearing.

"It's not random." Janet shut her eyes. "Some of the others here resented my relationship with Keith. They thought I was using him to get special treatment. I can't help it if he did nice things for me, can I? I never asked for anything, he just did it."

"Why attack now though?" Maiden asked. "Keith isn't an issue anymore."

"I told you he was probably drunk. Resentment runs deep," she replied sadly.

"That's still not a good reason to let this go unreported." Maiden shook her head and helped Janet to her feet. "If they get away with this, they'll only try again."

"I don't want anyone sniffing around in my personal business, all right?" Janet's eyes narrowed and her tone hardened.

"No, it's not all right," she said just as staunchly. "Has it occurred to you that whoever killed Keith is still on the loose? And now this? Come on, let's get out of this alley."

Janet went quiet after the mention of Keith's murder. Maiden took advantage of the lull, and with only the slightest hesitation, called Captain McAlister. She shifted a little and managed not to fidget as it started to ring; she wondered if he had her number saved in his phone and soon got her answer.

"You're actually calling me?" he asked wryly. "Something incredible must had happened."

"Attempted murder," she said bluntly, and gave Janet a firm but understanding look when she stiffened and turned to her sharply. "Are you at the fair by any chance?"

"Yeah, I am." He sounded much more alert now. "Are you serious, Harlow? Are you in danger?"

There are the good manners, well done! she thought churlishly but kept it to herself.

"I think we're okay, but someone attacked Janet." She glanced over and rested a hand on the lady's slender shoulder. "We're by the shooting gallery, if you could hurry, that would be great."

"I'm on my way," he said. "Stay there."

She hung up and put her phone back in her pocket. Janet dropped onto the nearest bench and was rubbing her throat as she stared down at the dirt. Maiden watched her quietly; she found it strange that Janet had resisted calling the police so strongly. She still didn't appear pleased about it, but sat there waiting. Of course, she didn't really have a choice.

It wasn't long before McAlister arrived with an out of breath Greg close behind. Maiden glanced over and raised a hand to flag them down. McAlister looked her over in an assessing manner as he approached, as though searching for any sign of injury before shifting his watchful gaze to Janet.

"All right, what happened?" he asked as he reached them. He scowled when he saw the angry red marks on Janet's throat.

"Nothing significant," Janet said firmly and gestured towards her. "Maiden saw a brief exchange with a pickpocket or something and got very upset. I've tried to calm her down, but she's not listening to me."

"Miss Harlow?" McAlister glanced at her.

"She was being strangled from behind by Timmy Gibson," she replied without hesitation. "I yelled and he ran off."

"What?" Janet blurted. "That's crazy!"

"He was wearing the same powder blue sleeveless shirt I saw him in yesterday. He was half drunk then." Maiden shrugged. "In any case, I recognized the tattoos on his left arm. On his shoulder there's a skeleton with a cowboy hat riding a horse. Under that is a wolf howling at the moon and on his forearm he's got a redhead in a bikini with a massive bottom."

"You can't have seen him that clearly." Janet was staring at her.

"There's also the two gold earrings on the ridge of his right ear," she rattled off easily. "Small scar on his forehead. And he runs like a three-legged squirrel, but he's probably still drunk."

"Stop showing off." McAlister smirked and pulled out his notebook. "Where'd he go?"

"He ran off down the alley." Maiden nodded towards it. "I neglected to follow him, sorry."

"How unusually sensible of you," he said under his breath and told Greg to have a look around. He then glanced back at Janet. "Any idea why Gibson would try to kill you?"

"He didn't!" She looked startled and appalled. "This is ridiculous! The man had a mask on, there's no way she could have seen who he was!"

"The mask covered a small portion of a very distinctive appearance. One that you no doubt recognized as easily as I did," Maiden pointed out, and then decided to throw her off kilter a bit more. "So, why didn't you want me to call the police? You were strongly against the idea."

McAlister arched a brow at Janet. She was scowling now and fisted her small hands angrily in her lap.

"Refusing to report a crime is serious, Miss Lee," he said. "What's the story?"

"This is all being blown way out of proportion!" she hissed, glaring at Maiden and then at him. "If I don't want to make an issue of it, why should anybody else?!"

"Because you might not be the only one in danger. And if I'd come along a few minutes later, you'd be dead," Maiden said plainly. "To be honest, you're arguing this a little too much; just something to think about."

Janet eyed her coldly but fell silent. As she thought it over, she finally started to calm. Whether it was genuine or because she understood that continuing to lie about the attack sounded suspicious was harder to tell.

"I...I don't want any more bad publicity. Okay?" she admitted with a sigh. "What happened to Keith was damaging enough; if this business has any hope of surviving we really need to keep some sort of good reputation. Rumors of muggings aren't going to help us."

"Hiding a criminal isn't an effective way to protect a business' reputation," McAlister said dryly.

"Especially when it was a targeted attack, not a mugging," Maiden added and gave Janet a curious frown. "Aren't you scared?"

"A little, yeah," Janet allowed in a subdued tone. "But not for the first time in my life. I'll be fine, I always am. Right now I need a roof over my head more than patronizing shows of fake concern."

"Cute. Thanks a lot," Maiden said with a humorless laugh. "For what it's worth, I rarely confront violent strangers just because I'm bored."

"Sorry, gorgeous." Janet frowned gently down at her lap. "I guess I'm a bit shaken up still. That came out harsher than I meant it to."

"I understand. Anyway, I'll leave you in the captain's capable hands," she murmured and stepped away. "Captain McAlister, my only advice is to look for a diabolical genius with 'Timmy' embroidered on his shirt. He's very slippery, don't let the masked scoundrel outwit you."

As she walked off, she could hear McAlister telling Janet not to move and that he'd be with her in a minute. She heard footsteps approach seconds later; she didn't stop or even slow her pace until she felt a tap on her shoulder.

Maiden turned to find McAlister standing kind of close. She honestly didn't mind that, but it surprised her, so she eased back half a step. He folded his arms over his broad chest and held her gaze steadily.

"Are you sure you're okay?" he asked.

"I think so," she replied ingenuously, patting herself down. "Everything seems to be where I left it."

"Fine. Are you going home now?" McAlister submerged a smile.

"Not right this second, no." She frowned. "Why do you ask?"

"Because either you find danger or it finds you," he said. "I have enough to deal with at the moment without you wandering around and getting into trouble."

"'Getting into trouble'?" she repeated with startled annoyance, resting her hands on her hips. "Are you aware that I just saved Janet's life? Which almost certainly makes it easier for you to question her."

"Yes I know, and it was very brave of you." He held up a hand in a calming gesture that was somehow more aggravating than his soothing tone. "But it's done now and this business is getting risky so I want you to go home."

"You think you can just spank me and send me to my room?—*Shut up!*" She pointed at him and raised her voice sharply as she processed what she'd actually said. "You know that's not what I meant!"

"Miss Harlow," he said after pausing to compose himself; he still rubbed his hands over his face in a fruitless attempt to hide his grin. "Please, you can't keep flirting your way around me."

"You are the most obnoxious person I've ever met!" she said tightly. "And I know a *lot* of people!"

"Stop it!" His voice was uneven as he struggled not to laugh. "I'm only flesh and blood!"

"I have to go," she muttered, feeling like a complete idiot now.

Maiden fumed as she stalked away from him. How that man managed to make her feel stupid after doing something heroic, she couldn't begin to understand. Whenever she was around him, she always seemed to say something dumb.

Her steps were swift and angry, but she felt a hint of relief and almost smiled when she saw Greg up ahead. He clearly hadn't found Timmy, but he offered a blessed reprieve from dealing with McAlister, as well as her verbal blunders.

Greg glanced up from his notebook and smiled at her, but looked beyond her shoulder and abruptly sobered. That meant McAlister was still following her; she felt her mood darken further and quickened her pace.

"Miss Harlow, wait up," McAlister called as he caught up with them. "I'm serious, I want you to leave this alone."

"Well, you don't dictate what I do, Captain," she retorted coolly as she glanced at him over her shoulder. "How about you keep me out of it by doing some work yourself?"

"Oh!" Greg exclaimed with a loud laugh before he could help it. He clapped a hand over his mouth and quickly looked away.

"What did you say?" McAlister stared at her incredulously.

"Didn't you hear me?" She turned to him, her dark brows lifted in gentle inquiry.

"*That's* how you talk to me, really?" He sounded more surprised than angry.

"Have you heard the way you talk to *me*?" she countered, not about to apologize for responding in kind.

"Is this because I wouldn't spank you?" he asked gently, and Greg whipped his head back around to stare at them.

You absolute toad of a spoiled brat, Maiden cursed the unwilling smile that curved her lips and quickly glanced away. *I can't believe you said that...and it was really funny. Do not laugh, Maiden. I'll give you a chocolate cupcake later if you don't laugh.*

She cleared her throat daintily, knowing full well that her cheeks had tinged pink. While his well-aimed retort secretly impressed her, she refused to let him win, and throwing insults at him would be handing him the victory on a platter. She did her best to ignore his quiet, sexy smile and pulled out her phone.

McAlister frowned a little as she started dialing. He glanced over at Greg when his phone rang. The long-suffering officer drew it out and put it to his ear.

"Hi, Maiden." He looked curiously at McAlister, who had turned back to her at this point.

She smiled wanly as she looked the captain in the eye.

"Hi, Greg," she said. "Could you do me a favor and tell your boss that he's being a *massive* jerk again?"

"Can't I just hand him the phone?" Greg rolled his eyes.

"No, you'd better not, he gets terribly jealous when I talk to other policemen," she said without looking away from McAlister's dark gaze. "So don't let him know it was me. Thanks, bye."

David was watching her with his arms folded and a remarkably patient look on his face. Harlow hung up the phone and shoved it in her back pocket before giving him a wink as she turned on her heel and sauntered away.

"It's times like this I wish you were less hot," he murmured quietly at her retreating back. He'd forgotten Smith was there until he spoke up.

"You don't really wish that, do you?" he asked with a puzzled frown.

"No, not really," David admitted as he leaned to the side to check out her bottom as she rounded the corner of a ticket booth. "It does make putting up with the sarcasm more worthwhile...All right, let's go."

Chapter Twelve

Maiden wandered around the carnival with no particular destination for a while to put any nosey cops off her scent. When she felt sure she was alone, she slipped off into the areas set aside for the workers.

The back lot was far less festive and colorful than the facade that the tourists enjoyed. A large portion of the parking lot of the local mall had been surrendered to accommodate Spencer and Spencer's numerous employees. Rows of trailers that housed them were interspersed with old lawn chairs and the occasional portable barbeque.

It was decidedly close quarters; she quickly saw why having an entire trailer to yourself would be a coveted privilege. The area was mostly empty as the fair was in peak hours; confident that she wouldn't be seen, she pressed further in.

It occurred to her that Timmy could be anywhere by now. There was a chance that McAlister and Greg had caught him already, but he could just as easily be hiding out somewhere nearby. She stayed alert and watchful as she wove through the rows of trailers.

She slowed her pace when she walked by one or two that were occupied. The smell of greasy food cooking mingled with cigarette smoke before being carried off on a merciful breeze. Maiden still held her breath until she had gotten away from the unpleasant smells.

She carefully skirted around a corner, ducked below a handful of windows and tried to look natural as she walked more briskly past an open front door. Snatches of conversations and the blare of a radio wafted out as she passed by unseen.

When she reached the outer edge of the crew's area, she saw a longer trailer sitting off on its own. It was a big silver beast of a vehicle with 'Workshop' stylishly emblazoned on the sides with green and yellow spray-paint.

She was definitely closing in on Oliver Armstrong. Apart from a stack of rusty steel drums near the door, the only other objects of note around the place were a few lawn flamingos fashioned out of scrap metal. She recalled Oliver's admiration of her dad's woodworking; evidently, his interest in unique and handmade décor was genuine.

She was working on a plausible way to open a conversation with him as she started towards the door, but she froze when she heard voices inside. She recognized Janet's throaty tones easily; she was a bit huskier since the attempted strangling.

Maiden considered her options for about half a second before hiding behind the steel drums. Eavesdropping wasn't a tactic she felt proud of, and she was a little surprised at how naturally it was starting to come to her. Perhaps it was because she was getting so much practice.

In any case, she didn't want to talk to Oliver and Janet at the same time; that felt risky. She crouched down low and listened intently.

"I can't believe you never told me!" Janet sounded hurt and possibly angry.

"And I can't believe you've stooped to reading my mail," Oliver replied dryly.

"What else was I supposed to do?" she demanded. "You've been acting strangely for weeks and now you won't even talk to me. What's really going on?"

"I'm just trying to do my job and keep this ridiculous show in working order," he said. "Which should be easier without your boyfriend skulking around loosening bolts and hiding parts."

"You know I had nothing to do with any of that," Janet protested sulkily.

"Really?" He sounded doubtful and disinterested. "Who got angry with him and made him think he'd find you in my room? And didn't he look like an idiot when he stormed in and found me alone. Not that it ended there; he was a huge pain in the neck ever since. So who was feeding those suspicions?"

"Keith was just a jealous guy, you know that." A big cloud of cigarette smoke billowed through the doorway as she spoke. "Look, not to sound crass, but he isn't our problem anymore. We can go anywhere you want, we don't have to stay here. We can start over with a clean slate, just the two of us."

"You know how I feel about that," he said more quietly. "Keith being gone doesn't change anything. I told you that already."

"But you didn't mean it!" Her voice grew louder and agitated. "You can't have! I've done so much to cover for you! Don't tell me that was for nothing!"

"I don't know what you're talking about," he muttered. "Look, I have my plans and that's it. I'm not going to shackle myself to another woman who's willing to cheat."

Maiden's mouth fell open; she couldn't imagine a devastating statement like that would go over well. The explosion of foul language that spewed out of Janet's mouth proved her right. Oliver didn't say a word in reply, and finally Janet stormed out with a frustrated shriek.

Maiden sat very still, hugging her knees to her chest in an attempt to look small and inconspicuous. She waited a few cautious minutes before she crept out into the open, all the while throwing nervous glances at the door of the workshop. She quickly decided that now wasn't the best time to talk to Oliver after all.

Maiden quickly headed back the way she had come. A part of her was tempted to stay at the carnival longer to spite McAlister a little, but she had thinking to do, and that called for peace and quiet. The attack on Janet had been disturbing in itself, but her refusal to do anything about it was even stranger. Janet said her attacker was one of the crew, so she must've gotten a look at him. She had to have known that it was Timmy.

She wondered what had driven Timmy to the point of violence, apart from too much alcohol. He really had meant to kill Janet, and that was a far cry from babbling about weak links and big problems. Something else must have happened, or there was a connection between him and Janet that she didn't know about.

She didn't get the impression that Janet had mentioned the attempt on her life to Oliver either. The woman was so determined to cover it up, but her reasoning seemed flimsy. Despite her claims of being desperate to keep the carnival running, she'd just openly offered to leave it all behind to start up somewhere else with the burly mechanic.

Maiden headed for Alfie's tent. She would see if he needed anything before she left for the day and then veer off long enough to get Vonny the caramel apple she'd promised her. A glass of wine and the quiet of her balcony beckoned to her; she hoped her father would tell her he was fine and that she may as well head straight home.

As Maiden approached his tent, her eyes widened and her stomach lurched. She saw her father stationed angrily in the doorway of his stall while Sam Chalmers pointed at him and railed like a maniac. It was both a comfort and a worry to see Captain McAlister and Greg standing nearby. Greg flicked her a nervous look and shook his head unhappily when he spotted her.

"What's going on now?" Maiden asked seriously as she approached and stood protectively at her father's side.

"*That man!*" Chalmers said through his teeth as he jabbed a finger in Alfie's direction. "Not satisfied with his unprovoked attack, he's escalated to sending me a death threat!"

Maiden looked at him like he were an idiot; it was preferable to blacking his other eye. The thought of Alfie threatening anyone was absurd. She folded her arms over her chest and arched a brow.

"Explain," she said.

"I received a menacing letter delivered to my office," Chalmers spluttered and turned to McAlister for confirmation.

McAlister stepped forward and held up the letter for her to see, but pulled back a little and gave her a look when she reached for it. It was in a plastic sleeve; she wasn't sure what he thought she'd do to it, but now wasn't the time to argue. Maiden just nodded and tucked her hands behind her back as she looked it over. The words had been cut and pasted onto a sheet of A4 paper.

Leave town or die! This is your last warning.

"You see?" Chalmers stamped his foot. "The attack was the first warning, and this is the second. Or the 'last', I should say!"

"You're loopy, Chalmers." Alfie rolled his eyes. "I don't need to threaten you and I don't care where you hang your shingle. You attacked me and I defended myself. That's the end of the matter as far as we're concerned."

"Not a chance, Harlow!" Chalmers grated. "For a start, I'm shutting your stall down. And first thing tomorrow I'm going to start the ball rolling to get you banned from Summerfest for life! Along with any other event in this town!"

"You can't do that. This isn't a dictatorship and you have no proof of anything." Maiden did her best to keep her voice steady. "All you have is an anonymous note with nothing to link it to Dad."

"We'll see about that!" he muttered darkly. "In the meantime, pack up all this junk and get it out of here!"

"I suppose it's no use to you, since you didn't get your kickback." Alfie sniffed at him and turned back to the tent. "You haven't heard the last of this, Chalmers. You're a snake and it'll catch up with you."

Maiden stepped to the side and draped her hands on her hips to block a furious Chalmers from storming inside after him. Her heart was thudding with anger and the unpleasant stress of an angry confrontation; she ignored it and kept her expression icy cold.

"You've served your notice, Chalmers." McAlister stepped closer to intercede. "You don't have much time to substantiate some very serious claims. Get out of here."

"I am coordinating this event, *Captain!*" Chalmers, already in a foul mood, turned to him and snarled. "I won't be ordered around and I won't leave until I'm ready!"

"Then I suggest that you make yourself ready *now*." McAlister took a step toward him. "You have no grounds to harass anyone, including Mr. Harlow."

Chalmers blustered but retreated. Maiden watched him stalk away, occasionally throwing a hand in the air as he continued the argument by himself.

Dad was right, she sighed inwardly, *he's a turkey.*

"I did ask you to go home," McAlister reminded her mildly as he shifted his attention back to her.

"Which would have helped my father how?" She turned to him, and he just shrugged. "What's the story with the stupid note?"

"I can't go into all the details," he said and handed the paper in question to Greg.

"You can't tell us the details of the note that my father's been accused of sending?" she demanded incredulously.

"I've already discussed all of that with Mr. Harlow," he replied without apology.

She stared at him and set her teeth as that sank in. He was refusing to discuss it with her, and with her specifically. Despite knowing that Alfie would confide in her, she was being *officially* excluded. She felt anger well up, but tamped it down brutally.

"Then we're done here," she said simply and disappeared into the tent.

She didn't look back; she refused to. She was pretty sure that she'd heave a birdhouse at him if he said another word to her. The turmoil of anger at Chalmers and now McAlister twisted with fear for her father and left her too on edge to tolerate much more at the moment.

Ignoring the way her hands were shaking, Maiden threw herself into the work that had to be done. She quickly helped her father pull out boxes and pack up his remaining stock. There was still a decent amount, but she was glad that he'd already sold well over half of his projects. It would make the mortifying process of being evicted a little quicker, if nothing else.

She glanced over and saw Alfie shaking his head and muttering as he packed up. He was such a kind and funny man; she hated seeing him treated with such disrespect. She felt tears of hurt sting her eyes, but blinked them away.

For the moment, she needed to help get her father out of the immediate danger of the situation. She wouldn't put it past Chalmers to hang around and come back to make sure they left, particularly when the police presence was gone. Once they were safely home, the family could sit down and plan their next move.

Maiden shook her head grimly; Chalmers had gone too far. He'd jumped to conclusions based on an encounter that he had personally escalated, and now he was using what meager influence he had to blackball her father because he didn't cave in to his greedy demands.

No, it was too much. They wouldn't stand back and let some crook taint the family's reputation or ruin woodworking for Alfie. Maiden was determined to expose the truth; her biggest hurdle would be figuring out how to do it.

But one thing was certain: Chalmers had made a huge tactical error; he'd chosen to pick on a man who had daughters.

Chapter Thirteen

As soon as they'd gotten home, Alfie called his lawyer again. They followed his advice to file an official complaint against Sam Chalmers. It was some recourse, but it wasn't a huge comfort or a guarantee of justice. The mood in the apartment was somber, and the evening was tense and uncomfortable.

Maiden had closed herself in her room straight after dinner, but sleep didn't come easily. She found it hard to believe that anyone would send Chalmers a death threat, and she knew Alfie certainly wouldn't.

Her thoughts went to Gabby and the brusque meeting she'd observed between her and Chalmers. Although wishing she could have heard what they were talking about, Maiden had to admit that Gabby had left looking smug, not murderous.

Of course, if Chalmers was in business for himself with some sort of extortion racket, there might be no shortage of people who wanted him run out of town. It wasn't a murder attempt after all; it was a threat. Someone was trying to scare him off, not get rid of him for good...hopefully.

By the following day, Maiden's mood had mellowed, but only slightly. She hadn't slept well, and she had no interest in breakfast. In hopes of avoiding listening to Gloria and Vonny fume over the situation and making her feel queasy again, she escaped downstairs and took up her post at reception.

It was mid-morning when Alfie finally ventured downstairs. As he rounded the corner and headed for the desk, Maiden started to stand so he could have the chair. Alfie smiled and gestured for her to stay put as he came and stood beside her. She sighed and gave him a concerned look.

"Are you okay, Dad?" she asked quietly.

"Yes, sweetheart, I promise you I'm fine. I'm not giving up on everything because of one greasy creep, don't you worry." He smiled affably and tapped his fingertip against his temple. "I'm already working on it."

"Awesome...what's your plan?" She was only slightly uncomfortable about what he might be hatching. "Keeping in mind that you can't punch him again."

"Once was enough." Alfie frowned down at his knuckles; they were still splotched with purple. "No, I have something else in mind, I'm going to get started today. I'll tell you about it later."

"Or you could tell me now." She gave him an earnest smile that she hoped would sway him. "Please."

"I have a few people I want to talk to," he allowed, but that was clearly all he wanted to say about it for the moment. "That young man of yours was quite helpful yesterday, it got me thinking."

"He's not my young man, Dad." Maiden ran a hand over her face. "He wouldn't even tell me what happened."

"It was hardly the time to stand around and discuss anything." He shrugged. "We'd just been told to clear out."

Maiden stilled and just looked at him; it was actually a quite valid point. She felt badly for being so surprised that it came from her dad, but in her defense he had a pen tucked behind both ears today.

"So, what exactly did he say to you yesterday?" She hadn't been game to ask him about the discussion last night since Vonny and Gloria had been hovering.

"He said the note had been pushed through the mail slot at Chalmer's office, no one saw who did it," Alfie murmured. "He also said they'll check for fingerprints, but he doubts they'll find anything useful. That dribbling moron Chalmers had already pawed it too much."

"Is that what he said?" Maiden gave him a doubtful look.

"I'm paraphrasing." Alfie waved it away. "Anyway, Captain McAlister got there first and advised me to talk to my lawyer before saying much, and not to engage with Chalmers if he tried to provoke me."

"Mm," she grunted thoughtfully. *That was actually really nice of him...darn it.*

She wondered if McAlister knew deep down that Chalmers' accusations were a complete crock. She hoped so, but hope alone wasn't going to pull her father out of this mess. And the way the captain kept trying to shut her out of everything didn't give her much to put her confidence in.

Her thoughts drifted to that note. She wondered if a spiteful Chalmers might have sent it to himself, just to get back at Alfie. Far-fetched, perhaps, but she wouldn't dismiss the idea completely, not yet.

"I'll be back later." He patted her on the shoulder and then walked towards the front door with purposeful steps.

Maiden watched him go with a fond smile. She had no idea what was going to happen, but she was glad to see him so upbeat about it all. A moment later Gloria walked in with a bag of groceries, doubtless more pie ingredients. At this point, Maiden had lost count of how many pies her mother had made. Gloria sauntered towards the stairs but detoured long enough to give Maiden a conspiratorial look.

"I found the fattest Granny Smith apples you ever seen!" She grinned as she pulled out an apple the size of a grapefruit. "Let Miss Fancy-la-dee-da choke on *that*!"

"You want people to choke on your pies?" Maiden asked with a trace of a smirk. "That's a different approach, kill the competition and then win every ribbon on offer? Dastardly."

"Don't tempt me, angel," Gloria cackled and continued towards the stairs. "Some of us don't need to spend years at college just to learn to cook! It's a bit pitiful if you ask me."

"Well, that's kind of mean, so it's a good thing I didn't ask you," Maiden mumbled to herself as she checked the doorway to the dining room to make sure Kylie hadn't been within earshot.

Another couple of hours passed uneventfully. Kylie wandered out at one point with a cappuccino, hoping to bribe her into tasting a cherry cream cheese pie with buttered brandy sauce. While she was there, Kylie also dropped a few less than generous remarks about her rival, although she was much more subtle about it than Gloria had been. Maiden smiled as broadly as she could, told her the pie was excellent, and then hid the plate in a drawer as soon as she walked away.

Maiden was sipping the coffee when she heard the clatter of a mop and bucket. Billie peeked around the end of the staircase.

Maiden couldn't hide her resigned sigh as she watched Billie creep cautiously into the foyer before setting her bucket down near the dining room. She looked as though she were hiding from sniper fire.

She spared Maiden a quick, anxious nod of greeting and then got to work. The fastidious cleaning lady started swirling her mop over the tiles, checking the doorway of the kitchen every few seconds, doubtless in fear of the same specter of baked evil that had been terrorizing them all. Maiden shook her head wryly as she considered the small but energetic woman.

Billie had worked for their family for years, and she worked hard. She could be a little too plain-spoken sometimes, but she was fiercely loyal.

She had been outside sweeping when Alfie and Maiden arrived home yesterday afternoon. Once she'd learned why they were carting boxes of his wooden creations back from the markets she ranted for an hour. She'd also thrown in some incredibly personal insults about Sam Chalmers, despite having never met the man.

Maiden had found the tirade frustrating as she'd been struggling with her own anger over the incident, but Billie had also helped them move the boxes back to Alfie's workshop. It was an instance of taking the rough with the smooth.

At the moment, Billie dropped her mop into her bucket and glanced over at Maiden. Her dark brows lifted, and her pale eyes were saddened.

"How's your dad today?" she asked uneasily.

"He's okay." Maiden smiled at the genuine concern in the other woman's gaze. "A little annoyed, but I would be too if my name was being dragged through the mud."

"I can't believe that idiot Chalmers!" Billie's nostrils flared, and she clenched her fists at her sides.

"Yes, I haven't forgotten." Maiden smiled again. "He'll get sorted out, don't worry. He doesn't run this town."

"He sounds too stupid to run anything," Billie muttered. "Including his fat, stupid mouth."

"So, we're agreed that he's stupid," Maiden chuckled, but was soon distracted by the sound of footsteps outside.

Both women glanced at the front door when it cracked open. Tony Ferris came in with a satchel of mail slung over his shoulder. A devious smile lit his face when he saw them, devious by his standards at least. He looked around to make sure no one else was in the foyer before creeping closer. Maiden sat a bit straighter; he was acting furtive, which meant he had news.

"Hey Tony." She eyed him curiously. "You're a little later than usual today."

"I know, some things have come up." He slid a handful of letters across the desk; he then rested his elbows on the polished wood and leaned closer. "Guess what."

"You've decided to give up the postal worker gig to be an astronaut instead?" she replied unhelpfully.

"Close, but no." He leaned in even more. "There's been another accident at the carnival."

"Are you serious?" Maiden gasped, her eyes widening. "When?"

"Today, and not long ago," he whispered intently. "The Ferris wheel broke down."

"Are you related to the guy who invented the Ferris wheel?" Billie asked in such a mild tone that it was hard to tell if she was joking.

"Yeah, Billie. I'm secretly a zillionaire." His serene smile quickly re-emerged; he rarely managed to look intense for very long. "That's why I drag this big bag around all day."

"How bad was the breakdown? Was anyone hurt?" Maiden ignored the disruption and tried to steer the conversation back on course.

"Not according to my sources, no. But a few of my regulars haven't checked in yet," he said in a perfectly serious tone. "The poor people stuck at the top have had a pretty terrible time though. Apparently, the ride had been working just fine and then ground to a screeching halt. They called in the police and the fire department. Last I heard, they were having to lower everyone down in harnesses."

"I hate carnival rides," Billie said with a sad shake of her head. "Those rickety outfits traveling from town to town; who knows how often they leave pieces of machines behind?"

"I've met the head of maintenance for Spencer and Spencer," Maiden mentioned, striving to be a little more open-minded. "He seems to know what he's doing."

"A lot of terrified fair-goers might disagree with you there," Tony pointed out.

"It's weird, that's for sure," Maiden said as she started sinking into thought.

Billie braced a hand on her narrow, well-toned hip. Apart from being a good friend and a dedicated wife and mother, she was mildly addicted to boot camp.

"I think that stupid, traveling clown-fest has been nothing but trouble since they scraped into town. They ought to be moved along, you know what I'm saying?" she muttered in a grim tone, lifting her dark brows once for emphasis.

"You're scary," Tony said simply and turned back to Maiden. "What do you think? Are you going to check it out?"

"Check what out?" She shook her head a little.

"The breakdown." He looked surprised at her confusion. "You're working on the case aren't you? Von told me that you and McAlister are all hotted up again."

"*What!*" Maiden stared at him in exasperated disbelief and then remembered that Vonny had been texting all night after they found Keith's body. "Never mind. As usual, Vonny's bored and exaggerating everything."

"I don't know about that." He smiled and pretended to study the backs of a few letters. "I talk to Greg regularly too. According to him, you and the captain haven't been especially subtle. It's not really fair to overtly flirt in public and then get upset when people notice. Just saying."

"If I may change the subject to something less imaginary," Maiden said with a hint of cranky warning. "I need you to do something for me, well, for Dad."

"What is it? What's wrong with Alfie?" Tony was suddenly all business.

Since his own father had died when he was a kid, Alfie had long ago become the nearest thing Tony had to a dad of his own. Maiden had walked in on one or two solemn, man-to-man talks over the years. She'd been young and overheard just enough to either bore her or gross her out; she typically scampered away as fast as could.

"Oh!" Billie turned red and angry again. "Don't get me started!"

Maiden hurried to explain the situation. Tony went from quietly amused at the thought of Alfie decking some swindler to outraged that he'd been thrown out of Summerfest so unjustly.

"All right, let's deal with this." He leaned against the desk again and lowered his voice to a conspiratorial whisper. "What can I do?"

"Do you deliver anything to City Hall?" Maiden asked.

"Yeah, sometimes." He inclined his head once. "Me and a few of the other guys alternate."

"Good. And do you know Chalmers' secretary?"

"Let me think." Tony considered that carefully, and then nodded. "Yes, a little redhead, I'm pretty sure her name is Florence. She's nice."

"Could you try to find out a bit more about that threatening note?" She held his gaze. "*Anything* that might give me an idea of who sent it...assuming Chalmers isn't lying about it."

"Maiden!" Billie gasped loudly and pointed at her. "I didn't even think of that! You're a genius!...Except you're clueless about when guys like you."

"No, she's not." Tony flashed his old friend a fond smile. "You just get embarrassed and deny it. Don't you, Maiden?"

Before she could try to deflect that annoyingly accurate assessment, they heard Gloria's voice echoing down the stairwell.

"I think I've got it this time!" she declared jubilantly, her southern accent thick with delight.

Groans of dismay escaped them in a quickly hushed chorus. Maiden didn't hesitate; she dropped to the floor and tucked herself under the desk. Tony pressed his lips together and scrambled to the front door with a speed that only terror could incite.

Billie was left alone and helpless; she glanced around with a hint of panic before it occurred to her to try to escape as well. She was tiptoeing towards her abandoned mop when Gloria emerged, looking flushed and victorious. Her eyes fastened on the first living, breathing thing she saw.

"Billie! Perfect!" She grinned. "Come try this pie!"

"Oh, gee whiz, Mrs. H." Billie's voice faltered. "I really should finish cleaning this floor before dinner."

"That's ages away, you silly little goose," Gloria tittered, her voice receding as she pranced into the dining room.

Just hit her with your mop and run, Maiden thought wryly to herself. *We'll tell everyone it was an accident.*

Despite the brazen defiance of her unspoken suggestion, Maiden squeezed her eyes shut and tucked deeper under the desk. She didn't budge until she heard Billie's defeated sigh, followed by the shuffling sound of her reluctant steps.

Maiden shook her head in wonder. How the usually genial Gloria and meek Kylie had managed to ruin something as wonderful as pie for everyone they encountered was staggering.

It wasn't that their creations weren't good, although a few of their efforts were a bit dicey, like the Peanut Butter Sandwich pie...with an actual sandwich baked into it. No, it was the ugly, competitive desperation that crackled in the air. Being forced to taste a dish while the baker and her sworn enemy stared her down, looking for the faintest twitch of a reaction. It was awful, and she refused to do it again.

Maiden peered over the top of the desk and, seeing no one, quickly stood and ducked into the office. She left her purse behind; it was upstairs in her room, and she couldn't risk being spotted. She had her phone and her car keys; that was enough. She slipped through the back door and ran away like a child.

Maiden found herself back at the carnival. She hadn't necessarily planned to go there today, but the Ferris wheel incident begged for a closer look. She looked it over as she approached, marvelling at how small she felt as she stared up at it. The giant structure was a somber vision, sitting still and empty. Her gaze dropped to the police officers who flitted around the area.

She didn't see McAlister, but he was certain to be there somewhere. She decided to give it a few more minutes before getting any closer to the scene; hopefully, they were packing up and would all leave soon.

She took a slight detour and headed straight for the manager's office. She knew that Gabby would have information about the breakdown and might be more likely to share it with her than a certain police captain would.

There was also that secret meeting with Chalmers that Maiden had observed. She was increasingly eager for details about that. Gabby and Chalmers had definitely argued about something, and Maiden was pretty sure now that she knew what it was. All she had to do was convince Gabby to confirm it.

She reached the plain white trailer marked 'Office' and knocked on the open door. She heard papers shuffling and the creak of a chair as its occupant shifted; she chanced a peek inside. Gabby peered back at her from behind a small but organized desk in the far corner.

"Hi Gabby." She smiled. "Do you have a minute? I need some advice, sort of."

"Oh, yeah. Hey, Maiden." She sat back a bit and waved her over. "Come on in."

Maiden walked in and glanced around the interior of the office. The walls were covered in so many flyers and vintage advertising posters that it was effectively wallpaper. The remarkable and stylish mix contained everything from maps of towns they'd doubtless passed through, posters featuring new and old-school rides, and even some circus and freak show advertisements.

There were several heavy steel filing cabinets bolted to the floor and a block of cubbyholes that looked to have come from an old post office hanging above Gabby's desk.

The desk itself was equally pieced together; each leg appeared to have come from separate pieces of furniture. They were all painted different colors and bore plenty of scratches that probably all told a story. Maiden smiled at the eclectic creation and took up the spindly chair that sat in front of it.

"What can I do for you?" Gabby interrupted her fascinated perusal.

"Well...this is kind of awkward," Maiden began slowly, now that it was time to ask it seemed a bit far-fetched. "My father is having some trouble with a local official. I have reason to believe he might not be the only target. I was wondering if you could help me confirm a few suspicions?"

"Go on." Gabby tented her stubby fingers and waited.

"I know this must sound terrible," she prefaced before diving straight in. "But Sam Chalmers physically attacked my father after trying to extort money from him. He's now trying to make my father look like *he* started the trouble."

"Oh dear." Gabby glanced away uncomfortably. "That's awful."

"It is." Maiden nodded and watched her carefully. "To be honest, I believe Sam Chalmers has been soliciting bribes from several businesses here. I was wondering if he's targeted the carnival at all?"

"Why would he bother us?" She wouldn't look at her at all now.

"You're one of the bigger fish to be had." Maiden shrugged and then cleared her throat. "And I saw him arguing with Keith Haynes the day he died."

"Did you?" Gabby snapped her gaze back to her again. "Chalmers never mentioned that."

She then shut her eyes when she realized her slipup. Maiden forced herself to stay calm. She was definitely on the right track, but she needed to put the other lady at ease before she got too nervous to talk.

"It's okay, Gabby." She lowered her voice a fraction. "It must be reasonably well known anyway, we won't be the only ones. But I think that in view of what happened to Keith, not to mention the sudden breakdown of one of the rides, maybe it's time Chalmers was reined in a bit."

"You think he had something to do with it?" She frowned.

"Not necessarily. Not directly anyway," Maiden admitted. "But I do believe that, at the very least, he's trying to capitalize on other people's problems. That's not okay, not in my opinion."

Gabby chewed at her upper lip as she considered that. She stared out the window for a long moment. When Maiden followed her gaze, she saw the Ferris wheel in the distance, sitting frozen and forlorn.

"It's not as though anyone working here is rich, or even comfortable," Gabby finally said; her tone was quiet and reflective. "We work hard, some more than others, but we get the job done. There are a lot of legitimate costs that go along with running any business, and there's rarely enough meat left on the bone to line some crooked idiot's pockets."

"That's exactly right." Maiden nodded. "So, did Chalmers approach you and demand money?"

"He...he approached Keith originally. And Keith being Keith," she rolled her dark eyes in disgust, "paid him out of profits that we couldn't really spare and thought that would be the end of it."

"But it wasn't?" Maiden arched a brow.

"Unfortunately no. The day Keith died, he came in here complaining that Chalmers was even worse than most of the dirty, cheating so-and-so's that he'd ever dealt with." She sighed and rested her chin on her fist. "The initial payoff was two grand, but we'd barely opened the gates when Chalmers came around again insisting on another three."

"Yikes, that's brassy!" Maiden stared at her and shook her head. "What was his explanation for that?"

"'Processing fees', he said." Gabby pulled an irate face. "Keith told him to get lost or he'd turn him in. He also demanded the initial bribe money back."

"That explains why Chalmers looked so angry that day." She nodded.

"Well, the best part is that Keith had something on him." Gabby smirked. "Chalmers was evidently very comfortable with his little racket, he gave Keith banking details to deposit the money."

"What?" Maiden's eyes widened. "Is he actually that stupid?"

"I'd say so. Heartless too," she muttered in disgust. "Keith's body was barely cold when he sent me a letter threatening action if we didn't pay up."

"You're kidding me." Maiden gave a hollow laugh. "Do you still have it?"

"Of course. That piece of paper is as good as an insurance policy," she chortled. "I'll let you look at it though."

Maiden sat forward, trying not to appear too eager, as Gabby pulled an open envelope from a drawer and pushed it across the desk. She thanked her quietly and opened it.

> *Dear Ms. Lopez,*
> *Firstly, please accept my sincere condolences on the*

passing of Keith Haynes. He was such an energetic and dedicated man.

I must, most regretfully, inform you that Mr. Haynes left one or two serious financial matters unsettled. There are a number of outstanding fees owing regarding the use of city property and utilities. These accounts are highly pressing and are at risk of accruing significant penalties if not addressed quickly.

I am here to streamline this process for you and assist in any way I can. Suffice to say that, with my help, these problems will all disappear. I'll be in contact to arrange a meeting to discuss this further.

Maiden lowered the letter and felt her dislike of the greedy man intensify. She glanced up at Gabby and asked a question she already knew the answer to.

"So, what happened?"

"I keep track of everything." She smiled, clearly pleased with herself. "I met him, as requested, and shut down every trick the rat tried to pull. He's done this before, he knew all the angles to try and catch me out, but he couldn't refute the paperwork. It was all present, current and correct. That's the last I've heard from him."

"That may be." Maiden eyed her watchfully; this would be the tricky part. "But I'm not so sure he's done with you. Even if he had nothing to do with this breakdown, do you really think he won't try to use it against you?"

"He can try if he wants." Gabby shrugged. "All our paperwork is in order, he has nothing to attack us with."

"I don't know, a lot of damage can be done before he's caught out. He shut my father's market stall down without any proof that could be definitely connected to him," she confided. "You might have to be a little bolder. And a little more proactive."

"What are you suggesting?" Gabby was suddenly tense and very guarded.

"Can I take a picture of this letter?" Maiden asked, lifting her dark brows a fraction. "If I can prove that he's crooked, he would have to back off and leave everyone in peace."

Gabby relaxed a little more than seemed necessary. She let out a low sigh and even smiled as she gestured for Maiden to continue.

Maiden stood and pulled her phone from her pocket. She snapped a couple of pictures, pausing long enough to make sure they were clear. She glanced up at Gabby.

"Any chance Keith held on to those banking details?" she asked hopefully.

Gabby chuckled wryly as she fished another piece of paper from the drawer and handed it to her.

Chapter Fourteen

Maiden felt like skipping joyfully as she headed back towards the entrance of the carnival. She maintained her dignity, however, as she brazenly approached the cordoned off area at the base of the Ferris wheel. She was too pleased with life in general to worry about McAlister seeing her there now.

She wasn't the only gawker either; a crowd of fair-goers were milling around and shaking their heads as they whispered to each other. A few took pictures, and one or two who had been rescued described their ordeal with sweeping gestures and breathless drama.

The ride was empty now, and the fire trucks Tony had mentioned were nowhere to be seen. The seats at the peak of the wheel sat idle; she could only imagine how terrifying it must have been for the poor people stuck in them.

Maiden disliked heights, particularly when swinging around in the breeze with nothing but a glorified metal bucket for protection. Rides like this had never appealed to her, and this incident hadn't strengthened their case any.

Grateful that at least no one seemed to have been hurt in the debacle, she glanced beside her when she saw movement. She wasn't a bit surprised to see Sam Chalmers strutting around like the biggest rooster in the farmyard.

The unpleasant man appeared smugly pleased despite looking at what should have been a major headache for him. He folded his arms as he gazed up at the dormant Ferris wheel. He flicked a sneering glance at Maiden but otherwise ignored her. She gladly returned the favor.

The sound of heavy footsteps behind her caught her attention. She looked over her shoulder and felt cool annoyance flutter over her at the sight of Captain McAlister approaching them. She did try not to scowl at him, but wasn't confident of her success.

While she did secretly appreciate that he had helped her father a little more than he had to, that didn't mean she wanted to talk to him. Certainly not when he had that stern, authoritative expression on his face, like he did now.

"What's going on?" McAlister asked as he looked between them.

"Nothing much, Captain McAlister. As the coordinator of this whole event I'm compelled to check into the carnival's latest disaster. It's amazing really, between derelict machinery," Chalmers gestured towards the halted ride and then flicked Maiden a sideways look, "and violent shopkeepers, this has been the worst Summerfest in living memory."

She felt herself bristle, but knew that it would be a mistake to let Chalmers provoke her into a verbal barrage. Instead, she kept her expression cool and draped her hands over her hips.

"It's also the first one that you've been assigned to coordinate," she pointed out dryly. "Isn't it interesting that you've found yourself in the middle of unprecedented trouble?"

"It'll get better once I've cleared out the riff-raff." He gave her a pointed look.

"You don't seem too heartbroken anyway." Maiden swallowed her anger and squared her shoulders. "But I suppose these little issues present a lot of opportunities for a mid-grade civil employee who likes to find creative ways to make extra money."

McAlister shifted a quietly startled gaze to Maiden, who ignored him. Chalmers had turned red and glared at her.

"More of your father's cheap lies?" he scoffed. "This isn't going to help his case one bit, Miss Harlow."

"What a shame. By the way, do you recognize this?" she continued relentlessly and held up her phone. "You signed it and sent it, after all."

Chalmers stilled, and his mustache twitched when he looked at the picture she'd taken of his letter to Gabby; he obviously recognized it. McAlister stepped closer and tilted the phone towards him so he could see it too. He read it over and turned to the suddenly quiet man.

"Anything to say, Chalmers?" he asked.

"It's a fake," he replied with badly feigned composure.

"I have access to the original," Maiden informed them. "It won't be hard to confirm your signature."

"That is a private letter, which you have no business trying to misuse!" he grated.

"So, you admit that it's an official letter that you sent?" She smiled. "I have the permission of the recipient, by the way. You'll find that people get a bit huffy when you try to force bribes out of them."

"How dare you!" he muttered furiously. "I'll sue you for slander!"

"I doubt that, Chalmers." She arched a dark brow, not about to let this creep harass her family any further. "I think you'll be too busy trying to explain to your superiors why you've been issuing infringement notices. And I also doubt there's any paper trail to support your claims of 'significant penalties'."

"You dirty little—" He started towards her only to be stopped in his tracks when McAlister stepped between them.

"What exactly are you planning to do, Mr. Chalmers?" the captain asked stonily. "You seem quick to resort to a physical attack. I may have to take a closer look at Alfred Harlow's claims of self-defense."

Chalmers clenched his hands into fists; his expression was thunderous.

"She goaded me," he protested, flinging a hand in Maiden's direction.

"You're the one that started throwing insults around. And that still wouldn't be justification for resorting to violence and intimidation." He didn't budge, and Chalmers finally took a step back. "Explain the letter."

"It's not what it looks like." Chalmers looked both annoyed and exasperated. "I found discrepancies and tried to warn the manager. If the festival fails it reflects badly on me too."

"Are you aware that the police can request your bank records?" Maiden's wry voice floated up from behind McAlister's broad back. "I wonder if there's a history of large and unexplained deposits."

"Easy tiger," McAlister murmured, glancing over his shoulder at her before turning back to the angry man in front of him. "I'll be looking into this more closely, Mr. Chalmers. But, for now, this is the scene of a rescue operation. You can leave."

Chalmers straightened his tie irately and, glaring once more at Maiden, turned and stormed off. Maiden watched him go with a sense of satisfaction. She wasn't a confrontational person by nature, but no one messed with her dad.

"Why?" McAlister asked with a loud sigh as he turned to face her. "Explain to me why you didn't come straight to me?"

"You're the same guy who refuses to discuss my own family's business with me, aren't you?" she reminded him, but then shrugged. "Anyway, Chalmers approached me. Was I supposed to ignore him?"

"You didn't have to get into an argument," he murmured, conveniently avoiding her other complaint.

"He's trying to ruin my father to cover his own corruption." She gestured in the direction that Chalmers had stormed off. "I take exception to that. Sorry if it's inconvenient for you."

"You do realize you've done nothing to disprove your father's motive?" he pointed out.

"Incorrect. I've proven that Sam Chalmers is extorting the businesses he's supposed to be supporting." She stepped closer and tipped her face up to look him in the eye. "That means my dad told the truth about what the argument was over. You also just saw for yourself that Chalmers reacts physically when he's angry."

"He's the one with the black eye," McAlister said, making no move to edge away from her.

"Which only means that he's slow and out of shape." She shrugged. "Dad's not exactly a karate master."

"He isn't the coolest head in the room either," McAlister pointed out.

"Was he supposed to do nothing while that jerk attacked him?!" she demanded as she scowled up at him. "Are you being deliberately difficult or what?"

"Why do you ask? Afraid I'll be stepping on your toes?" he asked in an infuriatingly impassive voice.

She set her teeth and held his gaze stubbornly, but she was standing quite close to him now. She was soon hopelessly distracted by the many hues of rich chocolate and caramel that glinted in his dark eyes. His brows were quirked inquisitively above them, and his clean-shaven jaw was square and stern. It was nice.

You really are very good-looking, Captain, and you smell in-credible. I wonder what cologne you use...I kind of want to spray my sheets with it.

Maiden was pleased that she managed to keep the wayward thoughts internal. She wasn't sure if he'd kept talking while her mind wandered, so she ignored his previous questions and forged ahead.

"So, are you going to follow up on this or what?" She shook her head.

"You mean you haven't called his bank yourself yet?" He folded his arms across his chest. "You're getting sloppy."

"Well, I do happen to have his banking details, but isn't that your job?" She pulled the scrap of paper from her pocket and held it up with an impudent grin. "Or do you *want* my help now?"

A corner of his mouth tilted upwards even as his eyes bored into hers. She wasn't sure if she'd finally pushed him too far and, somewhat worryingly, she didn't plan to behave herself even if she had. McAlister stepped closer still and lowered his head a fraction.

"Listen up, smart-ass," he said quietly and seriously. "You'd better be *very* careful. If you get so much as a parking ticket, your butt is mine."

It was clearly a threat, but she chose to take it as flirtation. Maybe because his smile was more cautionary than menacing. Either way, she had to respond somehow, and she might as well continue to be difficult.

Maiden pulled a curious face and glanced very obviously over her shoulder at her tush. As she faced him again, McAlister held up a finger when she would have spoken.

Are you shushing me? she demanded internally, but kept her mouth shut. She really didn't want to find a ticket on her car tomorrow.

McAlister grasped the paper from her hand, brushing his long fingers against hers far more than was required for the task. She shifted slightly and clasped her hands behind her back, ignoring the way her skin still tingled.

He held her gaze as he tapped his finger on his lips in a silencing gesture and then pointed her on her way. Maiden's eyes widened and her mouth fell open in startled disbelief.

Do. Not. Smile at him, she ordered herself, even as she felt her lips curve upward against her will. She glanced away and let out a breath that she knew darn well sounded both furious and interested. Finally, after a fierce internal debate and a large dose of self-control, she turned and stalked away.

"Text me a copy of that letter, please," he called after her. His tone was obnoxiously polite under the circumstances.

She threw him an unimpressed look over her shoulder and saw that he was watching her walk away with an appreciative smile. She quickly turned and kept going.

Later that afternoon, David was sitting at a table outside in the closed off section near the mirror maze. The area had remained cordoned off since the discovery of Haynes' body, so everything was quiet. But the entire carnival was quite subdued, as the majority of the rides had been shut down after the Ferris wheel malfunctioned.

Gabby Lopez had complained that the precautions were excessive, arguing that no one had been hurt and there was no indication of structural faults anywhere else.

David could sympathize with her position, but he wouldn't bargain with her. Not with the looming threat of sabotage still hanging over the carnival. They needed time for his officers to check the other rides for anything suspicious before letting people use them again. The best he could offer was to let them reopen tomorrow, provided the Ferris wheel was left unused.

It was cold comfort, and her tight-lipped agreement made it clear that she wasn't happy. It didn't help that the evening papers were referring to the Spencer and Spencer carnival as a disaster on stilts. That was beyond his control, however, and he had bigger problems to contend with.

He had already started following up on one of the many interesting curves that Harlow had thrown his way. They'd followed up on the bank details she'd passed along and found it to be a savings account that Chalmers had opened about five years ago. And just as Harlow had suggested, the account did reflect large and sporadic deposits, often two grand at a time. Apart from that, the warning notice he'd sent Gabby Lopez was fishy to say the least.

It offered strong reasons to suspect Sam Chalmers of professional misconduct and perhaps outright criminal activity. He'd have to dig into the details a bit more, but David was comfortably certain that Chalmers would drop the charges against Alfie Harlow without too much convincing. His thoughts again drifted to the man's feisty daughter, and a smile threatened.

Maiden Harlow was clever; he'd never argue that, but she really got under his skin. He was pretty sure that he got to her as well. At least he hoped he did; it was only fair. He'd had his actions challenged during an investigation before, and he had been hit on fairly blatantly too, but Harlow was a different experience altogether.

She mouthed off a bit, but she was witty and never genuinely insulting. He didn't mind it; in fact, he'd be lying if he claimed he didn't occasionally enjoy it. But she was smart and she was quick. He had no idea how she knew to get that letter from Gabby Lopez, but it was incredibly useful and came at a very handy time.

David knew he could've thanked her; he'd actually planned to until she kept talking. She was sneaking around behind his back, and that annoyed him a lot. When he got annoyed with her, he pushed, then she pushed back, and then things got...interesting.

Even so, his own behavior had startled him, threatening to throw the book at her and then sending her off without a word. It was heavy-handed, and that wasn't usually his style, but she'd been quite sassy. He knew the discussion wouldn't have stayed even remotely professional if he'd let it go on.

I can't believe I talked to her like that. He rubbed his eyes but smiled to himself. *And I think she liked it.*

He glanced up when he heard footsteps and saw Janet Lee striding purposefully towards him, swathed in a filmy, Giraffe-print dress. He was grateful for the distraction from his wayward thoughts and considered her critically.

Miss Lee was attractive in a flashy, attention-seeking sort of way. The consensus among the crew members he'd spoken to was that Janet used her body to get special treatment. The remarks might have been born of assumptions, of course, or pure spite. It wasn't a stretch of the imagination after the attack Miss Lee had tried to cover up.

When she had been more formally questioned regarding the incident, she'd implied more than once that she came from a rough background and it wasn't anything that she couldn't deal with. But the check David ran on her showed up nothing of note.

She talked tough despite seeming very stoic about her lot in life; it was a coping mechanism that he'd seen many times before. It didn't mean she was lying.

"Good afternoon, Miss Lee," he greeted her politely when she stood across the table from him.

"Captain McAlister," she said stoically, her expression was determined and her hands were clenched into tight fists. "I need to talk to you about Keith's death."

"All right. Have a seat." He gestured towards the chair in front of her.

Janet pulled out the nearest chair and sank down into it. Her gaze was distant, and her breathing was shallow. She drew a half-empty pack of cigarettes and a lighter out of her pocket.

"Don't smoke here," David said simply.

She glanced at him and then at the cigarette she was holding, as if wondering how it got there. She shook her head and slid it back into the packet before tucking it all into her pocket once more.

"Sorry, it's a bad habit that I can't seem to break," she chuckled weakly and brushed her white-blonde hair out of her face. "Look, this isn't very easy for me."

"I understand, Miss Lee," he acknowledged and tapped the end of his pen on the table. "What is it that you want to tell me?"

"It's about Oliver. Mr. Armstrong, that is." She took a deep breath and met his gaze. "I think he murdered Keith."

"You've changed your tune since the last time we talked." David quirked a brow, but that was the extent of his external reaction.

"Yes, I know." She nodded and sat up straighter. "But things have happened since then, things have changed."

"For instance?"

"I...I found out that he's been lying to me, he's been keeping secrets." Janet barely swallowed her anger as it threatened to bubble over. "He's had a getaway planned for months; he was probably scheming to kill Keith for a long time."

"Why would he do that?" David's expression revealed nothing.

"They hated each other, they always had. Long before I joined the company." She shook her head sadly and released a soft breath. "They argued constantly about the set up and tear down, Keith was always in a hurry and never wanted to pay extra people. Oliver was getting more and more aggressive towards him. I guess I can understand his frustration, but...it went too far."

"You were in a relationship with both Mr. Haynes and Mr. Armstrong, correct?" David asked frankly.

"No, not with Mr. Armstrong. I did think we had something at one point. It wasn't on purpose; I did love Keith. But Oliver acted so kind and showed me a lot of attention." Her gaze dropped to her hands, where they lay clasped in her lap. "Keith loved me, but he could be cruel sometimes. Oliver knew that and swooped in when I was vulnerable. I shouldn't have fallen for it, but I started to...and only to find out that he'd had different ideas all along."

"I take it these revelations have only recently come to light?" he asked carefully.

"Yes, Captain," she sighed loudly and rolled her eyes. "I know what you're thinking. You think he dumped me and I'm only here as the woman scorned. Well, you're half right. I'm not impressed to find out that Oliver Armstrong is a liar and a sleaze, but I'm here because someone murdered Keith and I'm honestly afraid that it was him!"

"There's no need to get upset, Miss Lee," he murmured and waited a moment while she settled down. "I'm not discounting anything you say. Do you have any evidence to suggest that Mr. Armstrong was involved in the murder of Keith Haynes?"

"Yes, I think I do." She reached into her pocket again and pulled out a piece of paper. "I found this in Oliver's knapsack the night of Keith died."

"And why were you searching through his knapsack?" David asked as he accepted the page she handed him.

"I was leaving him a note asking him to meet me." She shivered and hugged herself. "I changed my mind after I found that. I know I should have come and told you sooner, but I just couldn't believe it at the time. But now…now I realize that Oliver isn't the man I thought he was."

David read over what turned out to be a brusque letter of dismissal. It was from Keith Haynes and was addressed to Oliver Armstrong. He frowned pensively as he read it once more. The language was cold and bitter, and it was dated a week before the murder.

"Did you confront him about this?" David glanced up at her.

"No, I was afraid of what he might do." She shuddered again. "I found out that he's got a new job already lined up. I asked him about that, and asked why he had never told anyone about it. That's when he admitted that he'd been leading me on all this time; he was never serious about me. He's cold-blooded, Captain McAlister, very cold-blooded. Look at what happened with the Ferris wheel today."

"You think that was deliberate?" he asked in an unrevealing tone.

"It's never happened before." She shrugged helplessly. "And now, right before Oliver planned to leave without telling anyone? And him being the head of maintenance? It's too strange to be a coincidence."

Chapter Fifteen

Chapter Sixteen

David stood in the doorway of Oliver Armstrong's work-shop. His eyes narrowed when he saw that Harlow was not only there but was perched daintily on his filthy workbench like it were a piano in a nightclub.

She was leaning forward, braced on her palms. Her pale pink shirt was fitted, but still gaped enough at the top to reveal a lot more than he'd been prepared to find in a greasy workshop. His hands clenched at his sides; he forced them to relax.

She and Oliver were in the midst of a quiet and rather intent discussion. It annoyed him instantly; he told himself that it was only because she was butting in again and pressed on before he could call himself a liar.

"Good evening," he said coolly.

Harlow looked at him sharply and sat straighter. Her eyes were wide as they locked onto him; she swung her feet a little but stayed put. Oliver seemed completely undisturbed by his presence and met his dark gaze easily.

"Hello again, Captain McAlister." He inclined his head and started wiping his dirty hands on an equally filthy rag. "Come in, please."

"Thanks." He stepped further inside and kept an eye on them both. "I hope I'm not interrupting anything."

"We were discussing Keith's murder," Oliver said without preamble. "I was telling Maiden why I was behind the concession stands that evening."

"Were you? Interesting. I wonder that you didn't tell *me*." David folded his arms over his chest. "You had ample opportunity."

"She asked." Oliver shrugged. "And I wasn't ready to talk about it before now."

David gave Harlow a look; she smiled at him and nodded subtly towards Oliver. He took the hint and decided he could issue another pointless lecture on interfering with police business later.

"All right, so enlighten me," he sighed tolerantly. "What were you doing there?"

"Janet left me a note to meet her behind the concession truck she works in. So I did," he explained. "While I was waiting I drank a bit of my coffee and *boom*. The lights went out."

David studied Oliver as he listened. What he said directly contradicted Janet's story; the problem was he didn't trust either of them. He noticed too late that Harlow was watching him as he considered Oliver's account. She leaned towards him, bracing her hands on the edge of the table again.

"What's wrong?" she asked.

"I'm just listening to what Mr. Armstrong has to say." He flicked her a quelling frown that achieved nothing.

"I've seen that look before, Captain," she said as she studied him intently. "You've heard conflicting information, haven't you?"

"You're brutal, Harlow," he said under his breath and refused to let his eyes linger on her pale cleavage as he turned back to Oliver. "Fine, yes. Miss Lee told me that she never left you any note because, when she tried to, she found this."

He took a step closer and held out the letter of dismissal. Oliver pulled an uncertain face as he took it and read it over. He glanced at David and, to the captain's further annoyance, passed the note to Harlow.

"I've never seen that before," he said, but then frowned faintly. "Of course I can't prove that, can I?"

"Not really." David shrugged with little concern; Harlow spoke before he could elaborate.

"You don't need to," she mused as she pointed to the date in the top right corner. "This was dated a few days before the carnival reached Golden Glen. Obviously, Mr. Haynes knew you were still here so he hadn't fired you yet."

"Thanks for that, Miss Harlow. I also understand how a calendar works!" David muttered before he could rein himself in. "It doesn't mean he didn't know about it, only that it hadn't been acted upon."

Harlow met his gaze and lifted her dark brows a fraction; he immediately regretted snapping at her. She handed him the letter, and he took it back without a word.

Oliver shifted uncomfortably and cleared his throat as he looked between them.

"I'm sensing some tension here," he said quietly and glanced at the beautiful woman. "Sorry Maiden, I wasn't trying to cause you any trouble."

"She does fine with or without help," David cut in before she could respond. "Let's not get sidetracked. Why would Miss Lee lie about finding the note in your bag?"

"Because she's mad that I broke off our, kind of, relationship," he said easily. "She's mean, Captain. I know she looks sweet and delicate but, believe me, I've seen her angry."

"She said similar things about you," David informed him.

"I'm sure she said a lot of things about me." Oliver chuckled. "I invite you to find anyone that will claim they've ever seen me lose my temper. You're welcome to read her note if you want, it's not dated though, so it may not be of much help."

He dragged a worn and heavily patched knapsack from under the workbench and started digging through it. A moment later he pulled out a scrap of folded paper and handed it to David. He opened it up and read it over.

Meet me behind the ice cream truck at 6 tonight,
it's important.
J

"J for Janet," David murmured as he flipped the paper over. There were no other markings, nothing to suggest when it had been written. "Interesting, Mr. Armstrong. But it doesn't prove much."

Oliver gave a conceding shrug. David saw Harlow shift a little and braced himself for her next onslaught.

"Oliver," she said thoughtfully. "In that letter from Keith Haynes, he cited 'unsafe work practices' and 'equipment not maintained to industry standards'. Is that true at all? I mean, have there been any accidents?"

"No, because I know how all these rides work and exactly how they go together." He took noticeably less offense at the question than he had when David had hinted at it. "But Haynes was always on my case to work faster and cut costs by using fewer consumables. It was all a load of garbage that I never listened to. If he fired me, he fired me. I wasn't going to risk anyone's safety to save him a few bucks."

"Sorry, that's not what I meant." Harlow shook her head a little. "I believe that you did your job well; were there *accidents*?"

"Ah, I get you." He smiled and looked thoughtful. "No, there haven't been. But I did catch a few problems early on. Once there were bolts missing from a few seats on the merry-go-round. Not enough to hurt anyone, but it would have given them a heck of a scare."

"And people would've doubtless complained," David supplied. "And blame would have then fallen on you. Correct?"

"Yeah, correct." He smiled wryly. "I've been a mechanical engineer for almost two decades, most of these rides are tinker toys. They aren't that hard to manage."

"Yes, I checked up on you already," David said. "So why did you give up a much better job to travel from town to town putting up with a guy like Keith Haynes?"

"My boy died, then my wife left me, so I ran away," he explained. "Haynes was always a pest, but he wasn't too bad until Janet came along, and the work and constant change of scenery kept my mind off things. But I'm tired of this life now; I want to go home. I'm tired of being alone too, but there aren't that many genuine ladies like Maiden in the world." He gave her a fond smile. "And she's a little too young for me, sadly."

Harlow smiled and glanced away shyly. David knew he looked as unimpressed as he felt; when her big green eyes met his, she quickly sobered. He shifted his gaze back to Oliver and kept it there.

"Keith Haynes died, arguably, by a piece of equipment that wasn't in good working order." David steered him back to the matter at hand. "Is it possible that the mirror was sabotaged to implicate you?"

"It's possible, sure." He gave a conceding nod. "But everything breaks at some point, it doesn't mean that I did anything incorrectly. So, it's also possible that someone saw an opportunity to get rid of Keith without having to confront him."

"Would you be surprised if I told you that we found tools in Keith Haynes pockets?" He noticed the sharp look Harlow gave him but didn't react to it.

"No, that wouldn't surprise me," Oliver mumbled.

"Well, what about today's breakdown?" Harlow turned quite deliberately to Oliver. "Could that have been intentionally done?"

"Oh yes, I think it was, but I haven't been allowed near the sight to tell for certain." He folded his arms. "At the risk of pointing fingers, I believe Janet's out to get me. She's never acted uneasy or uncomfortable around me, a lot of people can attest to that. Any so-called suspicions were born curiously close on the heels of me telling her I wasn't interested in being with her."

"So, if she's sabotaging things to get back at you," she shook her head, "she could really hurt someone. Or, at the very least, damage the carnival's reputation and livelihood even more."

"That's right," he acknowledged. "And that's part of the reason I resigned this afternoon."

"You've actually quit?" David folded his arms.

"Yup, I already gave my letter to Gabby. Janet can snipe away all she wants, but if my name's not on the equipment any longer, then she gains nothing from it breaking down." He smiled serenely. "That should neutralize at least one source of trouble."

"That's assuming she was actually responsible for the breakdown," David qualified.

"Yeah, I'll let you handle that. It's not for me to say for certain and I wouldn't know where to start in trying to prove it," Oliver conceded. "Now, I realize that I'll need to stay in town until this is all settled, Captain. I'll find a room somewhere and let you know where I am straight away; will that be all right?"

"I suppose," he allowed cautiously. Once again he saw Harlow shift and knew she was about to butt in again. He took a deep breath and shut his eyes for a moment.

"Hold on, let me text Mom," Harlow said as she pulled her phone out of her back pocket. A few chirps from incoming messages later, and she glanced up at Oliver with a smile. "You've got a room, number 8. Just look up the Harlow House inn, my parents are expecting you."

"Oh, thanks Maiden. That's sweet of you." He smiled gratefully and then looked around the cramped trailer. "Well, I've put everything in order as best I can. That might make it easier for whoever replaces me. I've already packed, so I'll head out now. Hopefully Janet won't see me. She'll have steamed open my resignation letter by now."

Oliver gave David a polite nod, but Harlow got a smile and a wink as he gathered up his few possessions and slipped outside. They were both quiet for a moment and then slowly looked at each other.

Maiden didn't appreciate that McAlister had never told her about the evidence of Keith's sabotage. She knew she had no right to the information, but it still rankled. And now he was watching her with that same complicated expression he'd worn since he found her there. He looked wary, or maybe cheesed off; she wondered what he was thinking.

"Isn't number 8 the room right across from your apartment?" he asked at last.

"What? Um, I...I guess it is, yeah. Oh, come on!" She gave him a startled look. That wasn't the train of thought she'd been bracing for. "It was a vacant room, that's all. Mom chose it, not me!"

"Right," he said, just dubiously enough, and slid his gaze away.

"Are you serious?" she demanded incredulously.

"Were you here in his private space, hanging around him for no legitimate reason?" he retorted, looking back at her grimly. "And now you've invited him to stay at your inn?"

"But at least you know where he is," she pointed out.

"And that's massively comforting, Miss Harlow," he replied. "Thank you."

"Well, if you're that worried about it you can bunk in." Her cheeks flushed when he blinked at her. "I meant with Oliver!"

"Then forget it." He finally smiled a little. "You're kind of a tease, you know that?"

She mumbled under her breath and slid off the bench. After checking and finding no grease stains on her bottom, she walked past him and out into the brisk evening air. The sun was well on its way to setting, leaving a brilliant display of purple and gold streaking across the sky.

The season had been mild, and this evening was quite cool. Her shirt was short-sleeved and a bit chilly in the soft breeze, but she didn't mind; she loved being outside for a Michigan sunset.

The sound of McAlister descending the steps after her reminded her that this wasn't the time to admire the scenery. He stood beside her and folded his arms over his broad chest.

"So, you were in there hitting on Armstrong because—?" His joking words didn't fully hide the irritation lurking behind them.

"There were no cranky police captains available, so I had to make due," she said teasingly, but then pressed her lips together and refused to look at him.

I really do need to stop flirting with you. She rolled her eyes at herself. *But it's hard to stop something I've almost never done on purpose. And now you've stopped talking; that makes things nice and awkward for us both. Thanks a lot.*

"Miss Harlow," he finally said in a mellower tone. "What are you up to?"

"Can you be more specific?" She pulled a face and tried to think of an acceptable excuse for meddling. Nothing was coming to her, though.

"Why were you talking to Mr. Armstrong?" He arched a brow.

"Um...I was hitting on him?" she asked, realizing too late that it was idiotic to ask the person questioning her if her response sounded plausible.

"Seriously?" He scowled at her.

"No," she admitted, and settled her gaze on his open collar as she tucked her hands into her pockets.

"Could I get a real answer then?" He let out a huff of a breath.

"Captain, come on," she sighed loudly and dared to drag her eyes up to his again. "It's a lovely evening, there's an amazing sunset and we haven't met over a corpse. Can we please not spoil it by arguing?"

"You make that really difficult." He slid her a frustrated look.

"But never impossible!" She held up a finger triumphantly and was pleased to see him suppress a smirk.

Neither of them spoke for a few minutes as they started walking back in the direction of the carnival. Maiden glanced over to find him looking lost in thought. They wove through the rows of staff trailers and on towards the few lights that were on in the distance. The whole place was quiet.

"So, how was your day?" Maiden kept her tone companionable.

"Long and full of hysterical victims of the Ferris wheel disaster," he said wearily. "How was yours?"

"Hours of trying not to throw up worrying about Dad. Interspersed with listening to Mom criticize Kylie for daring to train as a chef." She smiled a little. "Followed by Kylie quietly mentioning that Mom doesn't know much about baking. After that I mostly hid under the desk whenever I saw either of them to avoid being force-fed more pie."

"Hard to say which day was worse." He almost smiled.

"*Mine* was worse," she contradicted.

"Mm, you're probably right," he allowed with a shrug, and then a mischievous grin spread across his face. "You'd have had plenty of time to read your dirty book though. I suppose you're used to hiding so no one will catch you."

"It's not a dirty book." She shut her eyes. "It's just stupid and aggravating."

"And yet you insist on finishing it," he chuckled as they stepped into the public area again. "You must like it at least a little."

"I do not. And at least I—" She stopped mid-sentence as she glanced over towards the funhouse. Purest horror seeped through her. "Oh no!"

"What's wrong?" he asked uncertainly when she ducked behind him.

"Don't move!" she whispered urgently. "*Please!*"

"Right," he said slowly and stood a bit straighter when she rested a hand on his back. "What are you doing, Miss Harlow? Am I aiding and abetting you in some fashion?"

"Yes," she said with a hint of exasperation. "Can you keep quiet for thirty seconds? Is that even possible?"

"That's a good way to ask for a favor," he murmured as he looked up to see what had sent her scurrying.

All he saw was a woman of indeterminate years wandering around with a bag of popcorn, looking at the posters on the side of the Tilt-a-Whirl. She was fairly short, with tightly permed hair in a muted shade of blonde and sporting a long, rather prim denim shirtdress.

David wondered what the problem was; she looked harmless enough. Regardless of that, he was happy to help Harlow, and she obviously didn't want this person to see her. He pulled out his notebook and pretended to look through it so no one would question him loitering, all the while he studied the woman near the tilt-a-whirl. He had no idea who she was, but Harlow sounded a little frightened by her; it was strange.

David's calm focus wavered when Harlow grasped the back of his shirt and edged closer.

You're touching me. Fine, that's completely fine. We're in a public place and none of this was my idea, he thought to himself but held his breath when she gasped and stepped nearer. *You really need to stop pulling at my clothes, Harlow. It's been a frustrating day, and I'm not made of stone.*

"What are you doing?" he asked, not daring to voice his other concerns.

"Hiding," she whispered. "Just stay quiet and act natural."

"So your master plan is that you press yourself against me," he paused for emphasis, "and I pretend not to notice?"

"Maiden?" The lady looked over and blinked eyes that squinted from behind large glasses. "Is that you, honey?"

"Oh hi, Ms. Adams!" Harlow leaned out from her hiding place with a perfectly natural smile. "How nice! Imagine bumping into you here of all places."

"Well, I've read so much about Summerfest in the paper every day. I thought I'd take a little peek around the carnival and the markets after work. I was just about to leave, in fact. Almost missed you!" Ms. Adams smiled cheerfully and then eyed David with quiet interest. "And who have we here?"

"This is Captain McAlister, the head of the police department." Harlow stepped out into the open and gestured towards him with a long-suffering sigh. She then met and held his gaze grimly as she introduced the lady. "Captain, this is Ms. Adams, one of the senior staff at the Golden Glen library."

Understanding dawned immediately. A slow smile spread across David's face as he did his very best not to laugh at her. Harlow looked so thoroughly put out and cranky as she glared at him, like he'd deliberately flagged the lady down and invited her to join them.

"It's not as exciting as it sounds," Ms. Adams said dryly. "But at least I get first crack at all the newest books. Speaking of which—"

"Oh please don't," Harlow whispered, but managed another sweet smile as she turned to take her medicine.

"I noticed you still haven't returned *Hero of the Heather*. Haven't you finished it yet?" Ms. Adams smiled so brightly and hopefully.

"Uh...not quite yet," Harlow said uncomfortably.

"*Still?*" The lady's eyes widened. "Don't you like it, dear?"

"It's not that!" she hurried to explain, shaking her head earnestly.

"You've had it for *two months*," Ms. Adams said with a hint of disapproval. She pulled her thick glasses down and eyed the younger woman over the top of them.

David was barely managing to suppress his amusement. Harlow looked so caught and guilty; he couldn't believe that this was the same woman who stood up to him about interfering with a murder investigation not even ten minutes ago.

"I know I have, I'm sorry. I've just been really busy with work and...dead bodies." Harlow turned helplessly to David and shook her head the barest fraction. "And stuff."

He grinned at her; it was the only way he could stop himself from laughing at her useless excuses. Somehow being chided by a grandmotherly librarian had reduced this witty little fox to an awkward mess.

When he didn't speak up on her behalf, Harlow's dark brows furrowed and she set her teeth; he somehow grinned wider but ran a hand over his face to at least try to hide it. The frustration of catching her with Oliver was starting to feel incredibly worth it.

He was enjoying Harlow's predicament too much to realize that Ms. Adams could well draw a different conclusion from their silent exchange.

"Oh! I see!" Ms. Adams' face lit up as she looked between them happily. "Who needs to read about it when you've got the real thing, right? Ha!"

"What?" Harlow's eyes widened. She turned back to the lady and started shaking her head. "No! That's not what I said!"

"Don't be so bashful, dear," Ms. Adams tittered and waved her obvious embarrassment away. "You've always been so picky about men, but I suppose a beautiful girl like you can afford to be. But that's all I'm going to say about that. In any case, please try to finish the book soon, it's not fair to keep it from others."

"Yes, I guess that's true," Harlow agreed and gave David an angry look, clearly unimpressed that he hadn't said a word since the affable librarian descended upon them.

"And besides," Ms. Adams gave her an eager smile, "there's more where that came from. It's part of a series!"

"Shoot me," Harlow muttered and pinched the bridge of her nose.

She caught herself an instant too late and, for reasons he couldn't begin to fathom, again looked to him for some kind of assistance. He clamped his mouth shut and shook his head; that was all the help he could give her at the moment.

"What was that, dear?" Ms. Adams' kindly eyes crinkled uncertainly at the edges.

"Shoot! Is that the time?" Harlow recovered admirably and glanced at her phone; she smiled sweetly and grasped David by the arm. "We have to go, but it's been *so* lovely talking to you, Ms. Adams! I hope you've enjoyed the carnival!"

"I have, dear. Goodnight." Ms. Adams smiled and backed away. "And it was lovely meeting you, Captain."

Harlow dug her little claws into his sleeve and dragged him back the way they'd come, glancing furtively over her shoulder until the terrifying librarian was out of sight. As soon as they were a safe distance away, she stopped and rounded on him.

"Nice 'helping', Captain!" she grated.

"You told me to keep quiet," he reminded her with a shrug, but then smiled broadly. "Was that more than thirty seconds?"

Harlow bowed her head and covered her face with her hands as she tried to muffle her begrudging laughter. She sucked in a deep breath and faced him again, draping her hands on her curvy hips.

"You realize that you've not only left me in the lurch for not finishing that stupid book but now she thinks we're dating because she can't tell the difference between flirting and being *deliberately useless.*" She arched a brow and tapped her foot. "And now I'm potentially on the hook for the rest of the horrendous series! And you stood there and did nothing!"

"What was I supposed to say?" he demanded with an incredulous laugh. "Besides, you were handling it so well."

"Total jerk," she informed him, but her threatening smirk let her down. "Just like in the book."

"Maybe I'll improve in the next one," he offered optimistically.

She sighed more genuinely and shut her eyes as she pushed past and skulked towards the funhouse again. He watched her for a second or two before he felt a niggle of worry that he'd pushed it too far; he quickly caught up.

"All right, Miss Harlow, I'm sorry," he said as he touched her shoulder. She turned to face him, and he smiled down at her. "I was caught off guard too, okay? As for the book, I don't know, throw it out or something and say its lost. It's not technically lying."

"I can't throw it out," she said miserably. "Its municipal property."

You are so adorable, Harlow. He closed his eyes and tried not to smile again. *Change the subject, David...you could always tell her she looks really good in those jeans. Brilliant choice. She's right, you're useless.*

Maiden noticed that McAlister had fallen silent. She realized she was going on a bit too much about the embarrassing encounter with Ms. Adams. The looming threat of another bodice-ripping nightmare was bad enough, but the kind librarian's assumption that she and the captain were dating had been the most mortifying part.

Her best bet at this point was to try to shrug off the entire episode and hope McAlister would buy it. She had just dredged up a serene smile and was about to tell him to forget about the whole silly thing, but she stilled when something else caught her eye. There was a flash of movement on top of the funhouse; she was certain of it. She frowned as she kept looking to see if it would happen again.

She could see the large structure clearly enough, despite the fading sunlight. It was among the larger attractions that had been shut down all day, ever since the Ferris wheel incident. But Maiden was sure she saw a person darting across the upper deck.

"What's wrong?" McAlister stood beside her and tried to see what she was staring at.

"I saw someone," she said softly and glanced at him. "Upstairs in the funhouse."

"Okay," he murmured as he trained his eyes on the darkened building. "Let's take a look; stay close."

They walked towards the funhouse, both of them studying it warily as they approached. The whole area felt eerily deserted, but then she saw it again. Someone ran back across the deck and then disappeared.

"Did you—"

"Yeah," McAlister whispered before she could finish. "Keep your voice down."

They silently approached the entrance. Within moments they were walking into the mouth of the giant clown. When she had seen it the other day, she'd found it all far more whimsical and fun. Of course, that was in the safety of broad daylight and with a crowd of other people around.

Maiden hugged herself and tried not to imagine the big, bright teeth dripping with gore and crunching down on them as they neared.

McAlister stepped through the façade just ahead of her and moved closer to examine the gate that sat behind it. Someone had thrown a heavy chain and lock around the gate to secure it, but as Maiden peered over his shoulder, she saw that the large padlock was open. They both looked at the doorway beyond, but there was no sign of anyone prowling nearby.

He grasped her wrist without a word and led her back through the hideous mouth and across the street. They ducked behind the ticket booth, and McAlister pulled out his phone.

Maiden chewed at her lip and stared watchfully at the upper level as she listened to him quietly call in a suspected break in. She could only wonder why anyone would sneak into the place at all. It was possible that some kids had swiped the keys to the lock and were poking around for a thrill and maybe bragging rights to impress their friends. Her gut told her it wasn't anything that innocently juvenile though; she was pretty sure something bad was happening.

"Okay, a team is on the way," he whispered as he put his phone away and headed towards the darkened building again. "I'm going to have a look around in the meantime. I won't be long."

Maiden gaped at his back and immediately started following. She was busy trying to peer into the surrounding shadows and had tucked herself fairly close behind him. As a result, she bumped straight into him when he stopped abruptly and glanced over his shoulder at her.

"Where do you think you're going?" he whispered.

"Someplace where I won't be standing alone in the dark in the middle of a creepy abandoned carnival!" she replied in a low, irritable voice.

"Fine," he sighed and held a finger to his lips. "But stay close and keep quiet."

CHAPTER SEVENTEEN

McAlister eased the heavy gate open and scanned the foyer. Maiden had never been in the funhouse, so she had no idea what to expect. McAlister didn't strike her as an amusement park kind of guy, so she doubted he was any more prepared than she was.

The interior was dimly lit by the pale moonlight that filtered in through large acrylic windows. She stared at the scene that lay before them and tried to make sense of what she was seeing. The room was a dizzying array of surreal staircases. They were on the floor, walls, and even the ceiling. All different sizes and colors, they twisted, swerved and spiraled off in every direction.

It occurred to Maiden that she and Vonny should have come there on their day out; she wouldn't mind seeing it all with the full lights and music. They stilled and looked up at the ceiling when they heard footsteps above them. She was immediately called back to the seriousness of the situation.

They exchanged a look, and Maiden bit the inside of her cheek to keep from suggesting that they leave; she had insisted on coming along after all. She gathered her wandering thoughts and peered around in the faint light.

McAlister started across the disorienting stairs; he stilled once or twice to get his bearings but managed without too much difficulty. Maiden was less graceful and almost fell a couple of times. She kept up, however, and they walked cautiously into the next room.

The floor became a minefield of inbuilt treadmills, wobble boards and what looked like water jets. The walls were strewn with distorting mirrors and different colored panels that no doubt lit up when the place was operating.

"I'm not sure how rolling your ankle counts as fun," McAlister said under his breath as he stepped carefully around one of the wobble boards.

Maiden agreed but didn't dare raise her voice for fear of letting the lurking stranger know they were there. She assumed the experience would be more enjoyable and perhaps longer lasting when everything was powered up and running. As it was, she was grateful not to be getting sprayed by the overgrown water pistols and followed McAlister as he led the way into the next room.

Striped punching bags and foam noodles that looked like barber poles were suspended from the ceiling. As they pushed pushed onwards, a giant spider's web of cargo nets and bungee cords confronted them. Despite not doing this sort of thing often, or ever, Maiden twisted through the netting fairly easily and glanced back at McAlister. He had to force his larger frame through some of the tighter spots, but squeezed past.

At last they came to a slanted and uneven staircase at the far end of the room and edged towards it. The large, demountable building creaked and groaned around them, adding to its foreboding ambience. She tried not to let her imagination run wild, but as the whole experience was designed to encourage exactly that, it wasn't easy.

We're going to die, she informed herself and then scowled. *Shut up, Maiden. Pointing out the obvious isn't helpful.*

They passed a few life-size plastic clowns that looked mean and evil in the weak light. Maiden reminded herself that she was a grown woman and resisted the urge to scream or kick them in the nuts and run for it.

She'd fallen behind but quickened her pace to catch up when McAlister glanced back to check where she was. They both paused when they heard more movement above them; someone was definitely up there. McAlister met her gaze and lifted his brows inquiringly; she assumed he was asking if she was okay to keep going. She was actually terrified, but pride came to her rescue; she inclined her head with feigned calm.

McAlister turned and led the way to the lopsided stairs. He gestured for her to stand back while he looked up into the stairwell for anything suspicious or dangerous. She doubted he'd be able to see much from there, and a moment later he nodded to her and started cautiously climbing.

They reached the second floor and were confronted by a long, dark passageway. The only illumination came from a large, stained-glass style window behind them. It was made from a more durable acrylic, but still cast a rainbow of colors across the room.

The light was a little too dim to give them much warning of what they were walking into. They both looked the area over anyway, but it was all too shadowed and silent. Her heart was thundering; whoever they'd seen and heard moving around had to be close by and might even know they were there. Maiden held her breath as McAlister started forward. She followed closely but kept looking to either side of them, waiting for an ambush.

It could just be a kid. A bored, adventurous kid who will be grounded for life if they get caught, she tried to reassure herself, but she didn't believe it for a second. *It isn't...it's some maniac killer with a sick sense of humor. This is bad; it's a trap.*

With only more scary clowns and what looked like a few green Martians to greet them, they stepped slowly into the passageway.

As soon as they'd walked a few steps in, she spied a large hole in the floor; like a piece of the walkway had broken through. Maiden gasped and grabbed McAlister's arm in case he'd somehow missed the gaping chasm.

He said nothing but raised a hand in a calming gesture. They eased closer; she looked inside the hole and saw a long drop to the ground. McAlister had begun ushering her backwards when the passage lit up brightly as the house came suddenly and noisily to life.

At the same moment a panel slid out of the wall behind them and snapped shut, blocking the way they'd come from. Maiden started and looked around sharply. Bright pink and purple lights shone mercilessly down on them while cheerful music mixed with demented laughter echoed from the speakers overhead.

The walls of the passage were all different colors and textures; some parts were raised and bumpy, others smooth like glass, while some areas looked like they were covered in fur. The textured panels moved forward and back, giving the entire hallway a strangely pulsating look.

Further along, the corridor narrowed to half its size to funnel people through a rotating barrel. It was big enough, but she suspected they'd have to crawl to get through it. Assuming they lived long enough to reach it.

"Kinda creepy," she ventured and shifted a bit closer to the large cop at her side.

"It's certainly interesting," McAlister replied as he tried to shift the panel and, when that failed, turned to size up the hole in the floor. "I think we can get through."

"What?" she gaped at him.

"It's not that far of a jump," he said reassuringly. "It'll be fine."

"No way! I hate heights!" she breathed.

"I'll go first," he promised.

Maiden watched anxiously as he turned to the pit and jumped over it with apparent ease. He stood on the other side and turned back to her with a smile. He gestured towards himself with a playful flourish.

"See? Nothing to it." He beckoned her forward. "Your turn, Miss Harlow. You'll be fine."

Maiden crept closer and looked down into the ragged opening again; the lights above her spilled down to the ground below. Aided by this, she now spied something at the shadow's edge. She frowned and peered down at it. It was a man's shoe, and she couldn't be certain there wasn't still a foot in it.

"Captain—" She glanced up at him with widened eyes.

"I know, I saw it too." He sounded calm, terrifyingly calm. "Come on over and we'll go back outside, it'll be okay."

He'd barely spoken the words when the lights cut out and the laughter and music died with a long, baleful moan. Maiden held her breath; a few seconds later she saw the flashlight from McAlister's phone shining over the space between them. It now looked much further and deeper than before. She wouldn't have been surprised if the edges of the damaged floor had grown grotesque fangs.

McAlister's steady confidence never wavered, and he never backed away from the edge. He set his phone up on the floor so it would light up the hallway, but kept his hands free. He beckoned her to him again.

"Just stay calm and jump to me, Miss Harlow," he said as he extended his hand towards her. "I won't let you fall, I promise."

"It's...pretty far down." She was aware that she sounded frightened; she was okay with that at the moment.

"It's deep, but it's not that wide." He sounded steady and confident. "You could easily jump that without my help, but I'm right here. It's safe, I swear."

Maiden closed her eyes and took a slow breath. Her heart was pounding and her palms were sweaty. She was terrified, but she knew with sickening certainty that they couldn't stay there too long. The person they saw lurking around may have tampered with that floor panel, and they could be getting away even now. Not to mention that the owner of that shoe might very well be lying dead on the ground below.

McAlister was watching her. She was sure he was running through his training for talking hysterical women down from high places. His obvious effort was both heartening and embarrassing; she could do this without his two hours of psychotherapy for beginners.

Maiden shut her eyes and let out a shaky breath. She stubbornly banished all macabre thoughts of plummeting to her death. She opened her eyes, gave a determined nod, and then ran the few steps to the edge of the hole and jumped before she could talk herself out of it.

An instant later she landed against McAlister with a tiny grunt. He wrapped his arms around her and dragged her away from the damaged floor.

Maiden slid her hands to the back of his neck and lowered her head to his chest as she took a moment to keep breathing. It was okay. She'd done it; she wasn't dead and was safely on the other side.

But her sigh of relief was soon replaced by a nervous intake of breath. He hadn't let go.

She raised her head and shifted her eyes up to his face. She was pressed against him, and his large hands were resting heavily on the small of her back; she'd never realized how sensitive that area could be.

He was staring at her; his intent and serious expression was barely discernable in the pale light thrown by his phone. She felt one of his hands slide slowly up her back and distantly realized that she still had her arms around him too. Their faces were close, and she was sure she could feel his heart pounding, although it might have been hers.

"Are you all right?" he asked softly.

"I think so." She didn't care for how breathless she sounded, but her lungs weren't cooperating.

"You did really well, Harlow." He shook his head and smiled appreciatively. "I could see how scared you were but you still did it. I thought you'd need a lot more convincing."

"Thanks," she said.

Her tone revealed her hopeless distraction, but he was holding her really close against him. She wasn't made of stone...and his muscles felt like they were. Maiden was sure she was blushing, but she was proud of herself for not collapsing in a gelatinous heap at his feet.

David knew he was staring; he knew he was holding her too tight and that he didn't need to hold her at all anymore. Somehow acknowledging those facts did nothing to help him let go.

It felt too good to hold her, and he didn't want to stop. That was the constant argument that hit back at him every time he tried to take his hands off her. Everything else had faded into the background, and he couldn't drag it back.

David, let go, he silently ordered himself, even as he relished the heat of her body soaking into his. *Yes, you're holding the most beautiful woman you've ever met; that's irrelevant. Don't think about it. Think about something that isn't soft and sexy. You have to get her out of here safely. That is your job; that's what you need to do.*

Harlow was holding his gaze, as though she knew what he was dealing with and was just waiting to see if he would crumble. He'd never seen eyes like hers; they were so deeply green and clever and curious. He felt her wriggle as she settled a little closer, her fingers brushing against his hair.

"You're sure you aren't hurt?" He flexed his hands a few times; it wasn't letting go, but it was a start.

"No...no, I'm okay, I think." Her eyes drifted to his mouth.

Don't kiss her. McAlister! Do not kiss this woman! If you kiss her, you can't go back. You don't know her. You only met her a month ago, and you think about her too much as it is. Let go right now! he ordered himself harshly, but then squeezed his eyes shut as his hands splayed across her back. *Damn it, Harlow, you feel incredible.*

David dredged up enough self-control to force his eyes open. He knew he needed to maintain some professionalism, but that was getting increasingly difficult; at the moment it seemed impossible. If she would only pull away or even look at all uncomfortable, it would be so much easier, but she didn't. She was holding eye contact and actually leaning into him. He could kiss her right now; she'd let him.

What are you doing to me, woman?

"All right." He took a breath and cleared his throat. "We should go then."

"Yeah," she murmured as she gazed up at him.

He slid his hands around her waist for the briefest moment before releasing her completely. Her arms slipped from his neck; she let her palms trail down his chest before she pulled her hands free.

David made himself glance away from her beautiful face and the undeniably interested look in her eyes. She'd touched him longer than she had to. He knew that. He was a cop; he analyzed evidence and drew logical conclusions.

At the moment, the conclusions were dragging him ridiculously far away from what he needed to be focusing on. He knelt long enough to collect his phone before standing again and finding her distractingly close. The space was suddenly quite warm.

"It may not be safe up ahead, so stay close." David's voice was softly unsteady for the first few words; he cleared his throat again and looked away from her, gradually sounding like his normal self. "Someone was here, not only to mess with the floor, but I don't know what that power surge was about."

As they made their way further down the strange hallway, David kept a sharp lookout for anything out of place, anyone who might be hiding nearby. He forced himself to pay attention to the obvious trap, who might have set it and who got caught in it before them.

There was no time to be distracted by Harlow, or the smell of her perfume, or how perfectly his hands spanned her waist.

They crawled through the now stationary barrel and found a door on the other side. This led them back out into the cool evening air. They were on the upper deck. He looked around but didn't see anyone else there.

As they walked over a small wooden suspension bridge and on to the end of the building, it became obvious that the only way down was a tubular slide that twisted down to the ground. He glanced over at Harlow; she did not look impressed.

"Well, we found the elevator." He smiled.

"And it's doubtless as safe as the rest of the place," she sighed.

"Don't be a baby." He elbowed her gently. "Come on, I'll race you down."

"Oh, grow up." She rolled her eyes.

A second later she turned and ran ahead of him. He scowled as she disappeared feet first into the large, fluorescent yellow pipe. He shook his head as he whipped down after her.

Maiden swirled around the spiraling slide and landed with a grunt at the base of it. Knowing McAlister would be close behind, she quickly rolled out of the way. Sure enough, he dropped onto the thick mat a few seconds later. Maiden, who was now sprawled out on her stomach, smirked up at him.

"I win," she said.

"That was a cheap victory," he protested wryly. "I thought you hated heights?"

"Only when there's no floor under me." She pushed up to her knees and shielded her eyes against a wash of bright light that suddenly poured over them.

They were confronted by two patrol cars that pulled in and shone their headlights across the front of the funhouse. Greg Smith climbed out of one of them and approached. If he were surprised to see them both there, he wisely kept his curiosity to himself.

"Good evening, Captain." He nodded respectfully and then slid a quietly intrigued look at her. "Hi, Maiden."

"Smith." McAlister gestured towards the building. "We need to find a way under the scaffolding, there may have been a casualty."

Greg was immediately all business. He looked over his shoulder and motioned to the other officers. Within seconds, they were following McAlister around the side of the funhouse, looking for an entry point.

Maiden brushed herself off and subtly followed as they circled the building. She was busy watching for any sign of the person they'd seen earlier while the others were searching for a door. It only took a few minutes for them to find a gate that was built into the mesh of scaffolding.

McAlister went in first, having availed himself of Greg's large flashlight, and swept the beam of light methodically over the area. They made their way under the highest portions of the funhouse and soon found what they were looking for.

There in the dirt, beneath the hole in the floor that she and McAlister had stumbled across upstairs, they saw a man's motionless body.

They eased closer. Maiden tried to stay as inconspicuous as possible to avoid being sent to wait outside. She'd gotten this far; she needed to know who the victim was. McAlister shone the light on the man's face, and Maiden's eyes widened. She instantly recognized his thinning hair and gray-flecked mustache, not to mention his bruised eye.

"That's Sam Chalmers!" she gasped before she could stop herself.

"So it is," McAlister murmured and glanced at Greg. "Call Doc Jenkins. The rest of you, fan out and secure the area."

The officers hurried back outside. Maiden's mind was reeling. She remembered the alleged death threat Chalmers had claimed to have been sent, although it could hardly be described as 'alleged' anymore. For one wild, terrified instant she desperately hoped her father was home and surrounded by people who could vouch for his whereabouts all evening.

She knew McAlister would be remembering him too; her time at the crime scene was almost up. Knowing this was her only chance, she quickly looked the area over as much as she could.

McAlister was examining the ground around the body; she watched him shine the flashlight over what had to be the chunk of floor that fell away under Chalmers.

She wondered what he was doing there, and how long he'd been dead. She wasn't about to go and touch the body to see if he felt warm, but the intruder they saw running around suggested this may have happened recently.

Had that part of the floor already been removed and the lights turned out, like what happened to her and McAlister? Or had the sabotaged section still been tacked in place? Maybe it looked normal and safe when Chalmers stepped onto it, only to fall to his death. It was a chilling thought either way.

Maiden edged to the side, hoping for a closer look, and accidentally sent a few pebbles skittering. McAlister glanced back at her and immediately frowned.

So much for getting a better look, she sighed.

"You should go home, Miss Harlow," he said quietly as he took a few steps toward her. He sounded more formal now, despite barely being able to take his hands off her when they were alone upstairs. "Did you drive here?"

"Yeah," she almost mumbled and rubbed her arms against the surprisingly cool evening air.

She gazed at him uncertainly; she wondered if he'd say anything about their brief but breathless encounter. She didn't claim to know a lot about men, but he had been as caught up as she was, even if only for a moment. But now he stood a little further than he had earlier and took a moment before he looked her in the eye.

"All right," he said tolerantly and braced a fist on his hip. "Look, under the circumstances, I won't make an issue of you going to see Mr. Armstrong behind my back."

"I beg your pardon?!" Maiden felt herself plummet back to reality as hard as if she'd fallen through that stupid hole herself.

"You had no business being there, or talking to him about the case," he told her, but then gave a conceding nod. "But, as I said, we won't worry about it this time. Okay?"

A wave of underwhelmed incredulity washed over her like a slap in the face with a cold, dead fish. As tempted as she was to verbalize her disappointment at his tepid attitude, he had reminded her that Oliver would be at the inn and perhaps full of further insights. She took a step back.

"That's so kind of you, thanks a lot, Captain," she said dryly as she turned and headed for the gate.

"Well, hey! Do you want someone to walk you out?" he called after her with a frown in his voice.

"Nope," she replied without sparing him another glance.

"Good night, I guess," he muttered as she hurried outside.

Chapter Eighteen

Maiden arrived back at the inn and walked in through the office door. She peered beyond the front desk and spotted Oliver sitting at a table in the dining room, surrounded by pies.

She sighed and shook her head, but wasn't at all surprised to see the poor man pressed into service already. He'd had a shower and changed into jeans and a blue flannel shirt; she almost didn't recognize him without the bare arms and greasy overalls. He had even combed his beard.

As she approached, she noticed that both Gloria and Kylie were standing beside the table, watching him intently. Both women looked pleased.

"I'm absolutely certain, ladies," Oliver said firmly as he pointed to two of the proffered pies. "Gloria's Butter Pecan Cream and Kylie's Chocolate-dipped Strawberry Whip. Those are your winners. No question about it, two of the best pies this town will ever see."

"I knew it," Kylie whispered to herself as she scooped up the pie as if it were made of gold and precious jewels. "Thank you *very* much, Mr. Armstrong. Now all I need to do is perfect the presentation."

She walked back into the kitchen with her chin held high and let the door fall shut behind her. Gloria wrinkled her nose and pulled a childishly mocking face in her rival's direction before claiming her own selection.

"You're a sweet boy, Oliver." She beamed at him and then gave Maiden an exasperated look. "You certainly know more about dessert than my daughters! I must've gone wrong with you girls somewhere."

"It's good of you to accept the responsibility, Mom," she replied mildly, even though the older woman swanned out without stopping to listen.

She turned to Oliver and shook her head in wonder. He looked very satisfied with himself, sitting there like a king surrounded by rich and decadent offerings. He gestured for her to sit down as he poked a fork into what appeared to be a cherry strudel that had been mashed into a pie shell.

"They're getting strapped for good ideas, I see." She wrinkled her nose at a pie made of half melted ice cream with banana spikes stabbed into the top.

"They *were*," he said smugly.

"How'd you do it?" She shook her head. "We've been dealing with the pie lunacy for more than a week, you've been here five minutes!"

"I just picked one each and raved about them. It made the ladies happy and stopped the onslaught." He sat back and folded his arms. "It's only pie."

"What if they both lose because you chose at random?" She arched a challenging brow.

"Life will probably go on," he laughed. "And I'll be long gone before next year's competition."

"Selfish," she chuckled, but then glanced around to make sure they were alone. "Listen, I need to talk to you about something serious."

"Then I suggest the Key Lime Meringue." He nodded sagely and pushed a plate towards her. "That's as serious as it gets."

"Knock it off, Armstrong." She eased closer and lowered her voice. "Sam Chalmers was killed tonight."

"Who's that?" He shook his head, but did look more serious now.

"You don't know him?" Her shoulders sagged. "I was hoping you did."

"What? Is this some kind of a frame up?" He lifted his sparse, orangey brows.

"Yes, Oliver. I came here to get your help in framing you." She propped her chin in her hand.

"Sorry, I'm a little paranoid these days." He shrugged and scratched his beard. "So, who's Sam Chalmers?"

"He was one of the event planners for Summerfest, he worked for the city," she explained. "I saw him fighting with Keith the day Keith died. I also saw him having a tense meeting with Gabby, but it looked like she handled him pretty easily."

"Yeah, Gabs doesn't fight," he said wryly. "She just steps in when she needs to and wins."

"Am I right in guessing that Gabby is the one that keeps the wheels of the carnival turning?" she asked carefully.

"Oh, Keith did his part," Oliver admitted. "But she could've managed without him. She did in fact, until he was signed on and started throwing his weight around."

"So how long were you working at Spencer and Spencer before Keith came along?"

"Four months or so." He searched his memory. "Gabby did a good job, she kept the paperwork in order and the bookings coming in. I have to admit though, for all his faults, Keith got us better terms than she ever dared to ask for."

"Terms?" Maiden shook her head.

"There are fees, permits and that kind of thing," he explained. "If visiting attractions don't play by the rules, they don't get to play. I got the impression that Keith was willing to make certain...compromises, that Gabby wouldn't stoop to."

"You mean he offered bribes?" Maiden asked plainly. He shrugged without offering an opinion and glanced away. "That sounds like a dangerous game. On both sides."

"Hard to argue that if you say this Chalmers guy has been killed," he said. "Mistakes tend to catch up with people."

"I guess so...Oliver," she waited until he looked back at her, "I got the impression from Janet that she was eyeing off Keith's job, what do you think of that?"

"Impossible," he said without hesitation. "She doesn't have the brains, the dedication or the temperament. She can't even keep the concession stands running."

"Yeah, they do seem to be stumbling along pretty badly," she acknowledged with a slight nod. "What about Gabby, though?"

"Gabby could do it." He inclined his head with certainty. "She was almost the complete package before and she'll have learned a few tricks from Keith; she's smart."

"Smart enough to get Keith out of her way?" Maiden asked. "And maybe Janet too?"

"What?" He could only stare at her. "*Gabby*?! No way! That woman is so clean she squeaks."

"Okay, you know her way better than I do." She saw no point in arguing it and forged ahead. "But why would Timmy have attacked Janet if someone else hadn't told him to? Someone could have put him up to it."

"It's possible, but you have to bear in mind that he's stupid, Maiden," he said frankly. "From what you told me he was also drunk. He probably convinced himself that this whole mess was

Janet's fault. Maybe he was afraid that she would take over from Keith, he always hated her. Most of the crew did."

"So I've heard." Maiden nodded. "Do you really think that's motive enough to kill her?"

"To the right person, absolutely." He looked at her as though it were a silly question. "Put yourself in the shoes of someone with nothing else to fall back on, no place else to go. Some mean and selfish woman breezes in out of nowhere and takes whatever she can get, no matter who already had it. And now she wants to run the place? How well is that going to turn out, and how would you feel about it?"

"Not good, that's for sure," Maiden conceded as she thought it over. "Okay, it's a start. Thanks, Oliver."

"Hey, Maiden. Listen, sweetheart, are you certain you want to keep getting involved in this?" he asked kindly. "You're dealing with some desperate people that don't have a lot to lose."

"You sound like Captain McAlister," she said as she pushed to her feet. "I have to help Dad. But I'll be careful, I promise."

Late that night, Maiden was lying in bed, staring up at the ceiling as she rehashed the events of the day. She'd told Alfie about Sam Chalmers' death; he'd been surprised but also annoyed. He finally admitted that his plot to thwart Chalmers had been to amass a crowd of his victims and confront him publicly.

Apparently, he had spent hours putting together a list of Chalmers' targets. He'd gotten most of them to agree to form a unified front against him in hopes of getting him replaced. He wasn't impressed that he had done all that work only to have the twit end up dead.

Maiden gently pleaded with him to be a little more tactful about it when the police inevitably questioned him. He assured her that he'd spent the day listening to Gloria prattle about pies and family traditions and how Kylie was too skinny to know anything about good dessert. He had his alibi and had certainly suffered to get it.

Maiden wasn't sure how strong an alibi that truly was, but she assured herself it didn't matter. Her father would never kill anyone, and whoever laid that trap for Chalmers knew their way around the carnival.

She sighed and stretched as her eyes drifted to the window. She splayed a hand across her stomach and wondered what Captain McAlister was doing. A glance at the clock confirmed that it was after midnight; he was probably at home fast asleep. She doubted he was lying awake in bed thinking about her.

She replayed their brief moment in the funhouse for at least the fiftieth time. She was afraid to allow herself to believe that he'd almost kissed her; it had felt like it at the time, though. He'd held her so close and struggled so obviously to let her go. It had been one of the most breathlessly exciting moments she'd ever shared with someone, and she hadn't even gotten a peck on the cheek to show for it.

After all the teasing buildup, he had been able to walk away, and all he could say in the end was that he wouldn't make an issue of her going to see Oliver, *this* time! He wasn't distracted by nearly kissing her; he was thinking about the case.

In all fairness, they had just found a body, but he knew it was down there already. He was annoyed that she was involved again; that clearly overrode everything else. It seemed terribly cold-blooded of him.

Maiden squeezed her eyes shut and sternly reminded herself that she needed to keep her attention on protecting Alfie. The confusing and attractive policeman was a dangerous distraction. Particularly if he decided to harass her father. She hadn't forgotten Alfie's parting shot at Sam Chalmers: *You're a snake and it'll catch up with you.*

While it was a hugely unfortunate choice of words, she knew he'd meant nothing by them. She was biased, though, and McAlister wasn't. And he had heard every word of the exchange. Maiden groaned and rubbed her face with her hands.

They were dealing with two murders now and possibly more to come if they didn't catch the killer soon. Something was missing from the picture, something important.

Timmy.

She sat up straight and stared into the darkness of her room. What happened to Timmy? No one had seen him since he ran off after attacking Janet. Or had they?

Maybe he was the person skulking around the funhouse. Someone had turned the power on long enough to trap her and Captain McAlister inside; it could very well have been Timmy.

She threw back the covers and slid out of bed. Walking to the French doors, she pushed them open and stepped out onto the balcony. It was a little cool, but the breeze had died down; her thin, strappy nightgown would be warm enough.

The moon was full and luminous in the night sky; she walked towards the railing and gazed up at it for a moment before settling into her favorite peacock chair.

The street below was quiet. There was a dim light shining in the window of the house across the road, but that was the only sign that anyone was awake except her.

She tucked deep into the chair and sank into uninterrupted thought. She stared into the distance and let the scenes she had witnessed unfold in her mind. Going back to the first day of the carnival, she tried to recall exactly what she'd seen.

Keith Haynes and Sam Chalmers had fought bitterly. Even without hearing their words, she could easily detect their mutual hatred. But they were both dead now.

Keith also humiliated Timmy Gibson, and before that he'd had another fight with Oliver. And then there was Daisy; he could hardly betray a person more extensively and intimately than he did her. A lot of people hated Keith; that was no secret.

As for Sam Chalmers, she suspected that a lot of people hated him too. She could only guess how many businesses he'd systematically fleeced with bogus claims of fees and charges. She'd had a brief look at the list of names her father had put together; there were a dozen listed and likely more that he hadn't spoken to yet.

She frowned thoughtfully; the suspects looked to be potentially quite extensive, but only at first glance.

The murders were both committed with pieces of carnival equipment. Both times the crimes could easily have pointed straight at Oliver Armstrong. Even Sam Chalmers likely died before Oliver had left for the inn. It was possible that he'd set the trap and stayed back long enough to use it against not only Chalmers but also her and the captain.

And yet, Maiden couldn't honestly believe that Oliver had killed anyone, but she didn't *want* to believe it either. She shut her eyes and sank deeper into the chair; she'd have to give it more thought.

Chapter Nineteen

The following morning, David walked through the front door of Harlow House. He glanced around the still and silent foyer and spotted Harlow sitting at the desk, staring dejectedly down at *Hero of the Heather*.

He felt himself smile, which eased some of the awkwardness of seeing her after that near miss last night. The encounter had been on his mind ever since and had made sleep incredibly difficult.

He had also dreamed about her again, and he didn't wake up as soon as he usually did this time. It had taken two cups of coffee and another run around the block to get straight in his head what had almost happened between them and what he'd imagined.

He had spent the time reminding himself that he was new in town and had just started settling into life in Golden Glen. The station needed a lot of work, and he was still getting familiar with his team. He hadn't even finished unpacking yet. This wasn't a wise time to start a relationship. He could only divide his efforts in so many directions, and if Harlow was among the options, he knew where most of his attention would go.

Besides that, things were moving too fast. Scary fast. It was getting out of hand; he needed to take charge of the situation.

He shut the door behind him and turned to her again. She looked beautiful; she probably always did. Her dark hair fell loose over her shoulder; it was shiny and smooth and she absently toyed with a lock of it as she struggled to read that stupid book.

After letting go of a tiny, unhappy moan, she glanced up at him slowly. Her clear green eyes locked on his, and a vivid flashback of his dream hit him hard. He cleared his throat and forced himself to keep walking towards her.

This is no different from any other time you've come here, he reminded himself. *This is just another day. Nothing happened. She didn't seem to think much of it anyway.*

Despite his tremulous new resolve to put the brakes on whatever it was that they had going, it bothered him that she had walked away with barely a word last night. He hadn't wanted to have a deep discussion about what almost happened, he still didn't, but he thought the way she ran out was a bit heartless, all things considered.

But the most pressing fact was that Sam Chalmers had been murdered; that meant he needed to talk to Alfie, and that also meant he had to deal with Harlow. Even now she was looking at him with watchful uncertainty; he suspected he looked the same.

"Good morning, Captain." Her tone was guarded; he didn't like that.

"Hello, Miss Harlow," he said as he approached the desk. "Sleep well?"

"I suppose." She shrugged and rested her chin in her palm. "Did you?"

"It was a late night; that's typical after finding bodies." He reminded himself that he had no reason to be annoyed with her, but kept talking anyway. "But you skipped out pretty quick so I guess you had more chance to rest."

"I left after being told to go." Her tone was flat, and her eyes had narrowed minutely. "Although you did generously decide not to make an issue of my being there in the first place. Thanks again, by the way, you're an angel."

Oh, you're cranky today. Good. I doubt you dreamed about me all night, and I bet you weren't standing in a freezing cold shower at 4am, he grumbled to himself.

"You were the one that left in the middle of the conversation." He gave a nonchalant shrug.

"You sounded like you were done with the conversation," she informed him and returned to the book.

"At least you would've had the chance to chat with Armstrong again," he said with deliberate calm. He could feel himself getting angry, but a more professional part of him wanted to know if she'd learned anything useful from the guy.

"He's not my type, Captain. You don't have to worry about that." She threw his earlier teasing back at him with a smirk, but didn't look up again.

Don't ask her what her type is, you idiot! he chided himself before the dangerously leading question slipped out. *Don't start hitting on her, she'll hit back and then what are you going to do?!*

"Right," he murmured aloud to himself, and then hurried to come up with something relevant to say when she glanced up. "How's the book going? Almost finished?"

"No, I'm closing in on halfway there, though," she sighed.

"How can it be *that* hard to plow through?" He shook his head. "What's it even about?"

"A jerk and an idiot." She met his gaze grimly. "I hate them both and I hope they die."

He laughed at the perfectly serious expression on her face. Harlow appeared to take exception to his amusement; she gave him a challenging smile and sat up straight in her chair.

"Fine, here." She pushed the book toward him. "Read a page. Read a paragraph even. I dare you."

"You blow things out of proportion," he chuckled at her and picked up the thick tome. "Where should I start?"

"It doesn't matter," she said dryly.

Partly to appease her and partly to show her up, he obligingly cracked it open in the middle and began to read. His confidence faded quickly.

It took only two paragraphs for him to start thinking about taking a match to the oppressively thick volume and rescuing them both. He cleared his throat as he skimmed over an indelicately descriptive passage about the heroine.

"Grizelda?" he asked politely.

"Oh yeah." She smiled happily, enjoying his slowly burgeoning despair. "Keep going, maybe it'll get better."

He did, but it got worse. There were a lot of references to longing glances, heaving bosoms and firm, ripe fruit. It was worse than garbage; even garbage had been useful once.

"Dang," he mused without thinking it through. "Sounds like she's stacked as high as you."

He froze and his eyes widened even as he kept his gaze glued to the page. Harlow had also gone still, but she was staring at him; he could feel it.

"Did you just say that?" Her voice was soft and startled and definitely amused.

"No." He shook his head, still refusing to face her. "You imagined it."

"Imagined what, Captain?" She was struggling to keep from laughing; he started to smile despite his mortification.

"Everything," he said with feigned calm. "I'm not even here right now."

"Impressive, you seem so life-like. And you look riveted to that," Harlow laughed softly and leaned forward, propping herself up on her elbows. "If you're enjoying the book that much, you can borrow it and tell me how it ends."

He snapped it shut and set it back in front of her. She was looking up at him with a wry smile.

This would be literally the worst time to stare at her cleavage, McAlister, he reminded himself and decided to ignore the way her casual pose inadvertently pushed her breasts together.

"I'm good, thanks." He cleared his throat and glanced around. "Anyway, I'm only here to ask your dad a few questions about his whereabouts last night."

"Yeah, I guessed that much." She was looking him over.

"So..." He forced himself to hold her steady gaze. "Is your dad here?"

"If he was, you'd know about it by now." She smirked, thoroughly amused by his obvious embarrassment.

David shut his eyes briefly, but felt a corner of his mouth tilt upwards.

"Are you done?" he asked patiently.

"With what, Captain?" Her tone was ingenuous.

"Do I go on like this when you accidentally—yeah I do, fine. Forget it." He caught himself as soon as she started laughing at him. "Your dad? Please?"

"Do you actually suspect that he sabotaged the funhouse floor?" She shook her head wryly.

"I won't bother asking if you remember that Mr. Harlow threatened Mr. Chalmers after being accused of sending an intimidating note," David said a little more seriously. "I have to follow up on the obvious leads."

Harlow's eyes widened with incredulous amusement. She looked quite pretty when she smiled like that. He gave her a quelling frown.

"'Obvious'?" she repeated. "Can you picture Alfred Francis Harlow slinking through that funhouse, without getting lost or tangled in the cargo nets, and somehow rigging that section of the upstairs floor?…Are you picturing it right now? Dad wrapped in bungee cords, flailing helplessly?"

David refused to be teased or flirted out of being thorough. In spite of that, he couldn't look at her without smiling like an idiot, so he locked his gaze on the front door, wishing he was safely on the other side of it.

"Would you please get Mr. Harlow so I can talk to him and get out of here?" he grumbled.

"Dad went out half an hour ago," she said without a hint of apology.

David stilled, and his eyes snapped back to hers as he took that in. The little monster had held him up, and even made him read her inane library book, knowing full well that his whole purpose in coming there was moot.

He exhaled slowly through his nose and leaned forward. He braced his elbows on the desk, matching her stance and looking her right in the eye.

"Do you enjoy wasting my time, Miss Harlow?" he asked quietly.

"I've certainly enjoyed it today," she admitted with a sexy little grin; she lifted her dark brows a fraction. "Didn't you? Even a tiny bit?"

Damn it. You have no idea, Harlow, absolutely none at all. I wonder what you'd have done if I'd kissed you last night. He held her gaze for as long as he dared. *Right. Time to leave, David.*

"I'll see you around, Miss Harlow," he said as he made himself stand up straight and turn for the door.

Maiden watched McAlister as he slipped outside into the bright sunshine. She hadn't set out to flirt with him or to chase him off, but even so, she couldn't help feeling like she'd won this skirmish.

She was doing her best to suppress her pleased smile, but then glanced down at her book and sniggered as she relived the captain's bemused horror. She sobered when she heard the doorknob rattle. Surely there was no way McAlister would dare to face her again so soon. What if he'd bumped into Alfie and was coming back to question him?

She watched the door swing open and felt a wave of relief when she saw Tony walk inside. Her relief was slightly tainted when he gave her a knowing smile. The chances of the eagle-eyed postman missing the sight of Captain McAlister leaving a moment ago were next to nil.

"Good morning, Maiden," he said affably as he walked over to the desk and tossed a few letters and a catalog off to the side. "Busy already?"

"Hey, Tony," she replied, and ignored his question. "Got any info for me?"

"You bet." He nodded and set his bag aside. "Did the captain tell you about Sam Chalmers?"

"He didn't have to, we both found his body," she sighed and sat back a little, admiring Tony's startled yet intrigued and rather excited expression.

"Are you actually working together on this case?" he whispered hopefully.

"No, we just happened to be in a sabotaged corridor in the abandoned funhouse at the same time, sheer coincidence." She smiled wanly. "Did you talk to Florence?"

"I...yeah." Tony shook his head and frowned a little before clearing his expression and forging ahead. "She was a mess, poor thing; she only heard about the murder this morning. I asked, but she said she didn't know anything about any bribes or threatening letters to local businesses. She insisted that Chalmers must have sent those out himself."

"I doubt she'd be in a hurry to admit anything else, but it is possible, I guess." Maiden shrugged. "If she had known about his scams he'd have had to cut her in on them to keep her quiet."

"Yeah, that's probably true. I also asked her about that note that Chalmers claimed Alfie sent." Tony folded his arms. "It was already sitting on the floor inside the door when she walked into the office. She read it and panicked. She didn't see who left it, but apparently it reeked of cigarette smoke."

"Definitely not Dad's style," Maiden murmured thoughtfully. *Sounds more like Timmy, or even Janet.*

"I don't know if that's enough to clear Alfie, though." Tony winced and shook his head. "The smell doesn't really prove anything and I would guess that it's faded by now."

"Possibly," she conceded. "But that wasn't the point anyway. It gives me a few ideas of who may have left it, that's what I was after."

"You are scary cool, Maiden." He grinned at her. "So why were you really with McAlister last night?"

Before she could answer, they heard a very heavy tread on the stairs. A moment later, Oliver turned the corner and glanced up from his phone.

"Good morning." He nodded politely to Tony, but his attention went straight to Maiden. "I have to go back to the carnival for a bit. Something's up."

"What is it?" Maiden asked, even as she pushed to her feet.

"Gabs just sent me a message saying that Daisy's made a very hostile tactical move," he said and shook his head. "She wants some muscle on hand in case things get nasty."

"Let's go. See you later Tony, thanks again." She gestured for Oliver to follow her through the office and then shouted towards the dining room. "Mom! We're going out! Watch the desk please!"

Oliver was fortunately able to fold himself into Maiden's car; they drove straight back to the fair and hurried towards Spencer and Spencer. They'd been making their way to Gabby's office but caught a glimpse of her and Janet standing behind the concession trucks. They immediately veered over to join them.

As she and Oliver approached, Maiden looked in the window of the ice cream truck and saw Daisy grinning as she strutted around, surveying the area. The man working there seemed more cheerful as well, and the line was moving steadily.

Maiden's gaze slid to Janet. She was lighting a cigarette, all the while watching her colorful rival with cold and furious eyes.

"What's going on?" Oliver asked with an impassive expression as they reached the ladies.

Janet looked at him sharply, and her countenance darkened further. Gabby edged away from the angry woman and turned to Oliver with an uneasy shake of her head.

"Daisy went behind my back and called the corporate office." Gabby scowled grimly. "She complained about Janet and the, uh, issues we've been having. Upper management insisted that she be replaced immediately."

"Oh, that would be...frustrating," Maiden said as tactfully as she could and glanced at Janet.

The diminutive blonde was tapping her foot and puffing at her cigarette as she glared at Daisy through the back door of the truck.

"It wasn't helpful." Gabby rubbed her eyes. "She also claimed that I wasn't taking care of business with Keith gone."

"Spiteful hag!" Janet hissed under her breath.

"Talking to yourself?" Daisy asked sweetly as she came to stand in the doorway. She was dressed in a bright pink and orange harlequin patterned jumpsuit today.

"Hey, Daisy." Oliver smiled. "Been up to mischief have you?"

"I'm just trying to make things right." She held up her hands innocently and flicked Janet a hateful look. "This place has gone to pieces thanks to the wandering minstrel over there. I have plenty to do to fix what she's ruined, so maybe it's time for her to move on again."

"You should have given me a chance to take care of things," Gabby said with an exasperated sigh. "What good has this done?"

"What good?" Daisy stared at her and then gestured around incredulously. "We're selling food again for a start! There were barrels of ice cream sitting in storage because her royal highness couldn't be bothered to go and check. She just had them put up 'sold out' signs because she's lazy! I've inventoried what we're actually out of so now we can get some stock moving and some money rolling in!"

"You shouldn't have pushed ahead!" Gabby scowled. "We have to work together."

"I tried working with you!" Daisy retorted, and planted her fists on her hips. "But you still act like Keith is here to push you around; that's *your* problem. Now, thanks to a little ingenuity and actual work, I have a job to do. Kindly excuse me."

Janet was glaring at her as she threw her cigarette to the ground and pulverized it under the toe of her shiny black pump. Daisy had turned to go but then stopped and leveled her heavily painted gaze on the other woman.

"Oh, one more thing, the advantages of the job come back to me too," she said with an icy smile. "Which includes my trailer. You have until the end of the day to clear out. According to the corporate office, that is."

Daisy smiled and waved at her before slipping back into the truck and getting to work. Janet took a deep breath and slid Gabby a furious look; the uneasy manager shrugged helplessly.

"She went over my head."

"Yeah, so I heard," Janet grated and stalked past. "Thanks a lot."

Oliver watched her storm off and then turned to Gabby and lifted his orange brows. She motioned for them to step away from Daisy's reclaimed domain. Maiden followed as they tucked back into the shade of a large storage truck.

"When did all of this happen?" he asked quietly.

"I got the call about an hour ago," Gabby muttered. "Daisy certainly didn't waste any time. She called up yesterday and told them all sorts of things about Janet and Keith. It wouldn't have been hard for them to check the sales records, they're all recorded electronically. I had a look after the phone call...it's not good. Sales have plummeted over the past four months and there's no valid reason for it."

"So Janet chewed through the supplies that Daisy had stocked up and never replenished anything?" He didn't sound surprised. "Keith never noticed that?"

"He never said anything to me about it." Gabby shrugged. "And I couldn't talk to him about Janet at the best of times. If he didn't want to hear it, he didn't listen."

"Were you actually planning to fire Janet?" Maiden lowered her voice discreetly.

"Hey, all of this *just* happened." Gabby's shoulders sagged. "People act like Janet was the only problem we had, or that the concession stands are the biggest source of revenue. They aren't! Right in the middle of a job, which is also right in the middle of a police investigation, isn't the ideal time to start restructuring things!"

"Sorry, I guess I didn't think that firing one lazy employee was so difficult or so deeply enmeshed in everything else." Maiden managed to keep most of the exasperated sarcasm out of her voice.

"It's a lot harder when you have to live with the fallout, okay?" Gabby gave her a look.

"I'm sorry," she said more genuinely. "It wouldn't be easy for you."

"It doesn't help when I have people standing over my shoulder and telling me what to do either," she grumbled. "But that's what keeps happening. Head office called and ordered that Janet be dismissed. I managed to get that changed to a demotion, but that's all I could do."

"So what's her new role?" Oliver asked.

"Ticket booth." Gabby quirked a brow at him. "How's that for ironic?"

Maiden watched the pair share a private chuckle. She couldn't help wondering why Gabby was trying so hard to soften the blow for Janet. She'd been handed the perfect excuse to get rid of her, but she chose to bargain her right back into the troupe.

She glanced over at Daisy when she heard her laughing and chatting with the guy working alongside her. She seemed eager to get her hands dirty, and it was obvious that things were already running better. While the concessions might not have earned a fortune, for a struggling business with a lot of employees to look after, every bit of revenue was important.

She thought back to what she'd overheard of Daisy's previous conversation with Gabby, including Daisy's threats to handle the matter herself. Seeing firsthand how hesitant Gabby was to deal with the problem, Maiden really couldn't blame Daisy for doing something about it on her own.

CHAPTER TWENTY

Gabby seemed a bit shaken up over the whole episode. Maiden suggested that the three of them have lunch at a café outside the fair. The stressed-out office manager agreed immediately and even led the way, clearly eager to get away for a while.

They ended up at the same jazzy café where Gabby had met Chalmers. Maiden found that interesting but didn't say anything; Gabby was unaware that she'd spied on her that day. They ate quietly as the frustrated manager wasn't in a chatty mood at first. Maiden bided her time and didn't broach the obvious topic until they'd moved on to coffee.

"Are you still angry with Daisy?" she asked with a gentle smile.

"Oh, well...yes, I am." Gabby sighed and ran her fingers through her thick hair. "I'm so sick of people treating me like I'm an idiot even as they sit back and let me do the tedious work that no one else wants to bother with. She jumped down my throat to start changing everything instantly. Keith died on Monday, for crying out loud, it hasn't even been a week!"

"Yeah," Maiden said quietly and gave a tiny shrug. "I suppose that, from her point of view, it's all been brewing for six months. Maybe Keith was the only obstacle she was aware of."

"Daisy can run the concession stands efficiently, I'll give her that. But ordering ice cream and dunking waffle cones in chocolate isn't enough to give a person a solid grasp of how a business like this runs. Nothing is that straightforward," Gabby grumbled. "Unfortunately."

Maiden glanced at Oliver, who let out a soundless whistle and looked away uncomfortably. Seeing that talking about Daisy wasn't a great idea at the moment, Maiden tried a slightly different line of questioning.

"That's true enough," she said mildly. "So, do you think Janet will stick around? Now that she's been demoted and has to watch a rival enjoy all the privileges she used to have?"

"She might; it's hard to say," Gabby replied with a shrug. "The biggest issue for Janet will be having nowhere else to go."

"Is that why you didn't want to fire her?" Maiden asked with an understanding smile that she hoped looked convincing.

"Yeah, I guess so," she said quietly. "It'll be tough for her if she does stay though. The rest of the crew despise her and won't make a secret of it, particularly now that she's lost all her authority."

"Did she really have much authority?" Maiden sounded deliberately dubious.

"When she was sleeping with the boss?" Oliver laughed. "Yeah."

"Oh, right." Maiden rolled her eyes at herself. "Well, maybe she'll just move on."

"Mm," he grunted and stared down into his coffee. Gabby noticed and rested a hand on his arm.

"You don't have to do anything, Oliver," she said earnestly. "You're not responsible for her, don't let her worm her way into your life."

"I won't, I promise." He smiled faintly and ran a hand over his beard. "But I don't look forward to possibly having to brush her off again. Especially now that she'll be desperate."

"I'm sure it won't come to that." Gabby patted his arm and brushed her thick, dark hair behind her ear. "Just try to avoid her."

"Yeah," he sounded subdued. He glanced up and met Maiden's enquiring gaze with a wary sigh. "She's asked me to help her move her stuff out of her trailer."

"When did that happen?" Maiden blinked at him.

"She sent me a text about fifteen minutes ago." He shrugged.

"Good old Janet." Gabby shook her head. "Never one to waste time."

"It's all right." Maiden smiled. "I'll go with you. That'll make it a little harder for her to push too much."

"You'd do that?" Oliver brightened. "Thanks Maiden, you're a lifesaver."

She just waved it away. Not only was she happy to help, but it was an opportunity to get a closer look at the conflict between Janet and Daisy. She was taking the last sip of her cappuccino when her phone rang.

She checked the display; it was Alfie. She mouthed a quick apology to her companions and answered it.

"Hi, Dad," she said. "Everything okay? What?...Yes, that nice young man with the beard is with me."

Oliver glanced at her and chuckled. Maiden pulled a face and then shook her head wryly.

"He wants to talk to you," she murmured as she handed him the phone. "He doesn't have your number."

Oliver gave her a wink and took the phone. Maiden watched with a smirk as Oliver mostly listened. She gathered from his side of the conversation that her father had gotten permission to reopen his stall and was looking for fit and willing volunteers to set everything up again.

"That's fine, Mr. Harlow." He smiled as he spoke. "We'll meet you at your car, let us know when you get here."

Oliver hung up and handed her the phone. Maiden took it back with a smile and distantly considered the sad plight of burly men, always being asked to lift and carry things.

"So who do you have to move first? Janet or Dad?"

"Let's start with Janet and get it over with," he replied.

Half an hour later they made their way to Janet's soon to be ex-home. Maiden hadn't seen it before and, having gotten a glimpse of where the rest of the crew slept, immediately saw where the envy and resentment would come into play.

The trailer was rather large, larger than the ones that housed multiple crew members. It was neat and tidy and looked newer than the others as well. Painted in a soft shade of cream, it had a little pink porch and matching lace curtains that fluttered in the windows. As they approached, she spied several pretty glass ornaments dangling from the tops of the window frames.

The door was propped open, and they could hear movement from inside. Maiden felt a tad awkward being there to witness Janet's fall from grace, but she glanced at Oliver and imagined how uncomfortable *he* must be. She focused on helping him and felt calmer.

A moment later, Janet appeared in the doorway. Her welcoming smile shrank when she saw Maiden standing there too, but she quickly recovered.

"Thanks for lending a hand," she murmured as she set a large pink suitcase in front of her. "I'm almost packed up."

"Sure," Oliver said in a bored voice. "Do you know where you're going yet?"

"To the office for now, Gabby promised she'd find me something today." Janet shrugged helplessly. "And considering that she's had months to claw me to shreds with her roommates, I'd rather not swap *everything* with Daisy."

Daisy probably felt the same when you swooped in and took everything from her, Maiden thought to herself but kept silent. The poetic justice of the situation wasn't likely to be lost on anyone; there was no need to harp on it.

Oliver had just grabbed the large suitcase when the woman in question sauntered into view. Maiden glanced from Daisy's smugly pleased expression to Janet's look of stoic tolerance and suddenly wished she was elsewhere.

"All packed and ready to go?" Daisy asked cheerfully as she stepped closer and rested a hand on the railing of the porch. "I have to admit that I'm so excited to get my little home back...I'll have to clean and disinfect it first, of course."

"Yeah, it's certainly seen more action than it ever did with you," Janet replied with an answering smile. "Ah well, nothing lasts forever."

"The time *you've* been hanging around like a bad smell has felt like an eternity," Daisy countered. "Are you finished yet? I'm pretty busy, *I* have a job to get back to."

"You said I had until the end of the day," Janet reminded her irately. "It's not even 2 o'clock. Why are you even here?"

"I'm only making sure you don't trash my house on your way out," she muttered. "You've taken enough from me already."

"The place looks fine, Daisy," Oliver strove for a patient tone in the midst of the ugly fight. "We'll take her stuff and go, okay? Can we just leave it at that?"

"Don't talk to me like I'm the awful one!" Daisy folded her arms and tapped her foot. "She's squandered and ruined everything else she took from me! Keith, the trucks, the morale of all the people that worked for her. Am I supposed to think she'd do any better by my home?!"

"I never asked for this place," Janet hissed. "Keith offered it. He *insisted* on it! He didn't say where it came from."

"Sure he didn't." Daisy rolled her eyes. "Rumors get around, honey. Everyone knows every disgusting thing you did to get what you wanted. Stop blaming it all on Keith. Yeah, he was a rotten pig to take you up on your offers, but *you* did the offering!"

"I am not going to stand here and listen to this bitter, hateful garbage!" Janet's voice faltered, and her eyes filled with tears. "You've got it all back now, can't you be satisfied with that?"

"Oh, I'm very satisfied," Daisy said ruthlessly. "And I'll be absolutely gleeful once your scrawny butt is out of my house!"

"Fine!" Janet sobbed as she pushed one more suitcase through the door and tucked a jacket under her arm.

She threw Daisy a set of keys and grabbed a small box as she stomped down the stairs. She stood in front of the other woman and thrust the box at her.

"Here! Have everything!" Her voice trembled. "The job, the house, even this. The last gift Keith ever gave me. Take them and choke on them for all I care!"

Daisy was thoroughly unmoved. She looked down at what turned out to be a box of chocolates. She smiled as she read the label.

"Oh, yummy! Exotic selections from around the world." She opened the lid and fished out a glossy chocolate. "And you haven't had a single one yet; another silly waste."

Maiden arched a brow at the sheer bad grace on display. She could understand the very real anger that Daisy would have been coping with for months, but it was horribly uncomfortable to witness the actual showdown. Daisy took a bite and closed her eyes. She let out a long, pleased moan as she savored the candy. Then she opened her eyes again and smiled meanly.

"Thanks, honey." She gestured behind her as she popped the rest of the chocolate into her mouth. "Off you go now. Buh-bye."

Janet set her teeth and stalked away without another word. Maiden watched her go with her head held high, but glanced back at Oliver when he spoke up.

"Always keeping it classy," he said dryly as he picked up both suitcases and followed Janet. "See ya, Daisy."

Daisy chuckled and reached into the box for another piece of candy. Maiden said nothing as the woman noisily devoured that one too. She hurried after the others, eager to get away from there as soon as possible.

Once they'd dropped a disgraced and sullen Janet outside Gabby's office, Maiden and Oliver got back to the markets just in time to help Alfie.

In stark contrast to Janet, the man was absolutely triumphant as he carried a crate full of birdhouses proudly in front of him. Maiden followed more sedately with a box of pens and bottle stoppers, while Oliver brought up the rear with the heavier items.

As far as helping people move went, this was certainly the nicest experience she'd had for the whole of Summerfest. Maiden ducked into the tent and set her box on the nearest table. She glanced around, pleased that none of the shelves or other displays seemed to have been touched during her father's enforced absence.

The day was half over, so they hadn't bothered bringing everything out just to pack it all away again. But Alfie had been eager to return to his stall and make a show of being exonerated.

They arranged his smattering of items on a few shelves and helped him get settled. Alfie pulled up his chair and eased into it with a satisfied smile.

"Thanks for the help, you two," he said happily. "To be honest, I don't care if I don't sell a thing this afternoon, I'm just glad to be back."

"That's an excellent attitude to have, Mr. Harlow." Oliver smiled at him. "If little things can make you happy, you'll be happy a lot more often."

"Exactly!" Alfie pointed at him in a gesture of agreement. "You've got a good head on your shoulders, young man."

Maiden smiled at first, but her enthusiasm soon waned as the discussion turned to the more minute details of wood and metalwork. It wasn't that she couldn't follow the gist of the conversation; she did know a little about it, she simply wasn't interested.

Over the years she'd heard her father talk at length about dovetails, mortises, and box joints. She had even given it a try herself when she was younger. Alfie had insisted that woodworking was in the blood and there was no chance that he could have two children without at least one of them being able to handle a chisel with the best of them.

Despite Maiden's best efforts, she wasn't genuinely devoted to developing the skill, and it showed in her work. Finally, even Alfie was forced to suggest that she go and do something more to her taste.

Maiden sniggered at the memory and slid her father a fondly amused look. He and Oliver were engrossed in a discussion about timber and end-grain; she was done. She was edging towards the door and about to excuse herself and take a walk when Oliver's phone rang.

He glanced at the display and frowned as he answered.

"Hey, Gabs," he said nicely but cautiously. "Are you all right?"

Maiden watched as his eyes widened and he pushed to his feet. She felt a worried frown settle over her features; something bad had happened.

"Okay...Yeah, I'm on my way," he said numbly. "You called the police? Good. See you soon."

"The police?" Maiden frowned questioningly at him.

"Yeah." He wet his lips and took a shaky breath. "Daisy never went back to the food trucks to finish her shift. Gabs went to check her trailer and found her...She's dead."

Chapter Twenty-One

M aiden and Oliver raced back to Daisy's trailer, but the police still got there first. Maiden felt a stab of apprehension when she spied McAlister standing outside the mockingly cheerful trailer, writing something in his notebook.

The playfulness of their last encounter meant nothing; he'd be all business now, and she was determined to be ready for it. The most likely obstacle she'd face would be getting sent away the moment he spotted her. There wasn't anything she could do about that, so she tried to observe as much as she could as they approached.

Her attention went first to Janet, who was sitting off to the side, hugging herself and rocking. She looked scared and lost; Maiden wondered why she was there.

Nothing around the trailer looked disturbed. There were no signs of damage to the door, no windows broken; everything seemed peaceful. But as she peeked through the open doorway, she got a glimpse of Daisy's bright purple hair on the floor. Her stomach tightened.

A flash of movement caught her eye as Doc Jenkins appeared, ever dazzling in his hazmat suit. His expression was grim and serious as he stepped through the doorway, but a pleased smile broke over his face when he glanced up and saw her.

He gave a happy wave that she returned despite sighing internally. As expected, his cheerful welcome immediately alerted McAlister that she was there. The captain glanced over at her and then at Oliver and quirked a brow before turning back to speak to Jenkins.

"I don't think Captain McAlister likes me very much," Oliver whispered with a faint smile.

"No, it won't be you. It's the case," she murmured. "But don't worry, you were with me and Dad all afternoon; you couldn't have done this."

He nodded, but said nothing. He folded his big arms over his chest and, just as she was, waited to either be questioned or told to get lost.

McAlister finished talking to Jenkins and then walked over to Janet. As the pair started to talk, Jenkins clasped his hands behind his back and edged over towards Maiden.

"Good afternoon, Miss Harlow," he said kindly, but spoke in a discreetly lowered tone so as not to disrupt the captain. "Lovely to see you, as always."

"I hope you've been well, doctor," she replied with similar care. "Summerfest has kept you pretty busy, I'm afraid."

"Yes, last year was far more docile, that's for certain." He smiled and sidled in beside her. "May I ask how you happen to be on hand again, my dear?"

"I helped Oliver move the previous tenant out an hour or so ago." She nodded towards Janet. "That's her over there."

"I see." He glanced at the lady and then at McAlister and smiled again. "Does David know that?"

About that time Janet wiped at her teary eyes and pointed to her and then Oliver. McAlister glanced over with an unreadable expression and then turned back to her as she kept talking.

"Yeah, he does," Maiden said wryly. "You can tell how thrilled he is about it too."

"Mm." Jenkins chuckled and eased closer. "Did you know the victim?"

"Not extensively, but we spoke a few times," she admitted. "She wasn't the nicest person I'd ever met, but she had reasons for that."

"Does David know who she is?" He slid her a curious look.

"The captain doesn't confide very much to me, Doctor," she informed him mildly. "He could know anything about anyone."

"I suppose that's true." He smiled.

"Yeah." Maiden didn't feel comfortable discussing McAlister at the moment, so she shifted the subject. "Any chance at all that Daisy wasn't murdered?"

"No, Miss Harlow," he murmured and shook his head. "None at all."

She wanted to ask him what had happened, but she hesitated to put him in that position; he was so nice. She slid her gaze to McAlister's broad back and tried to read his mind instead. Despite quickly giving up, she was soon rewarded when Janet's mouth dropped open and she started to gasp and shake.

"Oh yeah, you're great with women, Captain Smooth," she grumbled under her breath and shut her eyes briefly when she heard Jenkins chuckle.

Janet rescued her from the wave of embarrassment that had been looming. The woman stood on unsteady feet and almost fell a few times as she shrieked. McAlister watched her impassively and, perhaps having learned his lesson the last time, stepped back before she could pounce on him.

"The chocolates!" she screamed. "No! It's impossible! Keith gave me those! He wouldn't—"

She broke off the sentence in favor of hysterical weeping. A few daring officers edged closer and tried to calm her down.

"What else has he rigged? How many times have I almost died without even knowing it?!" Janet sobbed and dropped to her knees. "I loved him so much! How could he do this to me?!"

Maiden's thoughts raced even as the dramatic woman started hyperventilating. She ignored it and looked back at the tiny glimpse she had of Daisy's body.

The chocolates were poisoned? If what Janet said was true, then it was possible that Keith had been more than just jealous of Oliver. Was that why he hadn't bothered giving him that letter of dismissal the day he'd written it? Had he been pushed to even stronger measures?

"That is very interesting," she whispered to herself.

"Oh, excellent." McAlister's dry words dragged her back into the present. "I'd hate for you to be bored."

Maiden swallowed a startled gasp and stared up at him; she'd been too lost in thought to see him approach. She also noticed that at some point both Jenkins and Oliver had walked away, and McAlister was standing kind of close again.

His face was hard to read, but he didn't look too pleased that she was there, despite stationing himself near enough that she caught a whiff of his cologne. She took a deep breath and did her best to steady her nerves.

"You sure do get to hang around the carnival a lot. Must be nice," she said, immediately questioning the wisdom of being facetious.

"If only I had more useful things to do with my time," he replied.

"Maybe someday." She gave him an encouraging smile.

"I don't need attitude right now, Miss Harlow," he informed her grimly.

"Does that mean we can have a real, civilized conversation?" She draped her hands on her hips. "Or are you going to keep getting mad every time you look at me?"

"I'd like to not see you at every single crime scene I investigate in this town." He exhaled slowly through his nose. "I don't feel that's unreasonable."

"I happen to agree with you," she laughed ruefully. "This isn't how I wanted to spend my day."

"Ah yes." His expression softened slightly, and he folded his arms across his chest. "You've got your new friend in tow, haven't you? Did this inconvenient little murder spoil your plans?"

"Not at all." She shrugged and refused to rise to the bait. "It actually saved me from listening to Dad and Oliver debate the usefulness of hand routers."

"What's a hand router?" he almost sighed.

Maiden looked at him for a heartbeat. "You don't know much about woodworking, do you?"

"I know how to field strip an assault rifle," he replied with an unconcerned shrug.

"Wow, sexy." She slid him a wry smirk.

"I can't really help it," he said modestly, but continued on before she could retort. "So, how do you happen to be here this time?"

"Gabby called Oliver and asked him to come and help in case Daisy and Janet got into a fight," she replied, noting the incredulous look he gave her. "Apparently Daisy complained to the corporate office that Janet was letting the place go downhill."

"And Miss Lee found out about it?" He pulled out his notebook and started writing.

"She did when Gabby had to tell her she was canned." Maiden met his sharp gaze with a nod. "It didn't go over great, but it didn't turn violent...not that I saw."

"Right." He noted that too. "Miss Lee said you and Armstrong were present when she last spoke with the deceased. What brought that about?"

"She asked Oliver to help her move." Maiden lowered her voice and glanced at Janet; the lady was busy sobbing into a handkerchief. "I tagged along to make sure that was all she asked him for."

"You're everybody's little hero, aren't you?" he muttered down to his notes. "So, you're corroborating what she's claimed?"

"No," Maiden said frankly. "I'm saying that Oliver and I came here to help carry her stuff. Whether that was the last time she saw Daisy or not has yet to be determined."

McAlister tried to hide his pleased smirk as he kept scribbling, but she still caught it. He cleared his throat and faced her more impassively.

"How did the move go?" he asked.

"Nasty." Maiden's eyes widened briefly, and she shook her head. "Daisy was mean but, considering the history..."

"Yeah. I'm under the impression that Miss Lee moved in and took over everything she wanted? Regardless of who already had it?" He'd clearly gotten the story elsewhere, but did glance at her for confirmation.

"That's what I've heard." She nodded.

"The chocolates that allegedly killed Miss Brooks," he quirked a brow, "you saw Miss Lee hand them to her?"

"Yeah." Maiden rubbed her arms. "And Daisy ate at least two of them while we were here."

"Just as well she didn't offer to share." McAlister looked her over.

"She didn't come across as the sharing type." She suppressed a shudder at the thought. "And under the circumstances, I wouldn't have accepted even if she'd offered."

He watched her for a moment. Maiden tried not to shy away from his direct gaze, but it wasn't easy. She wasn't sure if he was actually worried about what could have been a close call for her or if he was just considering what she had told him.

"What do you think?" he asked at last.

That you smell really good and I wish we were back in the funhouse. She managed not to smile at herself and quickly searched for something plausible to offer him instead.

"I'm wondering if Gabby is around somewhere." She wet her lips and noticed his gaze drift to them. "She's the one that called Oliver and told him about Daisy."

"She's over there." He nodded to where Gabby was indeed standing and whispering to Oliver. "Why'd she call him?"

"She seems to turn to him. I get the impression they've been friends for a while." She shrugged. "I was still with him because he helped Dad carry some stuff, and I'd been here earlier so...yeah."

"Interesting that a fully qualified mechanical engineer is spending all his time carrying boxes around," McAlister pointed out dryly.

"There are more tawdry ways for a person to earn their keep." She smiled up at him. "And I dare you not to look at Janet while you think that over."

"Get out of my head, woman." He grinned at her. "I'm starting to wonder if I should save myself some hassle and hire you officially."

"Hilarious. Is that an 'earning my keep' joke?" she replied a little too cheekily. "I'm pretty capable, but I doubt there's much I could *officially* do for you on a regular basis."

McAlister stared at her as one of his thick, dark eyebrows slowly climbed. Maiden felt herself turn red, even more than usual.

"Oh crap." She held his gaze because she couldn't look away. "I said that out loud."

McAlister failed to stifle his startled laughter this time, which made everything extra awkward. She wasn't sure if she came across as a stubborn idiot or just a stupidly hapless one; either way, she was cementing the impression at every opportunity.

What is wrong with you, Maiden? she asked herself irately. *You've been attracted to men before without acting so stupid around them. Get a grip already!*

She refused to look around; she was sure that everyone was looking at them and wondering why an experienced cop was laughing when he was supposed to be questioning murder suspects.

You do have a nice laugh, even when it's aimed at me. She made herself focus on incidental observations in an attempt to act casual and not kick him. *Maybe it's the pressure of having a third murder on your hands, but you should really pull yourself together quickly. And...yeah, everyone's looking. Great. What a perfect day. I wonder if there are any of those chocolates left.*

McAlister took a slow breath and clamped his mouth shut for a moment. The resulting quiet was stark; even Janet had stopped bawling, Maiden resisted the urge to slink away and find a hole to climb in.

He glanced at her mortified expression and nearly lost it again; she died a little, deep inside. She saw him pinch his inner arm really hard; he winced and finally sobered. He then faced her as though nothing had happened.

"We'll forget that idea, then," he said with only the calmest smile. "And if you could please try not to flirt with me so aggressively, it would help things go more smoothly."

"Yeah, I imagine that might be easier on you," she said sardonically and was gratified to see him resort to another pinch. "Can I go now?"

He only managed a nod and quickly turned away.

Maiden didn't make eye contact with anyone as she walked from the crime scene. In her peripheral vision, she saw Oliver's massive form break away from Gabby and follow her.

She hoped he'd be polite enough to carry on as if he hadn't seen what everyone else had. In any case, she was determined to pretend that she hadn't just made a fool of herself. Oliver caught up to her easily but shoved his hands in his pockets and kept quiet. That suited her fine.

When they turned a corner and were out of sight, she relaxed a bit and glanced over at him. He looked somber, and she recalled that he'd known Daisy for a couple of years; this was probably hard for him.

"Are you doing okay?" she asked kindly.

"Hm? Oh, yeah I'm all right," he mumbled. "Just thinking."

"About what?" She slid him a curious look.

"How bizarre and sudden all of this is." He shuffled his big feet as he walked. "It's weird that Daisy stirred up all this commotion and now she's gone. Just like that."

"Yes, it's certainly a strange coincidence," Maiden agreed and stepped a little closer as she lowered her voice. "You sort of knew Keith Haynes; do you think he would have tried to poison Janet?"

"I wouldn't put almost anything past him," he admitted, but then pulled a face. "But honestly, he was more likely to slap her around and throw her out with nothing."

"What a sweetie." Maiden rolled her eyes.

"He was a slimeball," Oliver said with a sigh. "But he had more money than anyone else here; that led too many people to put up with more than they should've."

"Was he that harsh with Daisy?"

"I don't know." He shook his head. "She always wore a lot of makeup, so it didn't look like she was covering any bruises. And I never saw anything to make me wonder. I'd have flattened the creep if I had."

She smiled faintly but tried to get the conversation headed back to where she needed it.

"Do think that someone else here would have tried to poison Janet in Keith's name?" she asked, glancing sharply at an open window as they passed by; it was empty.

"I think that's more likely than Keith having done it," Oliver allowed, but he didn't sound convinced.

"What about Daisy?" she tried again. "Who all hated her?"

"Janet, obviously," he said as he considered the possibilities. "There were a few others that didn't like how she ran things back when she and Keith were together. That was mostly envy for the perks she had, though. There's always someone that wants what other people have."

"Gabby didn't seem too impressed that she'd gone over her head to the corporate office," she pointed out.

"No, she was pretty mad about it." Oliver nodded. "But Gabs really isn't vindictive."

"Mm," Maiden grunted noncommittally. "And Timmy's still on the loose, isn't he? I'm missing something here."

"What do you mean?" He glanced at her.

"How has Timmy stayed hidden for this long?" She stopped and turned to face him. "We're agreed that he's no super-genius. So how has he managed it?"

"You think he had help?" Oliver ran his fingers through his beard as he considered that.

"I do, I think someone's been hiding him," she murmured. "Any ideas?...Was he friends with Daisy, for instance?"

"Yes actually, they got along pretty well. They both hated Janet, and that was a strong point of common ground in this place." Oliver looked uneasy as he thought it over. "You don't think she hid him, do you?"

"Yeah, I think that's exactly what happened." She nodded. "And I wouldn't be surprised if Daisy nudged him in Janet's direction that day he tried to kill her."

"You could be right. But who killed Daisy then?" He shook his head. "Or that Chalmers guy?"

"Perfectly valid questions." She smiled faintly and started walking again.

Chapter Twenty-Two

That night Maiden again lay in bed thinking about the events of the day. It seemed strange that so much had happened so quickly. Oliver had been right; it was stark and sudden.

In the span of one short day, Daisy had finally asserted herself over her rival and reclaimed everything that had been hers, only to end up dead. Seemingly caught in a trap left for the other woman.

However, Janet had still been ousted. Even with Daisy gone, she wouldn't get her job back; not with the corporate office of Spencer and Spencer knowing about her bad habits and careless approach to the role. Dead or alive, Daisy's revenge had been enough to ruin Janet's cozy little setup and whatever ambitions she'd had for taking over from Keith.

So where did that leave them? The three murders had to be connected. Maiden shut her eyes and tried to relax in hopes that the answer would come. Refusing to let her unchecked thoughts wander to sexy cops with self-inflicted bruises on their forearms, she considered the common threads.

Timmy was certainly one. He was convinced that he needed Keith to protect the carnival; he'd been horrified when he saw him dead. And he was very likely the person who slipped the threatening note to Chalmers. Maybe Keith had told him about the bribes. Finally, he was friends with Daisy. She might have even coached him to attack Janet; she hadn't made her big move against the other woman until after Timmy's murder attempt failed.

Maiden returned to the day of Keith's murder. What else had happened? Something was niggling at the edge of her thoughts. Some little detail that she'd set aside and hadn't revisited yet.

She let her mind shift back and play through the day again. She recalled the arguments she and Vonny had witnessed: Keith and Chalmers, Keith and Oliver, Keith and Timmy. Janet falling in love with that birdhouse while Keith ignored her. Then the mirror maze.

She could almost hear the music and see the lights changing color above them as she relived their winding walk through the strange corridors. And then there was Keith's body; she saw it clearly in her mind. The grimace on his face and the blood that had pooled on the floor.

Maiden shivered and pushed on to when the police arrived. She didn't dwell on her banter with McAlister or the scent of his cologne, even though she would've sworn she could smell it again.

Janet and Gabby had come running; Janet had been hysterical, just as she had been today. She'd cried and screamed but also tried to climb Captain McAlister like a ladder. Maiden frowned up at the dormant ceiling light. It had felt like too much; it had felt fake.

Janet hadn't loved Keith; Maiden had seen and heard too many unguarded moments to take the woman's claims seriously. Her theatrical display of grief had been overdone...and she'd put on the same performance today. Was it because that's what she thought she was supposed to do? Or was she afraid of being blamed?

Maiden pushed on further, and something else occurred to her. Her eyes widened and she sat up in the midst of the soft blankets with a gasp.

Gabby's torn pant leg. She had forgotten about it in all the drama surrounding Alfie. It had stood out to her at the time, but what did it mean and what did it prove?

Gabby was another thread, perhaps a stronger one than Timmy. She had dealt with Keith for a long time; she'd also handled Sam Chalmers quite handily. Even Oliver had said that she didn't fight—she came in when she needed to and won.

Her dislike of Janet was obvious, and so was her fondness for Oliver. She had been frustrated and unhappy with how Keith had handled the carnival's profits and hadn't hesitated to slap away the greedy hands that he had yielded to only days before.

But she wouldn't deal with Janet for some reason. Daisy had come to her with a legitimate, if disrespectfully phrased, concern, and Gabby dismissed it. Firing Janet had been an obvious and easy solution; it was irresponsible *not* to, but she refused to consider it. She had even scrambled to salvage some kind of job for her when others stepped in.

Gabby was the key to this mess; she had to be. She'd had a fractious or outright hostile relationship with each victim, and yet she managed to stay tucked away in the background most of the time. She was more than she seemed, and she almost certainly knew more than she claimed.

Maiden stared out through the open French doors and into the starry sky. The soft, cool breeze soothed her and helped her to think clearly. A few suspicions were starting to crystalize in her mind. She was determined to get some answers tomorrow.

The following morning Maiden walked through the carnival once again. She had a clear goal in mind and headed resolutely deeper. As she passed the concession trucks, she noticed that there were a few people working today. She supposed Gabby wouldn't dare to let that corner of the business suffer now, even without Daisy there to point fingers.

Her gaze slid to the ticket booth for the funhouse, and she almost tripped. Not only was Janet not in her new post, but it was crawling with cops. Maiden felt herself start to smile and wondered if McAlister had reached the same conclusions about Timmy and Daisy that she had.

Content to leave the police to their work, she pressed on until the little white trailer marked 'office' loomed into view. A few moments later, Maiden was standing in the doorway. She smiled nicely at Gabby, even as she knocked on the open door.

"Oh, hello again," Gabby murmured when she glanced over at her. "What's up?"

"I wanted to have another quick chat with you," Maiden said as she took a step inside. "Is that okay?"

"Yeah," she shrugged and gestured to the chair before the desk, "I guess so."

Maiden ignored the unenthusiastic reception and settled carefully into the fragile seat. She had thought long and hard about the wisest way to handle this discussion. As time was a factor and people kept dying, she'd ultimately decided that a semi-direct approach might be best.

"You obviously realize the seriousness of the situation," she said solemnly.

"Yes, three murders onsite isn't great news for any business," Gabby sighed, but then met her gaze sharply. "And any loss of life is tragic, of course."

"Of course." Maiden almost smiled. None of the victims had been dear to Gabby's heart, and they both knew it.

"Is that why you're here?" Gabby shook her head.

"Sort of, I wanted to discuss something related...I noticed that you tore the leg of your capris the night Keith died, they were fine earlier in the day when we first met," she said mildly and even smiled again. "I was wondering how that happened?"

"What are you talking about?" Gabby gave her a look and arched a thick brow.

"The night Keith Haynes was killed, you and Janet came running to the mirror maze," she explained patiently. "There was a large tear in the leg of your pants, it wasn't there earlier. How'd you tear it?"

"What is this about, lady?" Gabby's expression and tone were suddenly less cordial, and her accent grew a bit thicker. "I'm busy, I don't need random weirdos busting in and asking about my *pants*."

"It's relevant though, isn't it?" Maiden held her gaze, cool and unperturbed. "Because you tore them in the mirror maze. There were a lot of sharp edges on that panel that crushed Keith."

"How dare you!" She stood and planted her fists on her full hips. "Get out!"

"I know you didn't kill him, Gabby. I'm not suggesting that." Maiden raised a calming hand but otherwise didn't budge or shift her gaze from Gabby's. "But you do know what happened."

"I'm outside of this whole mess, okay?" Gabby shook her head and waved her hands as though that would ward off her problems. "I just do my job and keep this place running, that's all."

"I don't buy that." Maiden folded her arms. "You have more information about this mess than anyone, and that's because you've been watching it all from behind the scenes. The question is, who's side are you on?"

"You're crazy, lady," Gabby grumbled down at her desk as she resumed her seat.

"How did you find out that Janet was planning to murder Keith?" It was a bold foray, but she was confident that she was right. Gabby's dark eyes widened.

"What?" she whispered.

"We both know it was Janet, but you've known for longer," she said firmly. "Why didn't you tell the police?"

"I haven't said anything to anyone!" Gabby huffed.

"Why not?" Maiden asked. "You keep doing everything you can to help Janet, but I don't understand why, I'm pretty sure you hate her guts."

Gabby looked angry at first, but the feigned indignation didn't last long. Maiden kept her expression mild as she waited, confident that she was on the right track.

"Look I...I have no proof," Gabby finally admitted. Her voice grew quieter, and she rested her hands on the top of the desk. "I tried putting that stupid birdhouse by Keith's body to make them wonder if Janet had been there, but it didn't work."

"Ah, of course." Maiden smiled and nodded; that was one question answered, at least. "Where did you find the birdhouse anyway?"

"In Janet's trailer. She was gushing about it and her grandmother, who she'd already told us was a violent alcoholic, but whatever. Apparently, that magical birdhouse was a portal to blissful memories," Gabby scoffed disdainfully. "I didn't find out until later that she sent one of the guys to get it for her, so she wasn't connected to it directly."

"Well, that's a shame, I guess," Maiden continued, determined to keep her talking while she was in the mood. "What made you suspect her?"

"She *told* me!" Gabby said with an exasperated sigh. "Not in those exact words, but about a month ago she started coming around when Keith was out and trying to be friends."

"But it was fake?" she asked.

"Totally fake! We barely knew each other and yet she came in acting like we're sisters or something. Talking about how hard it is for 'people like us'!" Gabby shook her head. "She's half Chinese and half Irish, and she's never set a toe outside this country. Suddenly that's the same as being Mexican? Does she think I'm stupid?"

"So, she was trying to manipulate you into forging some kind of bond?" Maiden asked as she thought that over.

"Yeah, never mind that she sits around painting her nails and smoking like a chimney while *I* work my fingers to the bone," Gabby said bitterly. "We're not white so we're exactly the same?"

"Ironically that's pretty racist," she murmured. "For what it's worth, I doubt she believes it."

"That's not really worth much," Gabby said dryly. "But her usual tricks wouldn't get her anywhere with me. She couldn't seduce me and I didn't feel sorry for her; a lot of us came from a rough background, that doesn't mean we get our way no matter what. It means we have to work harder. It's not fair, but it's real life."

"So, her next most viable option was to try and find common ground." Maiden nodded; it wasn't a question. "She's actually pretty clever."

"Yeah, for a selfish, murderous psycho." Gabby shuddered.

"So why do *you* think Janet killed Keith?" Maiden watched her closely. "If we know the motive, we have a better chance of finding evidence."

"She wanted Keith's job. The night he died she'd already started talking about 'keeping his dream alive'. She wanted everything he had. All the perks without having to put up with Keith." Gabby shook her head sadly. "He was pretty awful to her, but she knew what she was getting into when she started chasing him. And she got back at him by going after other men...it was pretty messed up."

"Sounds like it." Maiden exhaled slowly. "But when did she go from cheating on Keith to planning his murder?"

"Once she thought we were great pals she started making comments, talking about how much nicer things would be if Keith was out of the way." Gabby rubbed her arms as though she were cold. "She also wanted Oliver; but he's much too smart to get mixed up with her."

"You like Oliver, don't you?" She smiled faintly.

"Yes, I like him." Gabby shrugged. "He's a nice guy, too nice for someone like Janet. When I got his resignation, I was sad to lose him but happy for him that he was ready to put his life back together. He's been running away for a long time."

"You're the one that drugged him, aren't you?" Maiden asked calmly.

Gabby stared at her like a guilty child before letting out a soft sigh.

"How'd you know?" she asked quietly.

"Because I don't believe it was an attack," she said. "You were trying to protect him."

"I didn't know exactly what Janet was planning, but I suspected it would be something to do with Keith's sabotage. It was her best chance of killing him while making it look like an accident," Gabby whispered, glancing around to ensure they weren't overheard. "She'd been acting weird that day and kept asking where Keith was. I had a feeling something was about to happen. It had to be while we were in Golden Glen because Keith was going to fire Oliver before we went on to the next town. I wanted to make sure that no one would suspect him."

"What about the note in his knapsack?" Maiden asked. "The one asking him to come to the concession trucks at 6 o'clock."

"Oh, that was a note Janet had sent to Keith months ago, when she was first chasing him," Gabby said quietly. "He'd kept it; he was oddly sentimental about some things. It didn't mention him by name so I took it and put it in Oliver's bag. He wouldn't know the difference, but he might've recognized her handwriting."

"How did you find out Keith was planning to fire Oliver?" she asked.

"Janet told me," Gabby admitted. "She read Keith's mail and went through his desk regularly. I mentioned to Keith a few times that his stuff wasn't secure and he might want to lock up his sensitive papers, but he rarely listened to anything I suggested."

"But you didn't tell him about Janet's snooping?" She shook her head slightly.

"He wouldn't have believed it and it would've turned Janet against me." Gabby swallowed hard. "She's nasty and she holds a grudge. Anyway, she wanted to get rid of Keith and somehow convinced herself that he was the only thing keeping Oliver away from her."

"So, we're assuming that Keith was tampering with one of the panels to make Oliver look bad, so he could justify firing him. But Janet snuck in and, once he'd loosened everything up, pushed the panel onto him?" Maiden drummed her fingers on her arms. "Did you actually see her do anything?"

Gabby was silent for a long moment as she tried to gather her nerve. She clasped her hands together and shut her eyes briefly before answering.

"Yeah, I followed her and saw her run and push that panel as hard as she could. I was terrified so I hid. She watched Keith for a moment and then took off through the back door. I checked him, but he wasn't breathing and the blood was already spreading on the floor. It was too late." Gabby drove a hand anxiously through her thick hair. "After that I panicked, all I could think of was a way to put Janet on the scene. She'd looked really pleased about that birdhouse so I hoped that would be an easy connection. But when I was putting it next to Keith's body, I caught my pant leg on one of the broken bolts. I didn't see any fabric left behind and I didn't want to get caught there, so I ran."

"Wow, okay. Well, for a start, we can disregard the birdhouse from an evidence point of view," Maiden said carefully as she processed what all she'd just learned. "So why have you been trying to help Janet so much? She was almost out the door, but you interceded, why?"

"I'm afraid of her," Gabby admitted in a low whisper. "She's violent and willing to kill; I had to keep her thinking I was on her side."

"Does she know you saw her murder Keith?" she asked tactfully.

"No!" Gabby gasped and shook her head vehemently.

"Okay, good. So how does Timmy fit in?" she asked. "He tried to kill Janet and then disappeared. Was Daisy helping him?"

"Possibly," Gabby said as she considered it. "I'm not sure, but I can't think of who else could and would have sabotaged the funhouse like that. I wondered if Janet blackmailed Timmy into doing it, but I still don't know why. Unless Chalmers wasn't the intended victim."

"I believe he was. And Timmy might have been more willing than you think." Maiden tapped her chin thoughtfully. "When I spoke to him the other day he was babbling about corrupt politicians and weak links. I suspect he was talking about Sam Chalmers."

"Maybe." She nodded. "Chalmers *was* crooked."

"But when I saw him and Keith fighting, Chalmers looked angry," Maiden reminded her. "He didn't get anywhere with Keith the second time."

"Yes, but he tried again, remember." She smiled smugly. "He approached me with that stack of falsified infringements and I shot all of them down."

"Did Timmy or Janet know about that?" Maiden quirked a brow.

"About the fraudulent fees?" She pulled a face. "I don't know how they would, but they certainly wouldn't know about my meeting with Chalmers."

"But he did send that threatening letter," Maiden reminded her.

"Yeah, but I kept that in...my desk." Gabby slid her gaze to the drawers in front of her.

"Do you honestly think Janet would look through Keith's papers and not yours?" she asked patiently.

"Oh no!" The blood drained from Gabby's face. "That means Janet knew that he was threatening to close us down!"

"But she didn't know that it was an empty threat," Maiden finished the thought. "Or that you'd sorted it out already.

They'd both talked about being worried that the carnival would shut down; it was their bread and butter and they were scared. I'll bet Janet got Timmy to send that death threat to Chalmers. Whether she put him up to the murder or it was his own idea…who knows?"

"I feel sick." Gabby clutched at her stomach.

"There's no time for that," Maiden said seriously. "I think we're agreed that Janet and Timmy need to be stopped."

"Of course, but how?" Gabby shook her head.

"We have to focus on Janet first; she's the big fish. Well, debatably the most unstable one anyway," Maiden said pensively. "If she follows the same methods she's used so far, she'll play innocent and try to blame the man she's been using, in this case that's Timmy. If we can get him to talk, he might implicate her. But you're going to have to tell the police that you saw her kill Keith."

"But Janet will kill me if I do," Gabby said anxiously. "And I don't even know where Timmy is."

"He didn't go far," Maiden assured her. "I'm sure he's the one I saw scuttling around the funhouse that night, right around the time Sam Chalmers was killed. He's still here, he has nowhere else to go."

"But he can't suddenly reappear without having to account for himself," Gabby said with an anxious sigh.

"He might think he can if Janet's running the show." She gave her a speaking look. "And if *you* aren't there to turn him in."

"What?" she gasped.

"Without trying to sound too dramatic," Maiden pulled a sympathetic face, "I wouldn't be surprised if you'd been Janet's next target anyway."

"I'm gonna die!" she squeaked and looked around frantically.

"No, you're not!" Maiden glared at her. "Those two aren't going to get the better of all of us. Let's go, we need to talk to the police."

"Oh, this is too much," Gabby whimpered, but pushed to her feet. "I've only ever tried to do the best job I can and mind my own business!"

Maiden pulled out her phone and typed a message to McAlister. She hoped he'd respond fast.

Maiden

> *Hey, where are you?*

She waited for a few agonizingly long minutes until a reply came through.

McAlister

> *I'm in the markets. I'm busy.*

Maiden

> *It's important.*

She chewed at her lip and waited.

McAlister

> *I'm busy.*

Maiden scowled down at the screen, and then shoved the phone back in her pocket and turned to Gabby.

"Let's go," she muttered and headed for the door.

Whether he liked it or not, McAlister was about to get much busier.

Chapter
Twenty-Three

Maiden and Gabby ran through the carnival, ignoring a few of the workers who tried to get Gabby's attention as they passed. It was Saturday, and the place was packed, thanks in part to the recent sensationalized news reports. It also helped that most of the rides were opened up again.

They made their way through the bustling crowds and finally reached the markets. Maiden looked around anxiously for McAlister, or any other police officer, but didn't see any. Just a throng of laughing, chattering tourists.

Maiden gave an exasperated sigh. She was certain that they were running out of time before another 'accident' happened, and next time the victim could be Gabby, or even Oliver. She felt her determination grow and started off again with Gabby close behind.

There were people scattered everywhere, but they soon heard raised voices and found a crowd gathered. They forced their way through and saw McAlister along with a few of his officers. They'd cornered an extremely panicked Timmy.

He looked even filthier than usual. His eyes were wide and terrified as he tried to worm his way past some bollards that marked the edge of the markets. He didn't get far.

He'd thrown one leg over the top when McAlister grabbed him by the collar and dragged him back. A few other officers swarmed in, and Timmy immediately surrendered.

Maiden smiled with relief as the scruffy man was handcuffed. She looked around, positive that Janet would be nearby; she might have even told the cops where to find him. Getting rid of her accomplice while leaving him to take all the blame for the murders would have been a dream finish for the heartless woman.

Maiden scanned the onlookers and spotted Janet's platinum hair and tiger-print wrap dress. She was watching the police arrest Timmy and wearing the coldest smile Maiden had ever seen. Panic seized her as Janet started to back away unobtrusively into the crowd.

"Captain McAlister!" Maiden called out, even as she pointed at her quarry. "It was Janet! She was in on the whole scheme, stop her!"

Janet's eyes widened and she started backing up faster. McAlister frowned at Maiden and shook his head questioningly. Gabby stepped forward and pointed at Janet as well.

"It's true! It was all her idea, she told me she wanted Keith out of the way! I saw her kill him!" she shouted bravely.

The crowd erupted into gasps and parted, leaving a conspicuous gap around the diminutive blonde. Janet had gone still and was staring at Gabby, then her lovely face twisted with raw and frightening rage.

Gabby faltered and took an uneasy step away. Janet was seething; her fingers had curled up like claws, and her eyes were chillingly intent.

"*You backstabber!*" Janet shrieked and charged at her, pulling a folding knife from her pocket and flicking it open.

Gabby screamed and tried to run backwards but tripped over a basket of potpourri sachets. She fell onto her back with a loud grunt and a spray of scented bark and pinecones. Maiden didn't take her eyes off Janet as the angry woman neared.

As Janet darted past, Maiden jumped at her. She wrapped her arms around her and managed to wrestle her to the ground. But Janet was surprisingly strong; she clawed at the asphalt and inched them both forward.

The police were closing in fast, as were a few more courageous people in the crowd. Janet was screaming and thrashing wildly as she tried to stab Gabby anywhere she could.

Maiden was lying fully on top of her now, scrambling to pin her flailing arms down without getting stabbed herself. At the same time, a few helpful strangers were dragging Gabby out of reach.

A moment later Greg, Officer Briggs, and McAlister descended on them. Maiden was pulled off as carefully as such a thing could be done and deposited on the ground while Janet was disarmed and handcuffed.

The angry woman was still hurling threats and scathing insults at Gabby as she was hauled away behind a quietly smiling Timmy. McAlister flicked Maiden a bemused look over his shoulder; she shrugged helplessly.

In the resulting silence, Maiden sat on the street and tried to catch her breath and also ignore the perplexed looks they were getting from the startled crowd. She brushed the dirt from her hands and glanced over at Gabby.

"Are you okay?" she asked in a slightly breathless voice.

"Yeah, but just barely." Gabby nodded her thanks to the people who pulled her out of the basket she'd been tangled in. "What about you?"

"Ruined a perfectly good blouse," she said wryly as she looked down at the torn fabric on her elbows. "Otherwise, I think I'm good."

They both became aware of those surrounding them talking excitedly and snapping pictures on their phones. Phrases like: *That was incredible!* and *She's done it again!* rippled all around them.

A man approached and helped pull Maiden to her feet. She thanked him as she dusted herself off and waved away his admiring words. Before long the crowd was closing in and started bombarding them with questions.

"Sorry." Maiden smiled apologetically and pointed to the nearby police cars. "I think we're needed over there."

"I'll say you are!" someone said loudly, and more than a few titters resounded.

"The police did most of the work!" Maiden announced firmly as she grabbed Gabby by her wrist and dragged her away from the curious onlookers.

They hurried towards the telltale flashing lights in time to see Janet and Timmy being pushed into the backseat of separate police cars. Timmy looked exhausted and resigned, but Janet had gone furiously silent. Gabby took a shaky breath and stared at her through the window.

Janet glared hatefully back at her as she was driven out of sight. Gabby hugged herself and whispered something in Spanish. Maiden reached over and gave her shoulder a comforting pat. Gabby glanced at her and forced a weak smile.

"Are you all right, Miss Lopez?" McAlister asked as he approached them.

"Yeah, I think so." She nodded. "But I feel numb and awful. I've been waiting for Janet to blow for months, it seems unreal that she's finally been caught."

"If you knew she was responsible for Keith Haynes' death, why didn't you report it immediately?" he demanded mildly enough.

"I was afraid to," Gabby admitted. "And yes, I know that's cowardly, but without any concrete evidence, I was afraid it would be her word against mine. I didn't dare let her think I would turn against her. You saw how she reacted."

"Well, we'll have plenty of time to discuss the details now," he murmured and gestured toward Greg. "Officer Smith will drive you to the station and we can talk it out."

"Sure, Captain." She nodded and glanced at Maiden with a more genuine smile. "Thanks for everything, Maiden. You saved my life, probably a couple of times over, I won't forget that."

"Happy to help." She smiled and waved as Gabby trundled off after Greg.

She watched them climb into Greg's car and drive off. She was reliving the excitement of the confrontation with Janet when she glanced at McAlister to find him watching her.

"Good work finding Timmy," she said genuinely.

"Thanks. How'd you know to talk to the office manager again?" he asked. He leaned against his car and folded his arms across his chest.

"Everything always veered back to Gabby. At some point, she was involved with it all." She shrugged. "I remembered Janet acting like the carnival was in danger of falling apart, but that didn't make sense, Keith Haynes managed the show, he didn't own or fund it. Sam Chalmers sent that threatening letter, but Gabby blew him out of the water. Janet used to read Keith's mail, so it stood to reason that she read Gabby's too. The only ones that thought the show was at risk were Timmy and Janet. So, I kept asking and Gabby kept talking. It all eventually fell into place."

"I feel like a broken record," he sighed, "but you could have come to me."

"I did. Even though you were 'busy'." She smiled faintly. "We came straight to you, but then we spotted Janet in the crowd and well...yeah."

"So, your first instinct was the crash tackle?" He started to smile but quickly sobered.

"You weren't complaining when I jumped on *you*," she reminded him before thinking it through. She immediately looked away. "That came out really wrong."

When he didn't reply, she glanced at him to find him pressing a hand to his mouth and shaking with silent laughter. She smiled again, ignoring her flushed cheeks.

"How's your arm?" she asked.

"Bruised," he admitted with a chuckle. "Desperate times and all that. Considering your relentless attempts at seduction, I had to do something to protect myself."

"Awesome, thanks for that." She rolled her eyes but took the teasing gracefully. "I think I'll go now. Don't watch me walk away, I'll trip and kill myself. Actually, that'd be fine."

"Well, at the risk of inviting more trouble, come to the station this afternoon to give a statement." He smirked and opened the car door. "Thanks for your help, Miss Harlow. Don't watch me drive away, I'll hit something."

"Shut up, jerk," she laughed, shaking her head as she walked off.

Chapter
Twenty-Four

David was standing in the lobby of the police station. He'd just escorted Gabby Lopez from his office and was re-reading her statement. Her story fit in with the rest of the facts he had assembled and filled in a few gaps he'd been chasing.

He had already surmised that Timmy Gibson had threatened and subsequently murdered Sam Chalmers. It hadn't taken long for Gibson to admit that Janet had tracked him down after he'd attacked her and kicked him half to death for it. She'd also told him about the letter Chalmers sent and that he'd better do something about it or she would tell the cops where to find him.

He'd turned to Daisy Brooks for help, leaving Janet's name out of it, and she had happily obliged. Not only by helping him stay hidden but also by writing a note asking Chalmers to meet Gabby in the funhouse to collect his payoff. Gibson tampered with the floor, and Chalmers stepped right through it.

David had suspected a possible connection to Keith Haynes' death but was waiting until he'd questioned Gibson to reach any firm conclusions.

And then Harlow saved me the trouble. Again. He smiled to himself even as he shook his head ruefully.

As for the anonymous tipoff about the sabotage, they might never know for certain, but he was convinced that it had come from Haynes himself. It was likely intended to be another layer in his plan to discredit Oliver Armstrong.

David stirred from his musings and glanced up to find Nancy watching him. By far the best receptionist he'd ever seen in action, Nancy was quiet but observant. It had caught him out a few times, particularly when she witnessed his exchanges with Harlow, but he didn't mind. He trusted her despite having only known her for about two months; that was incredibly rare for him.

"What's on your mind?" he asked as he laid the statement on the desk in front of him.

"The third murder," Nancy admitted. "Daisy Brooks. What do you think happened to her?"

"Honestly, I think Janet Lee murdered her," David sighed and rested his elbow on the tall desk. "She was the only one that had a real motive or even a hope of benefitting from her death. Besides that, the chocolates were hers, she could've easily added the poison and then claimed they were a gift."

"True. So, are you going to charge her with the murder, sir?" she asked curiously.

"I'll try." He shrugged. "But I'm not sure there's enough evidence to make it stick. She might be scared enough to admit to it though; she's reasonably clever but very emotionally driven. It might work."

"Is it true that Miss Harlow physically subdued her?" Nancy smiled as she asked it.

"Do you think Smith would make that up?" he murmured dryly as he looked her in the eye. "Or are you just trying to make me admit it?"

"Officer Briggs told me, actually," she said with a shrug. "But if it annoys you, we can leave it, sir."

Before he could reply, the front door opened, and Harlow walked in. She'd changed out of her dirt-stained jeans and into a rather flattering green dress. He shifted his gaze a little too slowly to Nancy and found her smiling at him. He gave her a warning look, and she obligingly turned to greet the lady.

"Good afternoon, Miss Harlow. Quite recovered after the adventures of the morning?"

"I'm fine, I didn't really do that much," she said modestly and then slid David a look. "I hope I'm not late, I stopped by the library on the way."

"Don't tell me you plowed through the rest of that drivel already?" he chuckled.

"No," she admitted. "I skipped to the end."

"What a great idea! If only someone had mentioned that days ago." He smirked ungenerously. "And did the evil librarian sit you down and demand a detailed thesis?"

"She didn't get the chance, I threw it in the return slot and ran for it," she replied as she smiled at him. "So, it's available to borrow again, if you're interested."

"I'm good, thanks," he said with a quickly checked laugh. "You can tell me how it ended."

"They strangled each other to death," she replied without hesitation.

"Seriously?" He smirked at her.

"No. They defied the odds and got married." She rolled her eyes and glanced at Nancy. "It only took a thousand pages to get there."

"I'm sorry, I missed the beginning of this conversation." She shook her pale head.

"Trust me, you didn't miss anything," Maiden sighed.

David smiled down at his hands but glanced up when he saw Nancy shift. She was studying Harlow; he braced himself as a slow smile curved her lips.

"Miss Harlow," she began casually, "out of curiosity, who do *you* think killed Daisy Brooks?"

"Janet did it," she said as though it were obvious.

Nancy hid a pleased smirk; and David made a point of saying nothing.

"Interesting. Why do you say that?" she prompted.

"Her reaction to the murder was too much. And totally fake," Maiden explained. "It was the same when Keith died. Way over the top, considering."

"Considering what?" David asked carefully; he'd found Janet's reaction fairly convincing.

"That she was halfway in your shirt and ready to move on to your pants," Harlow said mildly enough.

He wasn't even drinking anything, and he still almost choked. He looked away sharply and felt his face grow warm. Stopping just long enough to clear his throat, he glanced back and did his best to ignore Nancy, who'd turned and pretended to type something on her computer as her shoulders convulsed.

"It wasn't *that* bad," he managed quietly.

"It wasn't good," she countered easily. "In any case, no one else had a reason to kill Daisy. And Janet actually gave her the candy. Who opens a box of chocolates and leaves them sitting around for a week without eating even one?"

"How do you know she'd opened it already?" David asked.

"It wasn't sealed," she murmured. "I saw her give Daisy the box."

"You actually noticed that it was unsealed?" He arched a brow.

"Yeah. And Daisy mentioned that Janet hadn't had any of them." She pulled a face. "I don't know how you'd prove it though. Might be worth charging her with it and seeing if she panics enough to give herself away. She's not coolheaded; it could work. Anyway, are you ready for me yet?"

She was looking at him calmly and expectantly. David was trying to absorb how close her conclusions were to his and didn't reply. Finally, Nancy, who'd returned to enjoy the rest of Harlow's hypothesis, leaned closer and cleared her throat loudly.

"Captain?" She smiled when he glanced at her. "Miss Harlow asked if you feel that you're ready for her. Do you, sir?"

"Yes, sorry." He pinched the bridge of his nose and nodded towards the hallway. "Go ahead and wait in my office please, Miss Harlow. I'll be in in a minute."

"See you later," she said to Nancy, and then walked down the hall.

David watched until she disappeared into his office and then turned a serious look on the smiling receptionist. He opened his mouth to speak, but Nancy smoothly interceded.

"It's a shame you two don't have more in common, sir." She held his gaze placidly. David shut his eyes and grinned. "Perhaps you'd prefer it if Officer Smith took her statement?"

"I think I can manage," he said dryly and gave her a teasingly stern look before walking away.

The following Monday, Maiden came downstairs a bit later than usual and took up her position behind the reception desk at Harlow House. She had slept well and was looking forward to life getting back to normal now that Summerfest was over.

Distantly noting that she'd missed Tony, she flicked the small pile of mail he'd left a disinterested glance and picked up the morning paper instead. As she had expected, the murder case was all over the front page.

And Maiden herself had made the headlines yet again. She pulled a face as she read the article; it wasn't quite as bad as the last time around, but there was still a lot of emphasis put on her efforts. The story featured a few first-hand accounts from bystanders who detailed her heroics not only in helping to catch the culprit behind two of the murders but also for her courage in wrestling the knife-wielding menace to the ground.

At least there was some mention of the police and how their dedicated efforts had led to the arrest of Timmy Gibson. But the majority of the kudos went to the local girl who once again 'saw through the shadows and found the truth'. She winced and sighed.

She wondered if Captain McAlister was angry with her. She sort of didn't blame him if he was, but she really did help, even he admitted that. If she hadn't confronted Gabby, she might never have told anyone about seeing Janet kill Keith.

As she read on, she found that Janet had confessed, even to Daisy's murder, and tried to paint a tragic portrait of an abused and neglected girl from the wrong side of the tracks.

Maiden thought about the coldly planned murders and her vicious public attempt to stab Gabby to death. She doubted that Janet's efforts to make herself into a victim would stand up under much scrutiny.

With another sigh and a shake of her head, Maiden turned to a far less sensational article covering the pie contest. A smile tugged at her lips as she looked at the official picture of the proud and boisterous winner.

Kylie stared back at the camera, looking as poised as a startled rabbit, even though her Chocolate Dipped Strawberry Whip pie had garnered accolades and a first-place ribbon. The shy cook hadn't taken into account the attention she would receive if she won; she was too focused on beating Gloria.

As for Gloria, she'd taken a respectable fourth place and accepted defeat quietly if not gracefully. She didn't speak to Kylie for a day or two while she cooled off. She then begrudgingly announced that they'd add the winning pie to the dessert menu. It was as peaceful a resolution as they were likely to get, and the horrible pie onslaught finally ended.

The Gazette had also run a small article featuring Alfie and his fight for justice against a corrupt local official. Once the lid was blown off the bribing scandal, other business owners started coming forward with stories of blackmail, physical threats and extortion at the hands of Sam Chalmers. He had apparently been running his dirty little side hustle for a few years.

The paper cited a public apology from the Golden Glen City Council to all the affected businesses. The spokesman promised a prompt and thorough investigation into all claims against the late Mr. Chalmers.

Alfie had enjoyed his moment of fame as a champion in the fight against local corruption. His newly reopened stall was now even more famous locally; as a result, he sold most of his remaining stock and all of his birdhouses.

The second week of Summerfest had been tame in comparison to the first. In the shadow of the far more dramatic events, the markets finished, and the carnival packed up and moved on.

It was hard to say whether this year's Summerfest could be judged a success. It had certainly been memorable, and would no doubt be an even bigger draw the next time around. The theory that 'no publicity is bad publicity' just might prove true in this instance.

Maiden shook her head and turned the page to another article outlining the perils and pitfalls of the beleaguered Spencer and Spencer carnival. Somehow the business had come out of the ordeal in a positive light. Now that there were cold-blooded killers and shameless saboteurs to blame for the equipment breakdowns, the carnival itself was treated as a victim.

She smiled wryly and hoped that it would all work out for Gabby. She had visited her one last time before the carnival left for the next town, Gabby confided that she had actually been appointed the new manager soon after news of Keith's death had reached head office. She'd kept it a secret because she was afraid of what Janet would do if she found out.

Grateful that the kind and hardworking woman didn't have to walk on eggshells anymore, Maiden's thoughts drifted to Oliver. He'd only left yesterday, after protesting Gloria and Alfie's refusal to let him pay for his stay there. Maiden agreed that the man had earned his keep and told him so.

He had remained with them at Harlow House until the end of the fair and had divided his time between helping Gabby by getting the Ferris wheel and the funhouse operational again, and showing his gratitude to the Harlows by fixing everything he could at the inn.

Maiden doubted there was a squeaky hinge or loose doorknob left in the building. He'd even changed the oil in Vonny's car, much to her delight.

Before he'd left, he had given Maiden a big hug and thanked her for believing in him. Then he was off to see his parents for the first time in years. She smiled at the thought; she was confident that he would be happy now.

She set the paper aside with a satisfied nod and turned to the stack of mail she'd been ignoring. A dark brow climbed when she picked up a fat envelope with her name on it.

She looked over the front of the parcel. There was no stamp and no address, just her name. Someone must have hand-delivered it when no one was at the desk. She opened the end and pulled out a thick book.

"Oh no!" She cringed and grinned at the same time as she read the title aloud. "*Hero of the Heather Volume 2: Heart of Thistles*...I take it you're a little mad at me, Captain McAlister."

She was still smiling as she flipped the envelope over and looked for a return address.

All it said was *Scottish Jerk*.

THANK YOU!

I hope you enjoyed A Fair Chance of Murder! This continues to be one of the most nostalgic books I've ever written. The fictional Spencer & Spencer carnival is a mélange of places that my sister and I went to in our single days.

The mirror maze and chocolate-dipped waffle cones were always favorites of ours, so I had to give both a mention in this book.

As always, I put a lot of time and love into this book and I really love the way it transports me back to those moments of fun, laughter and way too much ice cream.

If you feel inclined, it would mean so much to me if you'd leave a review. Reviews make a huge difference, especially for indie authors.

I appreciate your time and I hope you truly had fun coming along on Maiden's latest adventure!

Warm regards,

Camille

Also by Camille Sharp

<u>The Maiden Harlow Mysteries</u>
Murder Checks Inn
A Fair Chance of Murder
Pretty Little Princesses
Maiden of Honor
Treasure Hunt
Deathly Cold
Faraway Kingdoms
Voices From the Past
Old Scars

JOIN THE FUN!

If you'd like to receive updates, bonus content and a FREE copy of the mystery novella **Blood and Money,** a fun and twisty mini-mystery, please visit my website www.camillesharpbooks.com and sign up!

<u>Blood and Money</u>

A Maiden Harlow Mystery Prequel

When a beloved guest arrives at Harlow House carrying a dangerous secret, Maiden Harlow's peaceful life is thrown into chaos.

Maiden has always taken pride in running her family's charming, small-town inn, where every visitor is treated like family.

But when a favorite guest arrives acting anxious and evasive, Maiden's instincts tell her something is terribly wrong. The guest refuses to involve the police and won't reveal who's threatening her. As unsettling clues surface and danger creeps closer, Maiden must uncover the truth herself. If she can't convince her guest to accept help, the consequences may turn deadly.

Step into Maiden's very first brush with mystery and danger in this gripping prequel to the *Maiden Harlow Mysteries* series. Perfect for fans of dark cozy mysteries, amateur sleuths, and strong female leads who won't back down when lives are on the line.

A Little About Me...

I write warm and funny dark cozy mysteries filled with sharp-witted heroines, atmospheric small towns, and secrets that refuse to stay hidden. Storytelling has been part of my life for as long as I can remember; born from long car rides, a battered notebook, and a soundtrack of country, Motown, and 80s hair bands.

My writing journey amped up in my teens, hidden away in my room with stacks of handwritten stories and a determination to build new worlds. At nineteen, I bought my first laptop, an indestructible brick of a machine that felt like magic compared to my pencil-cramped hands. I've been creating mysteries, alternate realities, and complicated characters ever since.

I love writing from every angle—heroine, hero, side character, and sometimes even the villain. My stories often follow smart, capable, slightly chaotic women who solve crimes, navigate danger, and protect the people they love. While romance often threads through my books, I'm equally drawn to the bonds of friendship, found family, and the complicated ties that shape us.

I believe books are essential, imagination is sacred, and boredom is the birthplace of creativity. And when life offers no clear way to conquer or surrender, stories give us a place to escape, rebuild, and breathe.

If you enjoy dark cozies with heart, slow-burn suspense, quirky characters, and mysteries with emotional depth, you're in the right place.